A KISS IN THE DARK

Heading for the door, Pandora tossed over her shoulder, "You needn't see me out either. I'm using the back stairs, and that would certainly look bad for you."

"One moment!" The Viscount crossed to her side and, snaking his hand around her cloaked arm, drew her alongside him. "I do not allow ladies to go about unescorted."

"Oh, you don't? Well, this is one lady who is quite capable of caring for herself. I arrived under cover of darkness, and shall leave under cover of darkness. That's as plain as vanilla pudding, and unless you wish to continue our earlier disagreements, you will let me pass." She leveled her most threatening gaze on him and attempted to pull away.

"Not yet!" There was but a moment's warning before he dragged her against him and brought his mouth down on hers in a crushing kiss that startled him as much as it did her.

The Impetuous Pandora

Lydia Lee

JOVE BOOKS, NEW YORK

THE IMPETUOUS PANDORA

A Jove Book / published by arrangement with
the author

PRINTING HISTORY
Jove edition / October 1990

ISBN: 0-515-10424-8

Jove Books are published by The Berkley Publishing Group,
200 Madison Avenue, New York, New York 10016.

PRINTED IN THE UNITED STATES OF AMERICA

10 9 8 7 6 5 4 3 2 1

For my aunts—Edythe, Helen, Mimi, Florence, Bessie, and Marian—who, each in her own way, tried to make me a lady!

Thanks to:

My sister, Anne Weeks Hancock, and to my brother, Joseph Preble Weeks, for everything!

And to Michelle Ihlder, Bob Minter, Jon Kavalauskas, George Keister, and Earl Singleton for those early years on 42nd Place.

And a special thanks and remembrance to Major Murray Bayliss, whose colorful personality and tales of India under Britannia have been a continued source of delight.

Author's Note

As those of you familiar with the various aspects of Kali and the rites of the Thugs know, this cult was not widely known in England at the time of my novel. Thus I have used some poetic license with regard to historical chronology. There were, however, sketchy reports of the Stranglers (as the Thugs were also called) that did filter back to late Regency England.

My interest in India is long-standing, especially those early years of the Empire, and has served as inspiration for this tale of love and intrigue.

Chapter One

"We are headed for scandal broth!" Beatrix McClellan intoned. "Scandal broth!" she repeated, taking perverse pleasure in this prophecy. Lifting a dainty Wedgwood cup to her trembling lips, she awaited her niece's reply.

"More likely debtor's prison, and I, for one, shan't sit on my hands awaiting this fate." With a clatter, Pandora Tremantle set her teacup down on the silver tray that sat between the two ladies.

"Pandora, I do not like it above half when you use that tone; it always forbodes calamity. Please try to remember that you are a lady." Touching a lace-edged handkerchief to her brow, Miss McClellan added, "It is bad enough that your brother has taken to cards and drink. We, however, must remain stalwart, *not* foolhardy: cautious, not—"

"It is not in my nature to be cautious!" Pandora gave a toss to her fiery red curls, as if to emphasize the point, then narrowing her splendid green eyes to advantage, said, "And if I were of a placid nature—"

"Alas," her aunt interjected, reaching for a biscuit, "I fear you are too tall and outspoken to be even remotely mistaken for *placid,* though you do possess a remarkable countenance." With a wave of biscuit in Pandora's direction, and quite unmindful of her previous prophecy of scandal, she appeared on the brink of a recitation of her niece's social possibilities. It was a familiar digression which Miss Tremantle had endured countless times. The fact that she was three and twenty, had had two seasons at Almack's, three proposals, and numerous disappointed suitors, did not deter her aunt from hoping for a "brilliant match" for the girl. "Yes, my dear, a docile nature on you would not suit. But I digress. What were we saying?"

"That if I *were* placid, we would have long since gone to grass, or at the very least the pauper's house!" Sipping her tea with a precision that belied her impatience, Pandora continued, "In fact, it is because of Winthrop's latest folly that I fully intend to carry on with my plan."

Miss McClellan, reminded of the impending doom, hastily swallowed her biscuit, and managed to croak out once again, "Scandal broth! Think of what people will say if you accost Lord—oh, whatever his name is!"

"Cardew!" Pandora supplied the name as if it were poison.

"Ah, yes. Lord Cardew—a Viscount, I believe." The older woman shook her auburn curls, sending them into a frenzy about her cherubic face. "As for Winny's unfortunate gambling, it is to be expected in the Corinthian set."

"At the rate he is going, he shall be out of funds *and* his precious set."

"Child, you look perfectly fierce when you scowl like that; if you keep it up, it shall be permanent, and *no* man will have you." Beatrix made a little face of her own and reached for another biscuit, which she smothered in marmalade. "I do think you are mistaken about this whole episode. It is not as though Winny had taken up with the dregs of society. After all, Lord Cardew *is* a Viscount, and Winny is quite thrilled to have been befriended by him." Her tongue darted out, catching a dribble of marmalade as the biscuit made its way into her mouth.

"Oh, I am sure," Pandora countered testily, "but why do you suppose a respectable peer of the realm would be languishing in our lowly inn? Remember, Winny confessed to having lost to this so-called Viscount. Then there are those receipts from the moneylenders which Winny dropped the other day, and when confronted with them, he went off in a great furor."

Beatrix brushed aside this evidence with the wave of a hand. "Undoubtedly he has taken refuge at Boodle's in London, where he is surely at the mercy of unscrupulous creatures." She drew a weary sigh and, hand pressed to bosom, added, "You remember how Great-uncle Melrose was beset by the gambling demons, and lost all to some lowlife person in London. So, I wouldn't be so quick to condemn this Viscount." Her eyelids fluttered a bit. "As for *your* plan, I fear it shall lead to the vapors for me, and I daren't think *what* for you!"

"Nonsense! This isn't the first time I've had to step between Winthrop and the gaming table," Pandora reminded her aunt.

"No, and it shan't be the last. As you know, gambling is the fatal family flaw, and having skipped a generation, is most assuredly overdue. For it is said that when one is of the Blood, these irregularities *do* pop up. Deplorable, but there you have it. Why, your mama and I would have been quite undone had not our own mama taken a firm grip on Papa's finances." Miss McClellan's pointed brows inched up her remarkable forehead at this oft-repeated disclosure. Indeed, everything about Pandora's aunt was commanding and regal. One could well imagine this portly gentlewoman with a tiara upon her elaborately arrayed curls. Her countenance was well appointed, with the slightest excess of flesh about what in youth had been a most determined chin. Her chocolate brown eyes, however, sparked with merriment, and her mouth—a painted cherry—was as sweet as the bonbons she so loved. As a young lady she had been the toast of several seasons, and had made an eminent match with a Baron's son, who unfortunately had died in the American Revolution. There had been no one to replace her courageous fiancé, but rather than pine away, Miss McClellan answered her widowed brother-in-law's plea for a chaperon for his children. She threw herself into the position with the fervor of a saint, taking particular delight in the raising of the high-spirited Pandora.

"More tea?" Beatrix inquired, pouring as she spoke. She hastily plopped two biscuits onto Pandora's plate, then leaned forward, adding, "I cannot countenance this wild scheme of yours to liberate Winny; it is most unladylike. Surely if your papa were here instead of trouncing about India, he would put a stop to it." She sipped her tea as if testing for poison, then wrinkling her nose, quickly added more sugar.

"But Papa is *not* here, and if he were, it would be Winthrop who would be put on short rein, not I! Oh, the folly of Papa allowing Winny free access."

"Yes, pet, but I am certain all will be set to rights upon his return." Beatrix took a sustaining breath. "However, concerning your intentions of visiting this gambling Viscount . . ."

"There is nothing to fret about," Pandora interrupted on a swallow of biscuit and tea. "In any case, if we wait upon one of Papa's quixotic visits, Winny might well have gambled away Chatford Abbey!"

"Oh, no, no, my precious," she protested with a sigh of concession. "Though I'll grant you've undoubtedly helped keep this stately roof and all its furnishings over our heads." With a magnanimous gesture she indicated the voluptuous warmth of the gold saloon, from its rich Oriental carpet, marble fireplace and stained glass windows to its carved mahogany ceiling, stately ancestral portraits and delicate velvet couches. Beatrix nodded her head vigorously, setting her cap of curls to dancing. "Even so," she continued after taking a bite of scone, "It is not the thing for a young lady to race about the countryside! Ah, but I have said my piece." She uttered a sigh, then straightened in her chair. "Oh, I do hope your papa doesn't get it into his head to send us another of those . . ." Beatrix paused to look furtively about the drawing room, then in hushed tones, ". . . those tragic little ragamuffins."

"I think Jemnaz Singh is adorable," Pandora quickly said. "Papa refers to him as one of India's true jewels. And yes, another child *is* on his way."

"No!" Beatrix sputtered over her well-sugared tea. "When did you learn this? Mind you, I am quite fond of our little Jemnaz, but I fear your papa will go on a collecting spree like he has with all those dusty books. I am not as young as I used to be." She pressed a linen napkin to her forehead and daintily sank back in her chair to emphasize the point. "Naturally I care not a fig that the Wofford-Sydneys did not invite us to their last rout, though I did have it on the sly from Cook that it was indeed because Evelyn fears we might carry the plague. Imagine, the brass of that woman! If we *should* stumble upon her, I shall most certainly cough in her direction!—Ah, but tell me, when did you hear from your father?"

"This morning's mail; it was another box of books, with a cryptic message instructing me to study the volumes well," Pandora laughed. "As if I could read Sanskrit."

"But what of the child?"

"He went on to say that a 'second jewel' was on its way. I think he must have penned it on elephant back, for I could scarce make out his scrawl."

"Elephant back, you say? Tsk, tsk. I do think that dreadful Indian sun has done something to Horatio's upper story. It was understandable that he should lose himself in travel after your mama—my dearest sister—passed on. I can even see his fascination with the legend of the Snow Leopard Jewels. But to spend all these years searching for them—ha!—and then to go quite crackers over dusty old books written in a heathen tongue? Well, it is most peculiar! La, it wouldn't surprise me to learn he was planning on turning Chatford Abbey into a foundling home for Indian orphans!" With a shudder that rippled her purple silk bodice, she asked most solicitously, "By the by, where *is* little Jemnaz?"

"The 'little ragamuffin' is sequestered in the library with Nora, learning the alphabet."

"Oh? I didn't know your abigail knew her letters."

"I think they are teaching each other; for Jemnaz is determined to become educated. Last night when I tucked him in he told me he was going to be a professor when he grew up. Well, I had best be on my way if I'm to return by dinner." Pandora pressed a napkin to her lips, signaling that despite the fact Aunt Beatrix was still about the scones and jam, she was not to be deterred.

"Oh, but don't you want to be here when Cousin Chloe arrives?" Beatrix leaned forward, nearly spilling tea on her purple skirts. "You do remember she is due to arrive sometime this evening, don't you?"

"Hawkins can carry her portmanteau to my bedchamber. Rest assured, Aunt Beatrix, I've laid fresh linen out for her." Pandora smiled at her aunt's sigh of relief. "You can also be quite sure Aunt Statira will have sent her abigail, old Mrs. Pattybone, and a handsome retinue with her."

"A shame the country air makes Statira so dreadfully ill. And what a pity she won't be here for Chloe's ball!"

"Yes, Auntie," Pandora said patiently, well aware that Beatrix meant to stall her departure as long as possible, "However, we can discuss that later." She rose to leave, but halted at her aunt's parting request.

"Since you are so obstinate on this little matter of the Viscount, I expect to be amused with a verbal essay on him." Her cherry lips pursed together in profound satisfaction. "He might *actually* be eligible! And being as you are still . . . *available—*"

"Aunt Beatrix! Surely you've not been hoodwinked by Winny's description of the man? I beg of you, do not even imagine a match with him! I am quite surprised: one minute you're admonishing me not to go, and the next you're hearing wedding bells! Need I remind you, that aside from luring Winny further into debt, we have not—as you would say—'had the pleasure of being presented to him'!"

"Well, if the man *is* a bona fide Viscount, then introductions could be arranged, and certainly would be expected by his family as well."

"Auntie, you've been reading too many romances! This is quite different. If you must play Cupid, please aim your arrow in Chloe's direction. After all, you've a ball planned for her in a fortnight. She is far better material for such ploys than I."

"Nonsense! While it is true you are a bit tall, you were the nonpareil of your season. I recall the gentlemen positively buzzing about you like bees to a flower; you could easily have tied the nuptial knot with anyone of them. And even now, if you put a bridle on your tongue, I have not a doubt in the world that some delightfully acceptable young man, a Viscount even, would marry you in a trice!"

Pandora paused at the arched doorway, a smile playing about her mouth. "Aunt Bea, my manner, hoydenish though it may be, is as much a part of me as my red hair."

With a wink she slipped through the doorway, but not before her aunt called out, "Be sure that Nora is with you *every* minute!"

That Nora would remain behind, nicely ensconced in the library with the studious Jemnaz Singh, had not been revealed to Pandora's aunt. After all, there was only so much the dear lady could endure!

Settling herself on the riding seat of the open gig, Pandora gathered up the ribbons and set the gray to a smart pace down the carriage way, which curled a languid path through the majestic oaks and elms that lined the path leading to Chatford Abbey. The far horizon was streaked with the amber and gold of the setting sun. Overhead, dark clouds presaged a gathering storm, and the briskness in the air made Pandora thankful she had worn her dark green spencer over her muslin frock. She had been told green heightened her own coloring, and she had every intention of making a lasting impression on Lord Cardew. As far as her planned confrontation went, it was no more than the man deserved. Oh, but he would rue the day he tangled with the Tremantles!

Off in the distance thunder rumbled, and as the day darkened, so did her thoughts. Epithets hurled about her brain, chasing one another: gambler, liar, thief! Her mouth quivered in anticipation.

The gentleman to whom she mentally addressed this venom was at that very moment having equally dark ruminations as he considered the plate of venison and tankard of ale that had been set before him. Though it was an early hour to sup, he wished to have done with it that he might consider his next move without distraction. It would have to be planned carefully, for he did not wish to tip his hand to the enemy: or enemies, for in that narrow alley back in Bombay he had been set upon by three Thugs. His neck still bore the marks of the knotted scarf that had nearly choked out his life. They had robbed him clean, leaving him for dead, but it was most curious that they had searched and found a certain missive that could surely have held no value to them, if indeed they were Thugs. He had best be careful, for there were several lives held in the balance.

It had been a score of years since he'd left England; he had thought it was never to return, and certainly not under these conditions. Yet who was left to remember him?

"*Viscount Justin Cardew.*" He spoke his name to the four walls of the handsomely appointed private parlor as if enjoying an immense joke, then chuckling softly, raised the tankard to his lips and blew on white foam. It was a respectable brew, but then the Orange Crown Inn, similar to many that dotted the English countryside, was a respectable hostelry.

It was also a refuge for a gentleman who had spent the past eight years on the untamed subcontinent of India; years that had left their mark upon the Viscount, nearly stamping out all vestiges of aristocratic bearing. Still, beneath the darkened skin that stretched across the patrician planes of his face, a trace remained. Behind the piercing blue eyes lurked the barest hint of humor, and when Cardew allowed a smile to curve his lips, there was even warmth, albeit tempered by the tight line of a scar that cut a jagged white path across mahogany skin.

Who, indeed, would remember him? He raised his thick, dark eyebrows at such a query. More likely, who would recognize him? True, he was of a height one did not easily dismiss, but only that remained. His once-black hair had burnished under the fierce Indian sun, and he was thinner, tougher, and—at thirty-two years of age—more mature, or so he hoped. What he had lost in social graces he had made up in skills necessary for survival. All in all, Cardew's presence gave one pause. Since his arrival at the Orange Crown and his subsequent fits of cardplaying—at which he won hands down—most travelers and fellow gamblers gave him a wide berth and much obeisance.

Thus it was that Miss Tremantle, in high dudgeon at said gentleman for purportedly leading her younger brother Winthrop into gaming and drinking, requested of the innkeeper that she be led to the Viscount Cardew. The proprietor, if taken back by miss's conduct, flinched not a muscle, but replied that yes, his lordship was enjoying a light supper in his chamber, and would "miss" care to follow him?

Pandora noted the respect in the innkeeper's manner, and with an affirmative nod, followed him up the narrow staircase, then waited as he rapped at the Viscount's door. Obeying the summons, she entered the room as the proprietor swung wide the portal.

For several moments she could but stare at the swarthy face that greeted her expectantly, as two of the bluest eyes she had ever seen fastened on her, taking her measure. Then pulling her gaze from his she quickly made further inventory. That he was dressed on the very edge of fashion was no surprise—after all, he had invested himself with a Viscount's title. He wore a burgundy waistcoat handsomely fastened with pearl buttons, and his neck cloth, no doubt inspired by Brummell himself, was an elaborate waterfall of perfection. His waisted coat of dark blue superfine was tossed on the back of a chair: indolently he retrieved it, then easily shrugging into it, he rose to a height that caused an odd stirring within Pandora.

"I do not believe I have had the pleasure of the introduction . . . Miss . . . ?" The Viscount dangled the word like a carrot before a hungry horse, as a taunting smile teased his mouth, only to be followed by a resonant laugh that filled the chamber, chasing back the shadows.

"No, you have not had the pleasure, though *I* have most certainly heard of you, Lord Cardew. However, you may rest assured, this is not a social call. I am here to—"

"I shouldn't think it would be, yet why a lady of some breeding would . . ." He shrugged, purposefully letting the words trail off as he applied a napkin to the corner of his mouth, in pursuit of an errant crumb, or perhaps that irritating smile that was creeping onto his face.

"The question of my 'breeding' is of little concern to you, and I find it most ungentlemanly for you to . . . to—" Abruptly she cut herself off; the man was deliberately unnerving her, and she in turn was spouting hackneyed phrases more suited to Aunt Beatrix than herself. That this rakish Viscount deserved little more than the time of day was plainly evident, and Pandora had every intention of dealing with him and departing. "I am here to—"

" 'Ungentlemanly' is it?" He shot this unexpected query at her, much as he might have aimed an arrow at a fast-moving prey. "You storm into a strange man's chamber, unannounced and unaccompanied, then school me in manners?" His dark brows drew together in a dangerous V above his hawklike nose. "Ye gads, what a female you are!" he said with a laugh that heralded a lightning change of mood, which all but ripped the wind from Pandora's sails. "Mind you I am of a quirky nature myself, so let us not stand on formality." He made a sweeping gesture to include the chair opposite him, then added, "And since you are quite mindless of your reputation, perhaps you'll sup with me as you divest yourself of whatever errand brought you thus."

Pandora wrinkled her nose in evident distaste; for although what she could see of the dimly lit room with its mahogany tea table and delicate rosewood chairs was pleasant enough, its occupant was not. Her reputation indeed! With a defiant toss of her red curls, she said, "I fear not a jot for my rep, besides no one of social consequence knows I'm here—"

"Ah! You *are* a brave one, bearding the lion in his den, so to speak." Lifting a taper from the table, the Viscount slowly crossed towards her. "I'd say a better look was in order." He held the candle aloft, imprisoning Pandora in a tawny halo of light. Unexpectedly she felt the breath go out of her: all she could do was stare at the flickering shadows that danced upon the high, dark planes of his face—a face she knew she would not forget.

"More than passing fair," he murmured as his blue eyes made their inspection. "There's Scotch-Irish somewhere, and a fair temper to match; that is but on the surface, though." He reached for a lock of her hair, but Pandora nimbly stepped back.

"Do not think to trifle with me, for I know full well who you are," she fabricated blithely, "and what lies shrouded in your troubled past, *and* if you continue to lead my brother, Mr. Tremantle, into your gaming lures, I shall reveal everything!" Pandora's eyes kindled as she thoroughly enjoyed the startled look that flitted over the Viscount's features.

"You *are* an enterprising young lady." The lines about his mouth tightened, only to relax immediately, as once again he pressed a smile on her. "If only your father could see you now." Then in a dangerously soft voice, he added, "I would think twice before such threats if I were you . . . Miss Tremantle. It is *Miss,* is it not?"

"It is. But I am not here to discuss me, my reputation, lack of it, or my breeding! I want your solemn promise that you will cease gambling with my brother, or I'll—"

"You'll what? Denounce me as a spy? Murderer? Or have you dreamed up some other heinous crime to threaten me with?"

The Viscount, whose features seemed momentarily hard and sinister, moved even closer, until his breath ruffled not only the curls on the side of her face, but her composure as well. Her heart was pounding violently against her ribs and her breath was coming in little spurts. That he was hiding something, she was quite sure, for why else would a genuine Viscount be cooling his heels at the Orange Crown? Of a sudden she felt a compelling need to know what lay hidden behind his carefully masked eyes. Perhaps he *was* a highwayman or an escaped murderer. Fleetingly she glanced at the hand that gripped the candlestick; it was strong and dark with long, dexterous fingers—fingers that could wrap about a neck quite easily. Her head jerked up to meet his gaze.

"Why, I do believe I have gotten your attention," he said with maddening ease that was belied only by the pulsating white edge of the scar that ran down his cheek. He need never open his mouth for wild tales to be spread about *him.* Such was the imprint of his character.

"I stand quite firm," Pandora finally managed to reply, quelling her fantasies of murder and mayhem.

"So I see," he purred. "But you needn't fear; from this day on I shall leave off my friendship with your brother. After all a man in my position can't afford to have idle gossip hurled about. So, let us make an end of this brangle."

"Friendship with my brother, you say? What mockery this is!" She curled her lips derisively.

"Did he not mention me?" The Viscount's tone rang with a sincerity that took Pandora aback. Abruptly she shook off all thoughts of the man's innocence.

"Of course he spoke of you!"

"And did he tell you I'd taken great sums of money off him?"

"Well, not exactly. But I do know that he has been spending more and more time here, and frequently has come home quite foxed. Furthermore, he has apparently lost so much that he has resorted to the moneylenders." Pandora looked steadily into the Viscount's eye, and with a tilt of her determined chin, added, "It is plain that at one time you either *were* a gentleman or aspired to that station, so I am taking your word as such that you will deal honorably in this matter."

"Oh, most honorably, Miss Tremantle." A humorous glint settled in his eyes, "You have set my thinking in new directions. You don't perchance volunteer your time in charitable establishments, do you?"

"I can deal admirably without your mocking tone, Lord Cardew. Thank you for your time, and I bid you good day." With a nod as one might bestow on a prized servant, Miss Pandora Tremantle sailed from the room, then hurried down the darkened flight of stairs. Tallow candles positioned on the wall sputtered in her wake, sending shadows dancing all about her. As she paused at the landing between floors, she thought she saw a small figure with familiar eyes dart into a darkened alcove. She shook her head as if to dislodge the image, and hastened out of the inn to her awaiting gig. The sun was largely obscured by dark clouds, and only slivers of light touched the horizon. As she glanced behind her she noticed the inn seemed like a hungry beast shrouded in shadow: flickering tawny lights from diamond panes winked back at her. Shaking off the goosebumps, she climbed into the gig and gave a smart flick to the reins.

Journeying homeward, Pandora couldn't rid herself of a feeling of something familiar about the Viscount. But what? Fie on it! She would have done with this curiosity about the man! She had accomplished her goal; and for all she cared, the devil could take the hindmost, which he most assuredly would. Be hanged if she wanted to unearth the Viscount's secrets. He was but a strange nobleman who had quartered himself at a village inn and set to gambling. Aside from his rough manners, he had done her no actual harm. She slowed the horse to a trot as the image of the dimly lit chamber with its slanted walls sprang before her. What was it she had seen yet not seen? Something quite familiar, but what? Abruptly she pulled on the ribbons; it wasn't a thing, and it wasn't the Viscount, but rather the fleeting figure of a small boy on the landing, so quiet he might have been a ghost. Or had her eyes played tricks on her? He was dark and skinny with huge eyes. Suddenly she remembered the eyes, glowing at her, and looking so much like Jemnaz Singh, the little Indian boy her father had sent from Bombay last year.

Slowly Pandora gave the horse his lead, hardly noticing the distant thunder and gusty breeze that had picked up, whistling through the trees and sending ominous clouds scurrying across the darkened sky: her mind was elsewhere, caught up in puzzling thoughts centered on the gentleman who called himself Justin Cardew.

Whatever else she might have conjectured that evening was brought to a halt with her arrival home and Hawkins's announcement that Miss Beatrix wished her immediate presence in the drawing room on a matter of the utmost urgency. Even as the butler drew breath for yet another issuance, several servants rushed past, nearly colliding with a bevy of belowstairs maids coming in the other direction. It was as if a mop and duster war had been declared.

Pandora blinked but once, then carefully removing her gloves, said as an afterthought, "Miss Deeds has arrived, I gather?"

"Yes, Miss." Hawkins hesitated, as if pondering a great dilemma, but thinking better of it, merely indicated that she should repair to the drawing room, implying that news of great import awaited her. Then, as was his custom, he preceded Pandora down the length of the great hall. Undoubtedly he fancied this little ritual of delivering her to the gold saloon; then again, perhaps he enjoyed hearing the sound of his heels rap against the black and white marble squares of the floor. With Hawkins there was no telling what thoughts perambulated about his ancient brain. To Pandora, who had known him since childhood, he seemed a permanent fixture, much as the armor posted at the top of the lavishly carved oak staircase. As a child Pandora used to sit in fascination, waiting for the armored figures to come to life; what a clanging noise they would have made! and how they did enliven her imagination! But then everything about Chatford Abbey spoke of times long gone.

Originally, as the name suggested, it had been an abbey, and at the Dissolution of the Monasteries, Henry the Eighth bestowed the medieval cloisters and the title of Baronet upon the first Tremantle of any note, and thus it passed down, miraculously intact, and with all the descendants captured in portraiture and displayed to full advantage in the long gallery. The Abbey, an impressive pile of Jacobean origin, was divided into two wings and soared three stories high around an inner courtyard, which in spring and summer was a riot of fragrant flowers. That Pandora had known the Abbey all her life did not seem at all extraordinary to her; nor did it make her uppish in the least. They lived in a manner kin to modest, cousin to frugal. Indeed, some years ago it had been necessary to close off the north wing to spare expenses, and of course the staff had also been considerably reduced. However, they did manage to hold the necessary balls and receptions, though despite the ornate surroundings, one could discern upon close inspection that theirs was a slightly faded opulence, though heaven forbid anyone should be so ill-bred as to inspect: after all, they were the Tremantles!

The sight that greeted Pandora's eyes upon entering the drawing room was slightly more than she expected, for seated about Aunt Beatrix was a curious trio: Cousin Chloe, glowing radiantly in a peach velvet gown; Winthrop, looking more than undone, with mud-splattered pantaloons and thoroughly windswept hair; and an unknown but resplendently bedecked gentleman, who upon seeing Pandora immediately shot to his feet, and after clicking his highly polished Hessians together, made a splendid, if somewhat florid, leg. Everything about the stranger was so buffed and thoroughly polished that Pandora expected medals to fairly leap off his chest. On second glance it was quite obvious that he was not a member of the Dragoons, but a gentleman of some consequence. His costume of wine-colored pantaloons, matching waistcoat and a deeper-hued coat with silver buttons was the perfect foil for the intricacies of his Oriental tie. An ornate quizzing glass hung on a black ribbon about his neck, and carefully raising it to his eye, he surveyed Miss Tremantle, then letting it drop, quickly stepped back, as if he had forgotten himself, but the gleaming light in his gray eyes suggested other possibilities.

"Pandy, my love, come forward!" This regal command emanated from Aunt Beatrix, whose supine figure, swathed in purple satins, reclined on a red and gold velvet couch. The delight in her eyes attested that she was assuredly enjoying this preprandial gathering with her admiring audience.

"Yes, do," echoed Miss Deeds, pulling her adoring cerulean gaze from Winthrop's, and allowing it to settle fondly on Pandora. "We were just having the most interesting discussion with—" She quickly bit down on her lower lip and looked to her aunt to make proper introductions.

"The Marquess of Manakin," Beatrix trilled as if she had created the gentleman herself, then quelling her excitation, she added, "Edward Gales Conrad, you *do* recall his name! He is the *famous* gentleman explorer whose adventures we've read of in the paper! Oh, and that he should grace Chatford Abbey in person, and with such tales to impart!" There was a substantial pause, wherein Miss McClellan's lips pursed in delicious expectation. "Do come in, child, and stop standing there as if you'd been rooted. The Marquess will think you lack manners!"

"I should never think such a thing," the gentleman said, in a well-modulated voice. "Not after the glowing attributes Sir Horatio heaped upon you."

This remark propelled Pandora not only into the saloon, but onto the rose-colored settee with decided lack of ceremony. "You've spoken with Papa? Seen him?" In her excitement she indicated the Marquess might reclaim his seat. "When?" she demanded as he eased himself next to her.

"Pandora! You are being too forward," Beatrix scolded as she whipped her fan into play. "Our guest has just returned from the wilds of India, and has barely had time to catch his breath; you must not press him so. After dinner you can read the letter from your father—"

"Oh, but I would read it now!"—she shot an imploring look in the Marquess's direction—"for I shan't be able to swallow a thing, not knowing how Papa fares."

With a flick of his wrist, Lord Manakin silenced the sudden

murmurs that swept the little gathering, and producing the requested missive, leaned against the gilt back settee, a look of decided interest softening the planes of his face.

Pandora, hardly noting the stained and rumpled set to the envelope, tore at the wafer and withdrew the correspondence. That she had heard from her father that very morning hardly mattered, for she derived such joy from his adventures that she eagerly looked forward to all his news; and being hand delivered made it even more meaningful.

After quickly scanning it, a broad smile sprang to her face and with a laugh she said, "Well, Aunt Bea, looks like we shall have another 'true jewel' from India! Come, come, don't look so surprised."

Winthrop strained forward in his chair, "That shall be splendid! Especially for Jemnaz."

"Oh, dear no!" Beatrix's eyelashes fluttered considerably at this dreaded possibility, but Chloe clasped her little pink hands and cried, "Oh, famous! Another 'jewel'!"

The Marquess once again took to his quizzing glass, a thoroughly confounded look on his face; then with a great "Aha!" and a flourish, he presented Pandora with a small velvet box. "I had near forgot! Your father entrusted me with this, and said 'twas but a small token of his love for you."

"Oh?" Slowly Pandora opened the box and for several seconds merely stared at a rather impressive ruby pendant, the light from whose facets leapt like flames on a hearth. "Why . . . it's lovely!" she managed to say, for truly it was; still, she couldn't help wondering what had possessed her father to send this instead of the promised foundling. Most peculiar, especially considering that not once in all the years Sir Horatio had been in India had he sent home anything but old books and the little orphan.

Chloe and Winthrop exchanged puzzled looks, but Aunt Beatrix, vastly relieved at this fortuitous turn of events, said in dulcet tones, "Perhaps there is hope for Horry after all! I'd a notion he would eventually drop all that classical nonsense." She cast the Marquess a fetching look, and added, "My brother-in-law has sent us enough moldering books to start a lending library. Mind you I like nothing better than a good romance, but heavens, these tomes are printed in odd little scribbles. I can't imagine what possessed him to start collecting them in the first place. Though I suppose it was grief over the loss of his dearly loved wife, but that was years ago!" Beatrix tendered a sigh aimed in Lord Manakin's direction, then artlessly added, "Perhaps that ruby is part of the mysterious Snow Leopard Jewels!"

Pandora sent her aunt a darkling look; how could the woman be such a goosecap as to mention her father's search for the legendary cache of jewels that were reputed to be worth a maharaja's ransom?

"Ah, yes," the Marquess said quite unexpectedly, "Sir Horatio felt he was getting rather close to the source; of course it's been some time since we parted company. I daresay you have probably heard more news than I."

"We've heard nothing," Pandora said, as if to dismiss the topic, then on a light laugh, added, "And I for one do not believe they exist." With trembling fingers she fastened the gold chain about her slender neck: why the ruby instead of the expected orphan?

"Oh, the jewels exist, Miss Tremantle. Let me assure you of that," the Marquess countered in a droll voice that reminded Pandora of the sort of gentleman who might enjoy bearbaiting. Steadily she looked him in the eye; she was unflinching in her scrutiny, for there was something beneath all that elegance that uneased her. She was faintly reminded of the counterfeit Viscount at the Orange Crown, for they were of a similar height and build, and both of a complexion darkened by the sun, but there the similarity ceased. Where the Viscount's eyes flashed like blue lightning on a dark night, the Marquess's were dueling pistols, gunmetal gray and slightly obscure: they matched not the finery his lordship wore nor the impeccable manners he affected. Granted, the man could take a stance and appear singularly handsome. Even the curl to his lips could be mistaken for a smile, if he were in the shadows with a candle at his back.

"We shall have to hear more of the Snow Leopard Jewels at dinner," Pandora said, rising from the close-quartered position next to the Marquess. "Although I still say they are but a legend."

Whatever answer Lord Manakin might have given was cut

off by a shrill scream that echoed down the great hall, followed by the sounds of crockery breaking, a dog howling, and more screams, all building to a cacophonous crescendo that burst through the portal of the gold saloon, revealing a small and very skinny little boy, nearly as black as the dog to whose collar he clung. A flustered serving girl followed by Hawkins all but collided into the boy and the dog.

"Beggin' your pardon, madam," Hawkins addressed Miss McClellan, who had fallen back onto her couch, a near-quivering heap of purple satin, "but Jemnaz knows that animal is not allowed in the house. And as a result we have lost the berry pudding—smashed beyond all hope; and it is *his* fault!" Hawkins assumed an arrow-straight pose, all the while casting disparaging looks at the trembling child, who seemed quite cowed by the experience with the berry pudding and the screaming servants.

"Oh, that this should happen while we are entertaining!" Miss McClellan reached for her vinaigrette, then with a shake to her head, managed, "Jemnaz, you are excused, but you are never to bring Kublai Khan into the main house."

"Yes, memsahib!" The boy, still entwined with the dog, threw himself face down upon the carpet, then slowly craned his neck around, and after a moment's appraisal of the Marquess, gave a tug to Kublai Khan's collar, and together they scurried from the room.

"Forgive this distressing intrusion," Beatrix began. "He's not a *bad* boy." Thus recovered, she turned toward her nephew, "Winny, give me escort to the dining room, for we shall now sup, and attempt to forget this unfortunate incident with Jemnaz."

"The little chap's really most engaging," Winthrop said good-naturedly as he assisted his aunt to her feet. "And I might add, he's smart as a whip."

Quite innocently Chloe chirped out, "Uncle Horry calls him 'one of India's true jewels'!" She flashed Lord Manakin a smile. "Don't you think that's charming, your lordship?"

Pandora, who had fallen in step beside the Marquess, noticed this did give him pause, as if he'd just discovered the missing piece of a puzzle, and was not that pleased with the picture. It was then that Pandora felt an odd premonition ruffle her usually unflappable composure.

Chapter Two

"This is such an exceptional turn of events," Beatrix exclaimed. Having recovered her composure over a steaming bowl of fish broth, she was now quite prepared to hear the completion of the Marquess's tale, which had been interrupted by Pandora's arrival. "But then it's not all that surprising that Horatio should meet up with you; I imagine it was rather like a shared cultural oasis—and fancy you having such an interest in old books. I daresay," she continued as the soup bowls were whisked away and the second course presented, "you shall have a veritable literary feast in Chatford's library, for not only has Horry sent all those strange foreign books, we also have some splendid old English tomes." Beatrix's eyes sparkled and darted from their honored guest to Pandora, who looked quite fetching in her green frock, a fact not unnoticed by her aunt, who of a sudden said, "Why, I am possessed of the most splendid idea! After dinner we can have a little recital, with Pandora at the pianoforte and Chloe singing accompaniment; then afterwards perhaps Winny will be so good as to show you to the library before you retire."

"Sounds like a delightful evening," the Marquess said, presenting a smile designed to charm the most skeptical: one, however, that did not engage Pandora's sensibilities.

Swallowing a piece of well-disguised creamed vegetable, she said, "I am only tolerable at my music—lest you be led to think otherwise. However, we will do what we can to put you at your ease." She contrived an unconvincing smile. "But do continue your tale of adventure in India, for your exploits are very much the *on-dit,* you know. But then perhaps you are not acquainted with your far-flung fame?" She inspected his face for some reaction, but the wavering glow from the candelabra confounded his features, burnishing his skin to an even darker shade, and sent his iron gray eyes behind a veil of shadows.

"Famous, am I?" His laugh was edged with unexpected harshness. "I suppose when one survives that jungle and its murderous Thugs and unnavigable rivers, one does acquire a name in the process. Most wearisome, if I do say so!" He raised a forkful of lamb to his lips, and after brief contemplation, consumed it.

"You're all the talk at the clubs!" Winthrop said excitedly, tossing back a lock of flaxen hair. At nineteen, the boy affected the style of the Corinthian set, but his impetuosity and eagerness at proving himself a man of accomplishment caused him frequently to appear with his cravat somewhat askew and his coat slightly rumpled.

"In fact," Winthrop continued, hardly taking note of the laden plate before him, "if you're ever badly dipped and in need of some extra blunt, you could publish—"

"Winthrop! That will quite do!" Beatrix choked out, reaching for her goblet of wine, and after liberally refreshing herself, added, "One does not speak of such things. What must his lordship think?" Turning to the Marquess, she said, "Do excuse the boy. He gets rather carried away, though I must confess, we do wish to hear more of your adventures." She batted her eyes to great effect, then forgetting propriety herself, added, "*Thugs,* you say? Do they not strangle their victims as a sort of sacrifice to their pagan gods?"

"Ah," Lord Manakin murmured, setting his fork to one side, and giving Miss McClellan his full attention, "you are apprised of the cult of Kali? Most unusual, for very few English born even know of its existence."

"My brother-in-law has written extensive letters, and of course there has been all this talk of you being a cat with nine lives, and while it's true this heathen cult is not well-known, the grisly tale your bearer reported did trickle back to London. However, most people—fascinated though they were—thought it was sheer faradiddles!"

"Ha!" Winthrop interjected, "In the devil of a hobble, I'd wager you were. How *did* you escape them? We were given to understand you beat off three Thugs!"

"That heroic, eh?" The Marquess paused as if giving much consideration to the tale. "I daresay this is not proper chit-chat for table."

"But don't you see we're already in the thick of the soup? Why, just look: Pandora, Cousin Chloe and even Aunt Beatrix are on tenterhooks!" His sweeping gesture indicated that they would be quite put out if details were not revealed immediately. Chloe, taking up Winthrop's banner, declared that she *must* on all accounts hear the tale, whereas Pandora kept remarkably silent, and Beatrix torn between insatiable curiosity and proper decorum, nodded vigorously first one way then the other.

The Marquess, acquiescing to this command like an actor to a favored role, commenced with dramatic flair. "Thankfully my memory has been most merciful, and I recall very little of the incident, but that I was surrounded on three sides by the heathens, the knotted choke scarf about my neck and eternity a dash too close, when my man burst upon the scene and dispatched two of the assassins—to Kali's heaven, I suppose. The third chap, who held the strangle cord, escaped, and I survived with nary a mark for the telling." Indolently he touched the starched points of his collar, and allowed a tentative smile, thin yet potent as the wine before him, to touch his lips.

Chloe, enthralled with the tale, solicitously murmured, "How wicked these . . . these . . . Thugs are to set upon a gentleman such as yourself! Though I must confess some curiosity as to why you would prefer India to England. Why, little Jemnaz has said that he shall never return." Her gaze settled ingenuously upon the Marquess, awaiting his response to her query.

Beatrix, however, flushed to the roots of her auburn curls, pealed forth with, "Cousin Chloe, you must not presume upon his lordship's privacy: 'tis one thing to inquire of adventures previously made public, but quite another to—"

"Tosh!" the Marquess said, as he finished off the lamb. Then leaning back, he allowed the footman to remove his plate and place the sirloin before him. "I thought it common knowledge that I left England under a cloud—much to my discredit." He paused, then retrieving his knife and fork he contemplated the tender cut of meat on the gold-edged Wedgwood plate before adding, "I was a callow, green sprig, and though I committed an indiscretion of . . . uh . . . let us say unfortunate consequences, I am hopeful that my years in India have absolved me from that most aggrieved piece of behavior. I am only sorry my parents aren't alive, for I sense in my heart that all is forgiven." He cut and speared a thin slice of steak and ate it with relish that suggested, at least to Pandora, that he didn't give a fig if all was forgiven or not.

"Oh, Lord Manakin, you present such a puzzle to be solved!" Chloe pushed her plate from her, and inclining her head in his lordship's direction, added, "I am but in my first season, and had not heard a smidge against your name; but of these adventures on the Indian subcontinent, it is the most thrilling, and I must say you do not look like a man who has time and time again been set upon! More likely that you should entertain the ladies in the drawing room with droll tricks."

"Would you expect his lordship to appear in buckskin raiment, or whatever they wear on that beastly continent?" Beatrix enchanged sympathetic glances with the Marquess, "I think it a sublime testimony to your superiority that you have maintained your gentility, and I am only too pleased that Horatio has pressed you to stay with us until his return."

"Oh?" Pandora uttered as if she had forgotten that her papa had entreated Manakin to avail himself of their hospitality. That her father might well be arriving within the fortnight was great news indeed, but that this exquisite should reside at Chatford Abbey was quite outside of enough. Perhaps Chloe, Winny and Aunt Beatrix were impressed by the Marquess. She, however, could not share their enthusiasm. Setting her mouth in agreeable lines, she added, "We're really a touch provincial: I do hope you shan't get too bored."

"Nonsense!" Beatrix countered, indicating the footman

might bring on the next course. "In fact, I'm hosting a masked ball for my niece Chloe in a fortnight, which, Lord Manakin, you shall enjoy immensely for everyone of consequence shall be here."

"A capital affair, Auntie!" Winthrop interjected. "Which reminds me, I had rather hoped you could extend an invite to Lord Cardew."

"Lord Cardew?" Pandora echoed his name in disbelief, and would have undoubtedly said a deal more, had not the Marquess choked quite suddenly on his wine. Although he recovered quickly, Pandora noticed he was momentarily perturbed.

"Forgive me," Lord Manakin managed at length in a strained voice, as he tugged at his cravat. "But please, do continue. You were speaking of a Lord Cardew, I believe."

"Top of the trees chap!" Winthrop exclaimed. "And when Aunt Bea invited you to the ball, I naturally thought of him."

"A Viscount, isn't he?" Beatrix raised a knowing eyebrow at Pandora, then murmured, "Ah, yes, I seem to recall hearing of this young man, and I think it a splendid idea that he come to our Chloe's ball. In fact, I think we should have him over for tea as well."

"Capital, Aunt Bea!" Winthrop cried.

"Ah, but Lord Manakin," Beatrix continued, "I do hope you too will honor us with your presence; that is, unless following your arduous journey you wish to remain sequestered."

"One cannot hide forever," the Marquess declared on a firm note. "Since returning to England I've a mind to let the past go, and hope society will deal kindly with me."

"Oh, but I'm certain they will, Lord Manakin!" With a sigh Beatrix confessed that she too had known the sharp edge of society, and as they proceeded through dinner, she recounted the trials of being "slightly snubbed" by a certain neighbor who fancied that Jemnaz carried the plague. Over a dessert of questionable ingredients—the berry pudding having been smashed in the great hall—Beatrix prodded his lordship with all manner of questions in regard to Sir Horatio, then disallowing him any opportunity for reply, gushed on about the wearisome flow of foreign books to their library.

By the time they had repaired to the drawing room Beatrix, totally enchanted that this Marquess should grace Chatford Abbey, was practically tilting like a ship in breezy weather. Nor did Pandora misinterpret the lavish compliments her aunt aimed at *her*. Beatrix McClellan was obviously buoyed up by the possibility of her beloved niece marrying what she considered quite a catch. Pandora could almost see her aunt's brain feverishly at work as she listed her niece's innumerable accomplishments. *Tremantle* was a good name, she further stressed, with a line of baronets that reached back to the days of Henry the Eighth. An embarrassed Pandora quickly set to playing what proved to be exactly as she promised, a pleasing country tune, whose notes were sweetly sung by Chloe.

"I must beg of you another song!" the Marquess implored in a manner which suggested he frequently made such requests. Pandora nodded her head and set about the task, while Chloe, who had looked a trifle pink at the outset, commenced to trill out notes that would have put a songbird to shame.

"Ah, Cousin Chloe, that last was exceptional!" Winthrop exclaimed, and drawing Chloe to one side engaged her in a conversation, snatches of which wafted towards Pandora, interspersed with Beatrix's soliloquy on the history of Chatford Abbey.

". . . I had no idea you possessed such talent," Winthrop said enthusiastically.

"And it is rumored that a guest of that first Baronet murdered his wife in the chapel! Blood-stained marble remains there to this day!" Beatrix rattled on.

"You were just a twig of a girl last year, Chloe, and now . . ."

"I am a year older."

Thus the evening passed in exuberant conversation. Pandora, however, remained uncharacteristically silent, carefully observing the Marquess with growing interest, and would have continued to do so had not Miss McClellan, upon hearing the ormolu clock on the mantel chime eleven, exclaim, "Oh, my goodness! The hour is late, and I imagine Lord Manakin will be wanting to visit the library to select some reading material."

"I am most grateful."

"Winny!" Beatrix clapped her hands with imperial authority. "You must disengage yourself from Cousin Chloe, and see to our guest's needs and comforts."

It was Pandora's growing conviction that Lord Manakin never let anything keep him from his comforts. Perhaps Chloe was closer to the mark than she knew when she noted that he did not appear the sort who had endured such hardship in India. No, there was something amiss: he was a bit too polished, and not only that, he seemed somewhat confused at the mention of the *true jewel;* and yet he bore her father's letter, and seemed content to put up indefinitely at Chatford Abbey, despite the shadowy past that drove him from England so many years ago.

"I'm so glad Aunt Beatrix let me share your bedchamber," Chloe said, interrupting Pandora from further contemplation of the Marquess. "For we have so much to chat about—besides, every time Auntie tells that horrid tale of the murder in the chapel, I have nightmares. You know, I shouldn't be surprised if Chatford is haunted!" A tremulous sigh escaped her lips, and running a silver-backed brush through her cap of golden curls, she added, "And I'd hate to run into a ghost!"

"Well, you needn't worry, there are none. As for the chapel murder, Aunt Bea tells that story to any gentleman she thinks might offer for me. Pooh! She scares half of 'em off."

"I don't imagine the Marquess scares easily," Chloe said, placing her brush on the vanity. Then swinging around to face Pandora, she added, "You are not so keen on his lordship, are you?"

"Oh, dear. Was it that apparent? I really tried to put on a good show for Auntie, if no one else. Ah, but to answer your question, no, I was not that taken with Lord Manakin, for there's something about him that doesn't ring true." Pandora's brows drew together as she slowly added, "To begin with, why did he give me a ruby, when Papa's letter expressly referred to another 'true jewel'?"

"Perhaps your father fancied the ruby, and maybe he's bringing the orphan with him."

"Then Lord Manakin should have apprised me of that; for

he seemed to think this ruby—" Pandora touched the fiery stone with considerable hesitation "—that this ruby *was* the true jewel, yet just this morning I received a missive from Papa directing that this second child should be given a cot in Jemnaz's room as soon as he arrives."

"Well, this does present a puzzle; but then again, the child might arrive in a day or two." Chloe adjusted the ruffles on her night shift, and removing the lavender counterpane, slipped between the sheets of her canopied bed. On a yawn, she added, "If I were you, I shouldn't fret upon the matter."

"But I cannot help but wonder who this Marquess really is!"

"A man with a scandalous past." Chloe giggled and snuggled further into the bed. "But don't forget, he came with your father's letter."

"But Chloe . . ." Pandora paused, feeling a trifle guilty at her condemnation of their father's houseguest. "I still don't like it above half that Aunt Bea is practically eating out of his hand, and has obviously cast me in the role of his marchioness."

"You have eluded nuptials thus far: I am sure you shall continue to—that is, until the right gentleman comes along."

"*That* will be a miracle," Pandora replied, snuffing out the remaining taper as she climbed into the matching canopied bed. Outside the wind was picking up. Moonlight dappled the trees of the cool spring night, and slipping through the tall French windows, spilled across a Turkey rug and onto the lavender counterpanes.

"You see," Pandora continued after a moment, "I do not have your pleasing ways, and I fear I probably *am* too particular. Whereas you, if my guess is correct, will be wed by the end of your first season."

"Do you think so? Really?" Chloe's voice perked up through the haze of oncoming sleep.

"Assuredly, little coz." That Chloe was bursting to ask about Winthrop was painfully obvious, but Pandora—unlike Aunt Bea—knew better than to rush matters of the heart. No, as impulsive as Pandora had always been, she had never been one to fall willy-nilly into a love match.

Pulling the scented sheets up to her chin, her thoughts returned to the Marquess: for all his studious airs and magnificent show of manners, he was about as warm as the armored figures gracing the upstairs hall. What *had* he done that made him flee England? Aunt Beatrix might know, but then seeing the match making gleam in her eye, she would probably remain mute on the subject.

Pandora turned restlessly in bed as the hectic day's events pressed in on her. The unexpected appearance of the Marquess on top of the arrival of Chloe, Pattybone, and retinue was unsettling enough, but the most persistent disturbance to a restful night was the memory of the gambler at the Orange Crown. Pandora squeezed her eyelids shut in an attempt to purge the blue-eyed image, but it held with a tenacity which would assuredly keep her up half the night. With a sigh of exasperation, she threw the covers to one side, and stepping down from the tall bed, put on a wrapper and slippers, for the halls were drafty and the hour late. Some sherry or brandy would undoubtedly bring on sleep, and probably several interesting dreams.

She decided on the brandy and started for the library. She might even pull down one of Mrs. Hawkshore's latest romances and read herself to sleep right there on the settee. However, as she approached the tall doors leading into the library, she noticed a sliver of light beneath them. Heavens, surely Winthrop and the Marquess weren't still searching for books! Pausing, she entertained an odd presentiment. Then telling herself she was not a lily-livered chit, she slowly let her hand close about the doorknob. Still, she took care not to make a sound as she opened the door—though she need not have gone to such pains, for the Marquess, perched high on a ladder at the other end of the room, was quite absorbed in what appeared to be rapid perusal of a stack of her father's Indian books. Candles were positioned about the room and Winthrop was nowhere to be seen, but crouching behind Sir Horatio's secretary was Jemnaz Singh, his liquid gaze fastened on Pandora and a finger pressed to his lips. Seeing her assuring smile, the boy scampered to his feet, and would have cleared the room, had he not banged his head against an unseen leaf of the desk. His cry of pain brought the Marquess down the ladder and across the room in a trice, a look of rage on his face as he obviously restrained himself from collaring the boy, who, grappling with Miss Tremantle's wrapper, partially managed to hide behind her.

"The child needs lessons!" he said through tight lips. "I am surprised you would allow him in here, for there's no telling what damage he might do." His mouth eased into an abbreviated smile. "Some of these books are irreplaceable, and could be quite badly soiled by your . . . little charge." He fingered the volume in his hand with a great show of reverence.

"Lord Manakin," Pandora began, in what she hoped was a moderate tone, for she sensed it would bode ill to antagonize this man, "the boy's name is Jemnaz Singh, and he is considered one of the family, and as such is free to roam about the Abbey. In fact, we encourage him in his studies."

"*His studies?*" the Marquess queried, thoroughly amazed. "Pray tell, can the lad quote the Bard?" With this, he threw his head back and laughed. "My, my, Miss Tremantle, you *are* unique; I believe that was how your father described your character."

Pandora felt her face go scarlet. "This has nothing to do with my character, Lord Manakin." Putting a protective arm around the Indian boy, she added, "It is my father's wish that little Jemnaz be educated." Then allowing her gaze to rest on the tooled-leather-covered volume in the Marquess's hands, she said, "Do you fancy Sanskrit?"

"I do have an acquaintance with the language."

"Oh, of course, your years in India."

"However," he pursued, "this happens to be in Arabic, as I am sure you, being fully versed in your father's interest in that culture, must know."

Refraining from admitting that she steered clear of the foreign books, preferring works written in a language she could read, Pandora jauntily replied, "Yes, Papa is quite taken with the Eastern cultures, and I believe if he sends one more crate of books, we shall run out of shelf space."

"There are books you've not put out?" the Marquess inquired, crooking his neck about to gaze at the veritable wall of glassed-in volumes.

"A few." Pandora, unsure of just why, hedged on this

point. "However, Lord Manakin," Pandora continued, deciding to bring this midnight encounter to a close, "I doubt you would wish to go through them until they've been cleaned and placed on the shelves." Her vague gesture encompassed the entire library, whose vast collection of leather-bound volumes was set in a richly appointed chamber of dark mahogany paneling with occasional alcoves displaying delicate porcelain figurines and other treasures. French doors, leading into the rose garden, allowed the morning sun to fill the room, and throughout spring and summer a sweet fragrance mingled with the scent of leather. In the colder months a fire was set on the broad stone hearth, and numerous Oriental carpets would be laid down to seal in the warmth. For Pandora, this was a room of cherished memories, and the Marquess's presence seemed a harsh intrusion. Short of seeing him to his chamber, there was little she could do but bid him good night for the second time that evening, and return to her own bedchamber. This she did without further ceremony, *and* without her brandy. However, after tucking little Jemnaz Singh in for the night, she hastened to the drawing room, and though the smidge of sherry she found was too sweet, she drained the contents of the crystal decanter into a liqueur glass and swallowed it as one might swallow medicine—which indeed it was—then went off to bed, determined to sleep.

"Arabic?" She muttered this word as she passed the armored figures at the top of the stairs. What so intrigued the Marquess about an Arabic book that he would return in secret to the library for it? From the way he was flipping through the books it seemed more like he was searching for something hidden. But what? Jewels? In the library?

Entering her bedchamber, she headed straight for her jewel case, withdrew the ruby pendant, and in a shaft of moonlight studied the sparkling gem. *If* it was real, did this mean her father *had* found the legendary jewels? Then why no word from him? If it was fake . . . Pandora's thoughts snaked back to her father's cleverly worded note:

> Dear Pandy: Am packing off another of India's True Jewels for your collection. I trust you'll tuck 'em in at night.

Why then did the Marquess present her with a ruby pendant? She let it rest in the palm of her hand, noting its swirled gold filigree setting. Maybe it wasn't even Indian.

With decision she placed it back in its case; she would simply have to get it appraised. This resolved, she climbed into bed determined to go to sleep; she would not think about the jewels, Manakin, or Cardew . . . *Cardew.* Funny the way the Marquess reacted to hearing his name, almost as if he'd known him. Pandora mulled over this possibility for a moment, then closing her eyes, tried to evict all thoughts from her weary brain. But what if they *did* know each other? And why was Cardew at the inn in the first place? What purpose did he have in befriending Winny? Moreover, how did he know her father was away? Pandora sighed: obviously Winny had regaled him with the family history.

As Pandora's thoughts shifted back to Manakin, she again wondered at his actions in the library. True, he had come as her father's guest; still, he was a stranger to her, and in the very letter that arrived that morning Sir Horatio had cautioned that she be on guard with strangers. With a sigh, Pandora tossed aside the bedcovers, quietly crept across cold floorboards and retrieved her father's letter. Standing by the window she managed to peruse the second half of it.

> . . . and Pandy, though I know you to be of a trusting nature, I ask you take care, and in particular to be on guard against any stranger that might come inquiring of me. As you know, I am in search of the Snow Leopard Jewels, and though their legend decrees that only the pure of heart shall ever obtain them, I still send this warning.

Could it be the jewels *were* here? But surely her father would have said something more in the letter. Replacing it on her dresser, she retraced her steps and once again climbed back into bed. If anything, Pandora felt more confused, as again she wondered at Manakin's reaction to hearing Cardew's name. If the Marquess truly was her father's friend, perhaps he had warned him about Cardew. Still, she could not quite trust Manakin. But why did she find the Viscount so undeniably attractive? What if he were not just a gambler, but a real villain? Wasn't it just like her contrary nature to find him more appealing than Manakin, who was probably a sterling character, rich as Croesus, and a Marquess as well?

Pandora's thoughts continued chasing one another in a never ending circle of possibilities. Ha! Perhaps *both* men were after the jewels. Oh, would that Papa were here now! But he wasn't, and so the lot fell to her to unscramble.

Much to her surprise, in the middle of these tumultuous thoughts, Pandora slipped into a deep slumber and did not awaken until Nora appeared with her morning chocolate. This she set down with her familiar, "Up, up, like the sun; it's been shining for hours!" The sound of slippered feet padding across the floor was heard by a very drowsy Miss Tremantle, who yawned and stretched prodigiously, then through shuttered eyes watched her abigail push open the French windows.

"A body needs air!" The girl, who was but two years older than Pandora, intoned this with the importance of having delivered scripture. Then breathing deeply of the crisp spring air, turned back to her mistress and added, "And after what I have endured this morning, I feel most deprived of it." The frown that furrowed her pert forehead was most inauspicious. Indeed, her entire demeanor, usually calm and gentle, was bristling like a cat on a very hot wire. Nora was a slim girl with light brown hair, most of which was kept tucked under her cap: this morning, however, it seemed as if mice might be nesting there, and even more alarming was the sparkle in her hazel eyes and the spots of color on her cheeks.

"Whatever has happened?" Pandora asked, sitting bolt upright in bed.

"Well, and it's a good thing your sweet cousin and her abigail are downstairs at breakfast—for you know how hysterical old Pattybone can get—"

"Yes, yes—but what *happened?*"

"Well, Miss," Nora began as she seated herself primly on the edge of a high-backed chair, "the muddle started when the Marquess's valet—queer looking fellow, if you ask me—

got a bit friendly with the downstairs maid and tried for liberties! Well, Janet beat him with her broom, which started him cursing something fierce. Ha! 'Twas Janet's belief the man had been at the sherry, for there was not a drop left in the decanter. Well, next thing that happened was that his high 'n' mightiness, begging your pardon, came flying into the room, just as if he was the lord and master of Chatford Abbey!—Oh, my, I'm getting so excited that the words are just popping off my tongue, and Miss McClellan would die to hear me!"

"She's in her chamber, so fear not, and *do continue!*"

"And so I shall, Miss. Well, and this I did see with my own eyes because I was crossing the great hall heading for the kitchen to fetch your chocolate, when I heard this scuttle in the drawing room, and being of a curious nature, I made straight for the racket, slipped behind the door, and I swear on my dear mum this be the truth, I saw his lordship wrench the broom from Janet's hand and call her some terrible names that made her go white as a winding sheet! Then, it's like he remembered that this was not his house, nor his maid, but it certainly *was* his valet. So careful-like he handed back the broom, and got that funny smile on his face, put some gold coin into Janet's hand, and with his manservant took his leave, pretty as you please. I had scooted into the hidey hole beside the drawing room, so he never saw me." Nora took a deep breath as if the worst part of the tale had yet to be revealed.

"Go on," Pandora coaxed, understanding Nora's penchant for the melodramatic.

"Well, I rushed into the drawing room, and tried to console Janet—you know she supports her mother and that feckless brother of hers, so this position is very important to her—well, she would not say a word against the Marquess, for I do believe she thinks him to be as important as God himself, or at least the Prince Regent; but between you and me, I think she's not all buttoned up. So, I left her to the cleaning, and fast as ever I went toward the stable—the way I'd seen Lord Manakin and his valet go. And right I was. Oh, what a wicked-looking cove that valet is."

Pandora leaned intently forward, "Were there words between them? For I'm certain you could be excellent at keyholes, Nora."

Acknowledging this as a compliment, her abigail sported a ludicrous grin, and said, "So I crept forward and hid behind the edge of the barn. The Marquess was giving his valet a right good dressing down, and not words of a high-flown gentleman, more like one who knew the taste of Blue Ruin. And you best believe his valet understood, though he grumbled a bit, but then the Marquess told him to watch himself or he'd have to join the common files in London! Lord, that got the lackey's attention. 'Yes, Tribbs,' the Marquess said, 'that's the way it'll be, for I can't have you mucking things up; there's too much at stake!' With that, his high 'n' mightiness left! And a good thing, for my heart was crashing about my chest like I was fit to have one of Miss McClellan's swoons." Nora clapped a hand over that portion of her anatomy, and added on an heroic note, "Howsomever, I'll keep watch, for I believe they are not to be trusted."

Pandora's troubled silence prompted the abigail to add hurriedly, "Oh, miss, I do hope you aren't put out by my spying."

"Not at all, Nora; and you are quite right, for I fear they are *not* to be trusted. At the moment, it appears that you and I are the only ones to suspect this."

"And Jemnaz too, Miss Pandora; he told me last night there was something strange about the man from India, but for me not to worry, for he fancies keeping an eye on him." Nora's head bobbed proudly at this disclosure, as if Jemnaz Singh were her own child.

"Well, you both are to be congratulated!" Pandora said on a note of sudden triumph as she took her first swallow of chocolate. Then setting the lukewarm contents back on the tray, she fairly leapt from her bed. "I plan on gathering more information concerning this affair. However, you will at no time place yourself in jeopardy again, and we both must keep Jemnaz in line."

"That we will!" Nora said as she scurried to her mistress's side that she might assist in her toilette, all the while babbling of the nefarious goings-on in Chatford Abbey, and of course basking in the compliments Pandora had given her.

"Now, remember, not a word of this to anyone; not even to me—outside my chamber, that is," Pandora instructed, as they proceeded down to breakfast.

"Oh, torture wouldn't loosen my tongue!" Nora said on a note of drama. Just as they rounded the staircase, she whispered, "Besides, what with Chloe's servants, and most especially Pattybone, gossip would go all over the country. It's just a miracle no one heard the ruckus in the drawing room!" She closed her lips with the resolve of one destined to silence. What an adventure this morning had turned into, and didn't Miss Pandora look as bright as a new tuppence, her fiery curls coaxed about her face, and her sprig muslin frock with its capped sleeves and high waist as green and fresh as the spring morn.

At Chatford Abbey breakfast usually began around ten-thirty, which Sir Horatio said had been a tradition when he was a child and long before, and was considered by all to be most civilized. Steak and kidney pie, which Pandora loathed, was usually followed by fillets of salmon, biscuits, and small hot cakes. Dark, rich coffee or tea was served, and on those occasions when her father was in residence, a bit of ale. This morning's fare boasted an addition of roast beef and several partridges, which were being enjoyed heartily by the Marquess, who was fast in conversation with Beatrix. Winthrop and Chloe, equally engaged in one another's company, looked up as Pandora entered.

"You know, Pandora, our Cousin Chloe is a remarkable horsewoman. She insisted in riding Maiden's Prayer, *and* kept her seat!" With a scrambling motion, Winthrop stood up for his sister, and would have held her chair, but for the Marquess, who smoothly got to his feet and pulled it out for her.

Pandora managed a civil thank you, but was caught short by the glowing look in her aunt's eye; she was in obvious transports over every move the man made. Would that she would limit her matchmaking to Chloe and Winthrop, who were assuredly destined for each other, and leave off where she, Pandora, was concerned. Looking across the table at Chloe, she was suddenly struck with the possibility that her cousin's influence might well reform Winthrop, in which case, he would certainly not be returning to the Orange Crown. And yet . . .

"I had Cook prepare this especially for you," Beatrix said to Pandora, interrupting her thoughts as a salmon dish was set before her niece. "And speaking of which, I am of a mind to have a chilled salmon mousse at dinner preceding the ball for Chloe. Oh, but this will be a *fête fantastique!* Though I do wish Horry could make it back in time. But as the Marquess has said, that is most unlikely, especially given that the ball is but a fortnight away."

"Oh, Aunt Beatrix," Chloe said soothingly, "do not give up, for I am sure Uncle Horry will try his best to get here. And there will be other balls this season, though I daresay none so wonderful as yours. Why, it shall be quite a crush, with all sorts of people! And I'm particularly looking forward to meeting Lord Cardew."

"Oh, that reminds me," Beatrix said, pausing in the consumption of sliced partridge, "I must get those invitations out immediately: and I think tea in three days time would be in order, don't you, Pandy?" With the gayest of smiles that betrayed not a whit of their previous evening's contretemps with regard to Lord Cardew, Miss McClellan pressed on, "And my dear, we must embark on a little trip to London; for I daresay you and Chloe will be wanting some bits of frippery."

Pandora pressed her lips into a fine line and nodded. She should have been most annoyed at the thought of the Viscount coming to Chatford, especially having laid orders at his door to leave off all association with her brother. Somehow or other, she found herself surprisingly pleased at the idea of seeing him again. She justified this with the possibility of learning more about his motives. If he were indeed after the jewels, he would delight in an invitation to tea. Better, of course, to catch him off guard. Suddenly an outrageous notion struck her and she smiled to herself, imagining the Viscount's reaction to the scheme she was entertaining.

Chapter Three

Miss McClellan, while agreeing it a splendid idea to take Cousin Chloe into Kirk Cross village, cried off accompanying them, for she had much to do for the upcoming ball. Naturally, it was understood that only an expedition to London could possibly supply the essentials for the girls, though Beatrix did expect a few ribands could be had at one of the little shops that lined the main street of the village. Handing her niece some small change, she requested a box of her favorite chocolates. Sublimely content, she repaired to her secretary to plan further for Chloe's ball.

Not surprisingly, the Marquess also declined the venture, preferring the solitary pleasure of the library, which was just as well, for his presence would undoubtedly complicate Pandora's plans.

Everyone thus pleased, shortly after luncheon the party set out along the road that wound its way into the medieval village of Kirk Cross. Chloe, abandoning herself to the afternoon, waxed poetic over the charms of the countryside, with its broad rolling hills that gave way to shady thickets and gurgling streams.

"And to think we are so very near London!" Chloe exclaimed, holding fast to her chip straw bonnet as Winthrop took a narrow curve with finesse. Then flashing her blue eyes at him, she added, "You are ever so clever at handling the ribbons! Mama won't allow me to travel about in the open air. I should visit Chatford Abbey more often," she sighed as they crested a hill which afforded them a view of the village in the distance. Winthrop, glowing from her compliment, urged the bays to a fast canter, assuring Chloe that it was quite safe, especially since the road had widened enough to take three coaches abreast. She laughed gaily in return, saying that above all she loved an adventure, and alas, due to her mama's ideas, she had never really lived and, quite frankly, found life in Bath to be tedious.

By the time Winthrop tooled the gig into Kirk Cross village he and Pandora had learned of the trials which their cousin had endured; not that she sought pity—far from it—but her calm recitation of how her mama, widowed with a handsome inheritance, had embarked upon a career of taking the waters, sounded grim indeed.

"And even though I've never mentioned this before, I have always looked upon my sojourns at Chatford as bright spots. For Mama would not dream of coming to the country—it makes her sneeze, you know. Oh, I feel so free and adventuresome here."

Pandora, who until now had had few qualms about the charade she was about to thrust upon them, asked, "Does Aunt Statira know of your thirst for excitement?"

"Oh, no! But it needn't signify, for she will never come here, and need never learn of any escapades. Besides, Mama is most content to remain with her friends in Bath, though she will most certainly come to London when I am presented." Swiveling her head about, Chloe let out a peal of delight at the poke bonnet in the milliner's shop window. They would simply have to stop there, and yes, at the confectioners' for Aunt Beatrix's chocolate; and further down the street Chloe spotted several more establishments that demanded investigation.

By the time the afternoon was drawing to a close, they had visited nearly every shop in Kirk Cross, or so it seemed to Pandora, who was at the ready for her drama to commence. The scene was set: they were walking close to the Orange Crown, but just as she readied for her move, Chloe, not so accustomed to rushing about on an unseasonably warm afternoon, suddenly turned quite pale and without forewarning, noiselessly fainted forward. A startled Winthrop caught her, and heroically sweeping her into his arms, headed straight for the Orange Crown.

"She needs a restorative!" He tossed this observation over his shoulder at Pandora, who, stunned that Chloe had achieved the very faint that she herself had planned, dazedly followed in her brother's footsteps. That their little cousin actually *did* faint was hardly to be credited! Well, at least they were inside the inn, and if Pandora's timing was correct, the Viscount would be preparing for tea—for whatever his faults, he did seem as one who observed life's amenities.

Winthrop, on good terms with the innkeeper, was immediately led to a private parlor on the upper floor: this was followed by a string of commands given to the chambermaid, who bustled about with brandy, cooling cloths, and assurances that the 'miss' would be in fine fettle. Miss's eyes *did* flutter open, whereupon Winthrop clasped her hand and muttered endearments. Pandora, sitting beside Chloe on the divan, urged some brandy on her.

After obediently taking a sip, she managed to say, "Oh, that was horrid of me to interrupt our shopping that way!" Then in a faltering voice, she added, "How ever shall I manage when we go to London with Aunt Beatrix? Oh, I am mortified."

"Silly goose!" Pandora chided gently, "You shall do splendidly, for I've a notion this spell was due to your picky appetite at luncheon, but then I dislike grilled kidneys with a passion myself, especially since they were also presented in a pie for breakfast!"

Chloe laughed, admitting, "I am not overfond of them."

"Then we shan't have them again!" Winthrop announced, springing to his feet. He was about to add something of significance but for the rap on the door and the subsequent appearance of the innkeeper conveying my Lord Cardew's request to pay a call.

Winthrop turned to Pandora, his fear unspoken that she might allude to his gambling past with the Viscount. Instead he managed a taut, "I think it eminently thoughtful of the fellow to ask after us."

"Oh, assuredly," Pandora agreed, marveling that she hadn't had to *do* anything to bring about the Viscount's visit:

with an innocent smile, she added, "I daresay if Chloe is feeling better we should receive him."

"Yes! This is the greatest excitement!" Sitting up, Chloe immediately began to smooth out her sky blue frock, then as an afterthought took her bonnet from her head and put it to one side. "I do not look a wreck, I pray."

"Not at all, Chloe," Pandora assured her as she brushed a golden lock from her cousin's forehead. Winthrop, still concerned that his sister might say something untoward to or about the Viscount, began to pace the chamber in an agitated fashion.

"Winny, do alight some place or you shall have us all in the fidgets!" She pressed a knowing look on him. "We will have a most enjoyable time of it; perhaps Lord Cardew would care for some refreshment with us."

Relieved that Pandora was about her manners, Winthrop pulled the tasseled bellcord, and upon the chambermaid's inquiry, ordered an elaborate tea set, as the Viscount would be joining them. She curtsied at this intelligence and scurried from the room. Although the Orange Crown was a most respectable hostelry, courting the young bucks with its gaming rooms and private parlors, it rarely boasted a titled gentleman, and as such, much obsequious bowing and scraping did follow his consequence.

That Pandora's plan was actually under way brought her an instant flush of excitement, followed by an odd sensation of uneasiness: her palms, as she slid them over her jade-colored frock, were moist and trembled slightly; her heartbeat was both fast and irregular; and the high-ceilinged chamber suddenly seemed oppressively close. Like her cousin, she too had put her poke bonnet off and now imagined her curls to be in disarray. Oh, but what foolish thoughts! This was most unlike her, and no doubt due to the memory of her previous *and only* encounter with the Viscount. It was probably just as well it was Chloe and not she who had fainted, for Pandora sensed that Lord Cardew could see through a hoax just as rapidly as he could pull one off.

Just when she thought she might burst with anticipation, there was a rap on the door. Winthrop, perched on the edge of his chair, leapt to his feet, and with great ceremony opened the portal to present their esteemed guest, trailed by several serving girls carrying the resplendent tea.

Pandora's eyes locked immediately with the Viscount's, and to her mortification she felt her face go quite crimson. A glint of humor sparked in his vivid blue eyes, as if he could divine her every thought. Her responding heartbeat suggested that he probably could. Pulling her gaze from his, she chided herself for such idiocy.

This brief hiatus was quickly bridged and introductions were carried out with not so much as a raised eyebrow on the part of the Viscount. How delighted he was to make the acquaintance of Mr. Tremantle's sister and cousin, and he did hope Miss Deeds was feeling better. Naturally he made no reference to his gambling with Mr. Tremantle, and strike him from polite society should he mention having previously met Miss Tremantle! Thus, for the second time, Pandora was taken by the fact that whatever he might be now, he had at one time been a gentleman.

"Oh, and don't mind the lad," Lord Cardew remarked, indicating the same mysterious, dark-eyed child Pandora had spied on the landing of the Orange Crown. "He's my tiger, valet, *and* groom!"

"I expect he's kept quite busy," Pandora remarked as she poured out the tea.

"When I return to my estates, I shall divest the lad of so much responsibility, for Old Grimley will not take kindly to being replaced."

"Old Grimley?" The name leapt off Pandora's tongue as if it were a curse.

"Yes," the Viscount returned, "the old family retainer. He's a bit of a crusty chap, but soft as butter underneath. Now, this one—" Cardew indicated the dark-skinned boy behind his chair "—*looks* mild enough . . ." He let the words trail off, and accepting the tea from Pandora, added, "But don't let that deceive you."

"Where did you acquire the fellow?" Winthrop asked, passing the Viscount a plate of scones.

After a slight pause, he replied, "The south of France. Pleasant country, especially when we're not at war."

"How odd," Pandora couldn't resist saying. "The boy doesn't look French."

"Perhaps that's because he isn't," Lord Cardew countered, his dark brows forming distinctive arches above his hooded eyes. "The lad's originally from India, but I got him off a French fellow who was using him as a whipping post. I don't think he'll ever whip anyone again." He raised his teacup in a salutatory gesture, and allowed a rather remarkable smile to take possession of his lips, one which tingled Pandora from the tips of her slippered feet to the very roots of her fiery curls. And yet within a wink, the look vanished, leaving her bereft of speech. Winthrop and Chloe leaned forward in rapt fascination at what else this impeccably dressed peer of the realm would say.

Little did they know that the Viscount was about to expound on his smoothly crafted lie, albeit one nourished with a sprig of truth. "Chandro's his name: doesn't have a last name, so I've christened him with mine. Chandro Cardew."

"Oh, then you've adopted him?" Pandora sent him a decidedly devilish smile. Gads, he wished she wouldn't do that.

"Shall we say I'm indulging in a charitable whim?" He paused to estimate the extent of Miss Tremantle's knowledge. How in God's name was he to know Tremantle's sister was rabid on the subject of gambling? Cardew had considered it a fairly innocuous way to gather information. He was certainly not after the boy's blunt.

"Ah then," Cardew continued, "I suppose you're wondering why I didn't give him a Christian name, like Peter or Paul; though I doubt the Church of England would take to that, especially since he's probably a Hindu. What do you think, Miss Tremantle?" Dashed if he could take his eyes from her, and for the moment, be hanged the specter of his past, for he wished to enjoy this perusal: her hair was appealingly mussed, as if she'd just tumbled out of her bedchamber, and the growing spots of color on her high cheekbones heightened the flash in her emerald eyes. Pity that he didn't have more time to enjoy a flirtation with Miss Tremantle, for here was a lady to match wits with. Of course it could never go beyond that.

"Well?" he prodded at last, and setting his teacup on its saucer, he allowed his eyes to meet hers in a challenging look.

"Chandro is a charming name," she countered lightly, returning his challenge with aplomb. "Though he could be Buddhist or Muslim, you know. But then perhaps you're not familiar with India or her religions."

From the corner of the room a small voice said, "My name is Chandro Cardew. Hindu, memsahib!" His smile reminded Pandora of Jemnaz; the smile and the eyes were all you saw at first.

"Oh, do you speak English?" Pandora asked, forgetting her peckish banter with the Viscount.

"Very little," Lord Cardew answered a shade too quickly.

"Oh?" Pandora said with a tilt to her head, then turning her attention to Chandro was surprised by the way he imitated his master.

"Very little. But," the boy added confidently, "I learn quick."

The Viscount leaned back in his chair and laughed, "He's as smart as they come, but I'm afraid he has no use for English conventions, and due to his . . . treatment in France, he is loath to quit my side."

"How fortunate he is to have you for his champion," Chloe said, joining in the conversation. Her gaze settled fondly on Chandro, who, loving all this attention, grinned and repeated his name and religion several times as if he had discovered a magic formula.

This little interlude with the child put everyone, even Pandora, at apparent ease; and though enjoying her repartee with Cardew, she was still ever watchful of the man, for who knew what observation would prove a pivotal point in the future. That she should so immediately be rewarded was provident indeed, and once again it was her cousin who initiated the incident.

Yes, it was little Chloe, who in all innocence caused the Viscount to pale momentarily beneath his swarthy complexion. For Chloe, having lost some of her initial shyness, began to regale the Viscount with tales of Chatford Abbey, and how it had always been a haven for her. Lord Cardew seemed genuinely delighted with her narrative, and urged her to continue.

"And so I shall, for there is always something of consequence going on at the Abbey; why I expect you don't even know about the Marquess of Manakin, do you?"

It was then that Lord Cardew's color failed him. "There was talk of him some years back, I believe. But do continue."

"Blasted thing is," Winthrop interjected on a laugh, "we can't pry the tale out of him. He only alludes to some indiscretion." Turning to his cousin, he added, "Forgive my interrupting, Chloe, for from the look on Lord Cardew's face, you've quite swept him up in your tale."

"I am most curious; pray continue," the Viscount said, managing to compose himself on the instant.

Chloe, now thoroughly enjoying her role as story teller, paused dramatically before continuing in a voice filled with the portent of adventure. "The Marquess came straight from India to Chatford, bearing with him a letter from Uncle Horry—that's Pandora's and Winthrop's father—which introduced him as his dear friend, and further invited his lordship to remain as guest at the Abbey; but the greatest of gossip is that some years ago he *did* do something which evidently cast him out of society, though what it was we cannot fathom—as Winthrop was just saying. But of course Uncle Horry has never been one to give a fig about what is proper—which is probably why he and my mama do not get on so well. Oh, but I digress! What was I saying? Ah, yes, Lord Manakin will be staying until Uncle returns from India. Oh, Pandora, do show Lord Cardew the lovely ruby pendant your father sent you!"

"Manakin at Chatford . . . now?" The Viscount's eyes clouded over, and it seemed to Pandora he wished to hide something.

Once again she couldn't resist the temptation to speak. "Perhaps you know more of this Marquess than we do. What, for example, *was* the scandal surrounding him?" Her smile belied the look that accompanied this query.

"All gossip," the Viscount said on a perfunctory note, as he glanced casually at the ruby pendant. Pandora's fingers closed about the jewel, pleased with the immediate curiosity this gesture produced.

"Gossip drove the Marquess all the way to India?" she taunted playfully.

"It has been known to cause worse than that, Miss Tremantle." His jaw line tightened, and though the look he sent her was inscrutable and slightly dangerous, she felt herself unwittingly being drawn to him. She blinked her eyes rapidly in an attempt to ward off this spell. They were a chair's distance away, innocent teacups between them, and his eyes, glittering like ice chips, stared deep within hers.

"The ruby is lovely," he murmured.

"Pandora's papa is most generous," Chloe informed the Viscount. "Though he mostly sends old books no one can read, *and* children that apparently no one wants. Well, only one so far. But that ruby was supposed to be the second orphan!" She indicated the stone in question, then blithely continued her remarkable discourse. "The letter of introduction which Uncle gave the Marquess referred to another of 'India's true jewels,' which, you see, was Uncle Horry's way of indicating another orphan like Jemnaz Singh was on his way." She shrugged her pretty shoulders, "I suppose he couldn't find one this time, and sent a real jewel in his place."

"Pandora got a ruby, instead of an orphan," Winthrop summed up breezily, all the while his devoted eyes on Chloe, who nodded in agreement. "You do have a way with words, Winny," she added softly.

"You have painted an intriguing picture." Once again the Viscount's dark brows made their familiar arch above his eyes, with a sharpness suggestive of a gambler who held the winning card. "I would enjoy meeting this mysterious Marquess sometime," he said with an insouciance that didn't fool Pandora for a moment.

Sufficiently recovered from the unsettling looks he had given her earlier, Pandora said, "I expect he will be at tea three days hence; I believe that is when Auntie has invited you."

"We needn't wait so long, Miss Tremantle. In fact, it would give me immense pleasure to make a party of it sooner—say at Vauxhall Gardens?"

"Oh, how splendid!" Chloe cried, clapping her hands with childlike delight, then with an "Oh!" she pressed those same little hands to her mouth as if she'd just been caught at the sweets. Reluctantly she lowered them, her face crinkled with chagrin. "I have inherited one of the fatal family flaws," she informed his lordship, whose mood had shifted to one of unsuppressed mirth at Miss Deeds's conduct, "of talking too much and at the wrong time." She made quite a furor of her brow, adding, "Mama says I must break this deplorable habit, or Almack's will not have me; indeed, perhaps no one shall."

"Pray what are the other family flaws?" Lord Cardew asked with a laugh.

"Oh, Mama wouldn't tell me." She dimpled a smile at the Viscount, "Still and all, I must watch my tongue."

"I think your behavior charming," Winthrop uttered. Then swinging around, he met Cardew's gaze and added, "I but echo Chloe's enthusiasm for the venture, as I am sure does my sister."

"I think it would be delightful, and what a clever idea for you to suggest, Lord Cardew." Pandora tilted her chin and gave him what she hoped to be a knowing look, and though somewhat taken aback by the frank appraisal he tendered in return, she held her gaze.

"Then I shall make all arrangements; we could have a stroll about the gardens, then partake of supper and perhaps listen to a concert—or who knows but we might happen upon some fireworks." At Chloe's murmur of delight, he added, "I thought that might please you." Pandora noted, but questioned the smile that touched his lips.

"You are ever the sport!" Winthrop delivered in a tone of camaraderie, as if he had known this Viscount for an age.

"The pleasure is mine." Cardew's eyes lingered briefly on Pandora before adding, "The evening will be quite a daze."

"I, for one, am beside myself!" Chloe said in thorough rapture. "For you see, I've never even been to *London*, much less Vauxhall, where I'm given to understand light skirts mingle with the Ton." Biting down on her lower lip, she quickly added, "Well, that's what I've heard!" Emboldened by the merriment her remark caused, she gaily continued, "And on occasion Vauxhall holds grand masquerade balls wherein those same ladies might come disguised as quality! For example, an actress could aspire to duchess!"

"Or a villain to a . . . Viscount," Pandora added softly.

"Pity we shall be in dominos and not costumes," Lord Cardew remarked on a purposeful note. "Perhaps we could make a return engagement later in the season: I expect it should be rather amusing to play a 'flash cove.' "

"My sister did not mean to imply, my lord, that you are—"

"A *villain?*" the Viscount repeated for the incredulous Winthrop, who in turn was giving his unrepentant sister black looks.

"It was but a turn of phrase," Pandora said, smoothing over the wrinkle in the fabric of the afternoon. Once again she felt the heat of the Viscount's gaze as it settled on her. Then with an unconscious flutter of lashes, she looked into his ice blue eyes and wondered if he knew her suspicions, and if so, what he would do about it. How her moods did swing: bandying words with him one minute, and suspecting the worse the next. Abruptly her gaze dropped from the veiled look he sent her. That he had planned an evening of supposed gaiety at Vauxhall Gardens was probably a ruse, but for what she wasn't certain, unless he *was* after the jewels and intended to have an accomplice search for them while everyone was at Vauxhall. It would prove utterly fruitless of course, for Pandora was certain they were not there. Be that as it may, perhaps the Viscount was trying to gain information by wining and dining them. She could not conceive of any real danger in the outing, but none the less, *should* anything go afoul at Vauxhall, her brother's Forsythe pocket pistol secreted in her reticule would definitely come in handy.

Had Cardew known the extent of Miss Tremantle's inner drama, he might have entertained some reservations, instead of the intermittent pangs of damnable attraction that struck him like a craving for a rare and untried wine. The girl had spirit and a good mind, both of which engaged him, but there was something about the spark behind the emerald eyes that lured him far more than any jewel on earth could. Perhaps he was a fool to have suggested Vauxhall, but he wanted to see this *Marquess of Manakin,* and preferably before Miss

McClellan's tea. And he could not deny a certain attraction at the prospect of Vauxhall with Miss Tremantle, though he would no doubt roundly curse the gods for setting temptation in his path; for surely that way disaster lay.

The following morning gave no hint of its tumultuous climax. Pandora was not surprised that Lord Manakin declined the invitation to Vauxhall; having pleaded the headache he retired to his chambers before the Viscount's arrival. Was he, in fact, acting on her father's behalf, guarding the Abbey, as it were? Or did he have reasons of his own for staying behind? Once again she remembered Manakin's startled reaction at Cardew's name. Well, if the Marquess was up to no good, he would be in for a surprise: for at Pandora's request, Nora was keeping a watch over him.

Pandora was thus assured that all would go smoothly that evening. Their party looked handsome indeed: beneath dark cloaks—for the evening presaged a slight chill—the ladies were decked out in their finery. Pandora sparkled like a gold coin, outfitted in a silk gown that flowed unadorned to the prescribed length in a classic line that suited her tall, slender frame. A gold domino concealed her identity; and Nora had tamed Pandora's unruly locks into several thick curls that lay like tongues of fire against the tops of her ivory shoulders. Around her neck she wore a black velvet choker which held the ruby—*and* Lord Cardew's gaze.

Chloe, in gentle contrast to her cousin's fiery presence, was charmingly arrayed in a pale blue satin frock with a plethora of bows, and a darker blue satin domino, and looked—as Winthrop assured her—good enough to eat. It fell to Aunt Beatrix, however, to command center stage, resplendent in what could only be described as a 'costume' of puce velveteen, which did grapple the woman's body with a life of its own. Indeed, beside this vision, the gentlemen fell into the shade, though even Pandora had to admit that Lord Cardew—attired wholly in black save for the immaculate, if somewhat severe, neckcloth—presented a picture of quiet elegance, though his black domino added a sinister touch. Winthrop was more nattily spruced up in yellow pantaloons, matching waistcoat, and a deep green long-tailed coat; his highest achievement, however, was the intricate stock at his neck, from whose folds gleamed a single diamond.

Thus it was that this exquisitely arrayed party did arrive at Vauxhall Gardens just as dusk was settling its peach glow across London. The Viscount had engaged one of the more festively decorated booths, which afforded not only an excellent view of the orchestra, but of other couples, too, as they strolled the gardens. Colorful paper lanterns positioned about the lush grounds spilled a roseate glow on peasant and nobleman alike, for whoever could pay the few shillings entrance fee could take his pleasure. Chloe was the first to give vocal appreciation of this fact.

"Look!" she whispered in hurried tones, as a gawdy creature with quantities of brass-colored curls and face paint sailed by them in a bit of scarlet satin that revealed more than it covered.

"My dear," Beatrix intoned, rapping Chloe with her ostrich plume fan, "we do not notice *them;* I should have thought Statira would have taught you that." Then with a swish of her remarkable puce skirts, she entered the booth and accepted the chair which the Viscount held for her. "Do come and sit down, child," she added more kindly; for her niece, enthralled at the passing sights, stood stock-still at the entrance of their booth. However, as Winthrop stepped forward to remove her cloak, she whirled towards him, eyes glowing with an expectancy which announced she'd much rather be mingling with the throng than sitting down to supper.

Lord Cardew, helping Pandora out of her wrap, allowed his hands to pause longer than necessary on her shoulders—or was it her imagination? His touch was cool, and she felt a shiver pass through her. Averting her gaze from his scrutiny—for his eyes had rarely left her all evening—she sat beside her aunt at the small table provided for refreshments and tried to collect herself as Lord Cardew spoke quietly to the waiter. He was being quite charming, but then many a villain played that role to perfection. Idly her fingers went to the ruby at her throat: only today she'd arranged to have it appraised. At least if someone was ransacking the Abbey, they wouldn't find the ruby! Her thoughts were interrupted as a bottle of chilled white wine appeared. Lord Cardew, after ascertaining the vintage to be sound, proposed a toast to the ladies.

The conversation that followed was as light as the supper, which consisted of clear broth, white fish in an herbed sauce, paper-thin slices of ham, and a brandied fruit compote. Despite the excellence of the dinner, Pandora found her appetite somewhat lacking, for the Viscount's presence was more disturbing than she would have imagined, and in a way she could hardly credit. How different he suddenly seemed; or was it the two glasses of wine she had consumed? For his rough edges were softened by lantern light, the jagged scar not quite so menacing, and yet the easy smile his lips possessed waged a private battle with the hooded, veiled eyes. There was more to this man than met the eye. Off in the distance she heard the musicians tuning their instruments preparatory to further dancing, and as waiters whisked the empty plates from their table the Viscount requested the pleasure of a dance with her.

"Certainly do!" Beatrix urged on a jubilant note, then with a nod at Chloe and Winthrop, added, "And don't imagine I shall pine away if left alone. Just remember, Chloe, you haven't been presented, so no waltzing for you. But I expect the sights, which so captivated you earlier, will be sufficient reward." There was a twinkle in her brown eyes, and her mouth curved in a generous smile.

Since there was no escaping the inevitable, Pandora politely acquiesced to Lord Cardew's invitation, praying her inner turmoil wasn't too apparent. Nothing, however, had prepared her for the experience of being taken in the arms of a man who knew how to hold a woman. Not in her two seasons at Almack's had *any* gentleman literally swept her off her feet, the way the Viscount did! No sooner had they reached the rotunda where the dancing was held, then he slipped one powerful arm around her waist and in a fluid motion drew her onto the floor. His other hand tingled against her palm as skin touched skin. Then, as if a magic wand had been waved over them, they seemed to float in time to the waltz music: around and around they spun as colored lights twinkled above. She felt a little dizzy, and breathing deeply took in the scent of him: woodsmoke and leather. He had tightened his arms about her, drawing her slender form with its pounding heart against him; he was lean and hard and oh so warm, and his heartbeat was steady. She wanted to look at him, into those eyes, and see if the veil was still in place, but she daren't, for he was too close. It would not be seemly. Ha! Seemly indeed! Would that her thoughts followed a logic, rather than the erratic pendulum swings she was experiencing.

Yet in the warm circle of his arms, her thoughts came in a jumble of confusion: was he villain or Viscount, or both? Her slippered feet hardly touched the ground, she might have been a feather captured on the wind, spinning higher and higher, but that the music concluded, and for one dizzy moment she held to his sleeve before stepping from his embrace.

Whatever moonlight magic he was weaving was quickly dashed to pieces, as she felt him stiffen beside her, but before she could say anything, he had her firmly by the elbow and was steering her from the floor.

"There is a matter I must attend to," he managed with civility, his gaze searching out the shadowed paths leading to the dancing arena. "I just saw an old friend, and must speak with him, so I will return you to our booth—"

"But—"

"When my business is concluded we will all seek out a favorable spot to view the fireworks. I shall explain later." His eyes darted to the ruby at her throat, then gripping her arm, he abruptly led her back to their box, and after repeating these same excuses to Miss McClellan, made a hurried departure.

"I think the man is touched in his upper story," Pandora said after a stunned moment.

"Oh?" Beatrix drawled. "Your last condemnations were merely gambler and impostor; tut! He is a gentleman of the first stare, and I cannot impress upon you how fortunate you are to have him dangle after you."

"*Dangle* after me?" Unwittingly Pandora's pulse raced at the suggestion. But with a contrary laugh she added, "I doubt he dangles after anything but the turn of a card. He's naught but a crack-brained gambler." Feeling her cheeks glow with a betraying flush of color, she wished she had kept her own counsel. The evening was not progressing the way she had planned.

"Pandora!" her aunt scolded. "Why, Lord Cardew has been bestowing burning looks on you all evening."

"Perhaps he's trying to burn me—as a witch, no doubt!"

"Tut! Why, it wouldn't surprise me if he is at this very moment arranging a little tryst in some secluded spot in the gardens." Her fan was unnecessarily engaged in cooling her brow, her eyes glazed with the rapture of a budding romance. She would have expounded further, but for a messenger who appeared with a sealed missive for Miss Tremantle.

"It's from him, is it not?" her aunt uttered in transports of delight. "Importuning you to meet with him!" Impatiently she leaned forward in an attempt to read the message.

"How perceptive of you," Pandora said on a distinct note of sarcasm. Tossing the hastily scrawled message on the table, she added, "This quite puts the seal on his madness."

"Nonsense!" Beatrix snatched the note. "He is in the throes of love, which *is* a madness of sorts. Why, here you have it, clear as glass." Holding the note some distance from her, she practically warbled the message: " 'My dear Miss Tremantle, I entreat you to meet me in the fifth summer house by the Cupid fountain on a matter of the utmost importance. You know who I am!' "

Beatrix clasped the love note to her as if she herself had been the recipient. "Oh, too divine! Naturally, you won't go: still, how clever of him. You know, Mrs. Hawkshore's latest romance, *The Dangerous Duke,* employs this very device; of course you must not do what her heroine did, for she was cut from all the lists, and had not the Duke—"

"I am going!" Pandora smiled, sprung to her feet, and without giving her aunt a chance to further protest, pulled her dark cloak about her like a raiment of the night and hurried out of the booth.

Having been to Vauxhall several times she knew exactly where the summer house was, and was so engrossed in rehearsing her diatribe against the Viscount that she hardly gave a thought to where her slippered feet carried her. The full moon sliced through thick clouds, then rolled lazily like a silver coin onto the velvet fabric of the night; above an arch of dark trees only a smattering of stars could be seen. But Pandora, whose breathing echoed her rapid heartbeat, noticed none of this, and though there was a cool breeze, she felt quite warm; too warm, almost out of breath. She slowed her pace, and noted that the area, save for a few couples strolling arm in arm, was practically deserted. A prickle of irrational panic inched up her spine; she tossed this off, and gripping her reticule *and* the Forsythe pistol hidden within, assured herself there was nothing to fear. Still, a small voice posed unanswered questions: why had the Viscount left so abruptly? Surely not to arrange this rendezvous! That was utter poppycock . . . unless he *did* intend to lure her there for other purposes. But what?

Up ahead the stone Cupid baby shimmered in the moonlight. A stream of water gurgled from his mouth, and an arrow pointed at the summer house. Would he be inside . . . waiting? She paused for a moment, listening for some clue, but only distant music, faint sounds of revelry, and the wind in the trees filled the air. With a defiant toss of her head, Pandora crossed the damp grass, passed the Cupid baby, and entered the summer house.

"Lord Cardew?" Her voice sounded odd in the little gazebo, and she hated the way it quavered. In an attempt to quell her fears, she stepped further into the enclosure and repeated his name in a somewhat stronger voice. It was then she heard the footfall behind her—too late. Panic closed in, followed by a curtain of darkness as she crumpled beneath the blow to her head.

Chapter Four

"Miss Tremantle! Miss Tremantle!" Pandora heard her name through layers of blackness as she struggled to open her eyes, but even that minor exertion brought awareness of the throbbing pain at the back of her head.

"Oh," she moaned, as her hand instinctively reached for her head, only to fall back limply.

"Easy now," the concerned voice counseled. "It could have been worse, though."

Slowly her eyes opened and stared at the blurry outline of a man's face. "What happened?" she heard herself ask.

"You were hit upon the head, knocked out, *and* robbed." At this, Pandora attempted to sit up, only to be struck back by a wave of dizziness. After a moment she opened her eyes, and recognizing the Viscount, said, "But you were—" Abruptly she cut herself off, then quickly added, "*Robbed,* you say? They shall find very little save for Winny's pistol in my reticule." She winced in pain. "Did they have to hit me quite so hard?" This time her hand *did* tentatively touch the back of her head.

"They were not interested in your reticule *or* your pistol," the Viscount said, his voice ringing with sharpness. In a gentler tone he added, "Do you think that with my assistance you could walk back to our booth? For Miss McClellan was quite upset when I left her."

Pandora's eyes flew wide open at this remark. "You saw her?"

"Of course. She had some strange idea that I had sent you a note to meet me in one of the summer houses."

"But didn't you?"

"No, Miss Tremantle, I did not: I leave off such theatrics." Gently he brushed a lock of hair from the side of her face, and with an odd smile, he said, "We should get you back home as soon as possible, for I imagine several days' bed rest is what you'll need."

"Do you mean to say," Pandora began, quite ignoring his medical advice regarding her unfortunate condition, "That you *didn't* send me that message?"

"Heavens, Miss Tremantle, would you prefer that I had?" A hint of amusement laced his voice.

"No. Of course not!" Pandora winced again, and after a moment, she said, "It's just that no one else knew I was here, and so naturally Aunt Beatrix and I thought . . . well, that it was you!"

"Well, you may dispossess yourself of such fancies; though I would most certainly like to know who *did* send it." The moonlight masked his face in silver, but the dangerous glint in his eyes was plain to see. Then, of a sudden, it vanished and he was all solicitousness.

"Miss Tremantle, I think it best if we start back, for I truly believe your aunt capable of rousing the Bow Street Runners if we dally much longer."

Biting back a grimace of pain, Pandora allowed the Viscount to assist her to her feet. Then pausing at the steps leading to the walk, she suddenly reached for the ruby choker. "It's gone!"

"Yes, I'm afraid that's what the thief was after. You needn't worry about your reticule. I've got that." His arm tightened about her, and without saying another word, he led her carefully down the steps.

"I can't believe that anyone would . . ." She groped for the words which the Viscount neatly supplied.

"Knock you over the head for a jewel? I would quite believe anything these days. Watch your step," he warned as they navigated the flagstone path surrounding the Cupid Baby. "We wouldn't want another mishap."

Pandora fell silent. She wished her head didn't hurt quite

so much, for there were a great many things that needed explanations. But for the moment, feeling slightly woozy, it was all she could do to get back to their booth. As far as Lord Cardew's assistance went, she was beginning to think she would be safer without it. Yes, he was attractive, solicitous, and even handsome—in the way novelists portray highwaymen and pirates! But her ruby was gone, and was possibly on the Viscount's person. But why? Why would he have stolen it? Perhaps it *was* part of the Snow Leopard collection; but surely her father would have warned her and the Marquess to take greater care. Unless of course Cardew and Manakin were working together. If so, had they meant to lull her into trusting them? If only her head didn't ache so much. Could it be that the Viscount had indeed just accosted her? If that were the case, he certainly was a good actor. Too good. For despite everything, she found herself strangely attracted to him. Even now, with his arm encircling her, she felt a strange longing deep within her for this mysterious Viscount.

By the time they reached their booth, Pandora's emotions were in such a jangle that she had almost forgotten her sorely abused head, and perhaps might have, were it not for Beatrix, who, having attracted quite a little scene with her near hysterics, shooed her concerned audience from the booth and descended upon her niece like a mother hen upon a chick.

"Oh, my precious!" she wailed, drawing Pandora into a chair, then with a shudder and a tiny step back, she managed, "Your . . . your coiffure!" Gingerly she touched the back of her niece's head, then withdrew it immediately. "Great heavens! Whatever has happened?"

"Just an accident," Pandora fibbed quite simply, then seeing the look of horror on Chloe's face, added, "But I am recovered; thanks to Lord Cardew's timely appearance."

"Oh, this is not to be credited!" Beatrix announced. "We must immediately fetch a surgeon to our box!" She waved a lace handkerchief in midair as if the doctor were a footman for whom she might ring.

Cardew, who had kept quiet counsel during this drama, interrupted: "It might perhaps be wiser to remove Miss Tremantle to a quieter place, for though you've sent the curious on their way, they still linger outside." With a nonchalant gesture he indicated the knot of people who were viewing the little scene as if it were an interlude at Covent Garden.

"Lord Cardew is absolutely right," Winthrop volunteered, then stepping forward inspected the back of his sister's head. "Nasty blow that. Egad. Did you truly fall, Pandora, or were you set upon by footpads?"

"For my ruby," Pandora replied somewhat wryly. "And yet they left my reticule alone."

"Oh, my sainted mother!" Beatrix gasped. "Set upon!" Collapsing into a chair next to Pandora and looking thoroughly rumpled in her puce velveteen, she managed to add, "It is nearly the end of the world when one cannot enjoy an evening abroad." Her hand trailed a vague gesture in the air, then suddenly clasping it to her bosom, she cried, "We must call for the Bow Street Runners!"

"Allow me to handle that, Miss McClellan," Lord Cardew hastily replied. "But in the meantime, Miss Tremantle should probably be transported back home, so if you will excuse me, I'll see to having the carriage brought round to the gate."

"Lord Cardew, we are so indebted to you," Beatrix said with genuine gratitude, rising as the Viscount withdrew from their box. She then settled her concerned gaze on Pandora, "It is of the highest luck that the Viscount rescued you, or heaven knows how long you would have lain in that summer house! And to think we believed he sent you that note!"

"It is all very extraordinary," Chloe said. "But if Lord Cardew didn't send the message, who did?"

"One of my secret admirers, no doubt," Pandora replied with a feeble laugh. For the time being, she would keep her suspicions to herself.

"Of course you jest," her cousin said with a shake of her blond curls. "But to think, that somewhere out there is a very wicked person who accosted and robbed you! And under the pretense of an assignation!"

"I went out of stupid curiosity," Pandora, tiring of this talk, blurted out. "Not for an amorous tryst, I assure you."

"I was rather hoping it *was* the Viscount," Winthrop offered. "For the chap does seem keen on you, and I daresay he'd make a *demned* fine protector for you."

"Oh, that he would," Beatrix interjected.

"I do not need a protector!" Pandora said with a firmness that sent a sharp pain through her head.

"You do if you insist on traipsing about unescorted!" Pressing a handkerchief to her brow, Beatrix—having nearly forgotten her niece's injury—was about to launch into a lecture on decorum, when Pandora leaned forward and thoroughly alarmed her by cradling her head in her arms.

"Oh, mercy!" her aunt cried. "Speak to us!" Catapulting out of her chair, Beatrix sloshed the last bit of wine into a glass, and standing over Pandora, thrust the goblet at her.

"Are you feeling very sick?" Chloe asked in a most concerned way.

"I shall feel ever so much better after a night's rest." Accepting the wine from her aunt, she threw her a grateful glance, though in fact it was the last thing she wanted.

"In that case, I would suggest you stay in London tonight." This advice came from the Viscount, who along with an older gentleman had just stepped into the booth. "Wouldn't you agree, doctor?"

The physician, a florid man of remarkable rotundity, who sported several chins and a burgundy waistcoat with buttons which threatened to pop with every breath he took, was in complete agreement. Thus, after assuring Miss Tremantle that her wound was superficial, he instructed the Viscount on proper cleansing of the abrasion. After stressing that two days' bed rest was mandatory, he took his leave.

At that point Pandora would have agreed to almost anything; for in truth, her head was beginning to throb incessantly. They would definitely spend the night in London. Then, if Pandora was feeling up to it, they would return to Chatford Abbey on the morrow.

Pandora didn't even mind the Viscount's ministrations, though she was somewhat surprised at his expertise in tending to her head wound. Naturally the skeleton staff of the town house on Grosvenor Square buzzed with curiosity about Miss Pandora's "accident," but were shortly put to work with various imperious commands, which Miss McClellan was quite adept at issuing: a message was to be sent to the staff at Chatford informing them of their unexpected stop in London; the maids were to prepare several chambers immediately; and when the housekeeper looked somewhat askance at Chandro, who hovered near his master, she was informed that the Indian boy would naturally be quartered belowstairs. Furthermore, laudanum would be required for Miss Pandora, and she was not to be disturbed until ten-thirty at the earliest the following morning.

Thus it was that Pandora, having been tended to by the man she suspected responsible for her injury in the first place, drank her sleeping potion and drifted into a dreamless sleep.

Upon awakening, however, with naught but a whisper of a headache, she marveled at the series of incidents involving the Marquess and the Viscount.

While drinking her morning chocolate, which arrived promptly at ten-thirty, Pandora rethought the various possibilities. That the Viscount's behavior had been strange last night was surely a fact. But would he go so far as to lure her into the summer house, knock her out, steal the ruby, and then don the hero's mask and not only revive her, but tend to her wounds as well?

Not waiting for Nora's assistance, she performed her ablutions, then slipped into a simple morning dress of pale pink, from a wardrobe kept at the ready at their town house. With a sigh of regret she glanced at the gown she had worn to Vauxhall: the gold silk fabric was not only crushed and torn from her fall, but there were dirt and grass stains that would never come out.

Throughout breakfast, which thankfully did not include kidneys in any form, Pandora attempted casually to make a study of the Viscount; but every time she looked in his direction, he caught and held her glance with one of his own. At length she gave up this line of investigation, and turned her attention to Chloe and Winthrop, who—if possible—were more deeply involved with each other than the night before. It appeared, at least as far as Pandora could tell, that Chloe had worked a miracle on Winthrop, for snatches of conversation she caught included his avowed antipathy to gambling! And from the grateful look he shot the Viscount, it was obvious that he had been apprised of this new situation.

After breakfast and preparatory to their departure for Chatford, Lord Cardew, within earshot of Pandora, asked

Miss McClellan if she still had the note that had lured Miss Tremantle to the summer house. Yes, indeed, she replied, and withdrawing it from her reticule, presented it to the Viscount as if it were a great prize. There was a curious look about his face upon perusing it, then after a moment he returned it to her, and with a sudden chuckle said the message was a bit dramatic for him. Beatrix beamed at his lordship and declared that he had truly been their savior that evening.

Savior, indeed! Pandora thought, as Lord Cardew helped her into the carriage. It was obvious that Aunt Beatrix was thoroughly bewitched by the man, to such an extent that, were it in her power, she would have bestowed not only Pandora upon his pleasure, but their lovely town house too. As it was, Aunt Bea had arranged a dinner invitation for him that evening at the Waverlys'. Why, indeed, he appeared to have supplanted the Marquess in Aunt Bea's affections. Pandora preferred *not* to think about the effect Lord Cardew was having on herself; the man definitely had more charm than should be allowed, she decided, settling in her seat opposite him for the journey home.

"I trust you're feeling better?" he inquired after a beat, his features drawn in magnificent concern.

"Yes," she replied, all too aware of the brittle smile that threatened to crack her face.

"I hope you are not too upset about the ruby."

"I shall miss it," she managed to say, her fingers straying to the plain choker she had put on that morning. *And I shall find it too!* she thought, suddenly possessed of a desire to search his lordship's belongings *before* he returned to the Orange Crown. And although Pandora applied her considerable talents towards this end, she was quite frustrated by Lord Cardew's hasty departure upon their arrival at Chatford Abbey.

Aunt Beatrix, seeing her peeved expression as the Viscount's carriage disappeared in a trail of dust, clapped her hands ecstatically, and barring her niece's passage to the upstairs, said in a most indicting fashion, "You *do* hold a tendre for Lord Cardew!"

"Nothing of the sort," Pandora countered, thoroughly displeased that she should display *any* emotion whatsoever concerning the Viscount. With a shrug of her shoulders, she added, in a voice loud enough to reach Winthrop and Chloe, who had withdrawn to the next room, "I assure you, seeing the Viscount's tailcoat, if anything, should put me in fine fettle!"

"Well, in the carriage you seemed rather friendly towards him. And when he declined my invite to luncheon, you looked positively grieved!" Beatrix sniffed the air as if she had achieved the last word.

"It was the headache that elicited that response, nothing more, I assure you." With a dramatic gesture worthy of her aunt, she touched her brow, and murmured, "I do believe I *will* take the doctor's advice and rest a while."

"Oh, of course, my precious!" Fluttering forward, the older woman put a comforting arm about Pandora's shoulders, and leading her up the stairs, added, "How thoughtless of me to be chattering away after that dreadful battering you received last night. Still, I must say it was a stroke of luck that Lord Cardew came upon you when he did."

"Pity he didn't get there sooner."

This last sailed over Beatrix's head as she expounded on the mysterious assailant, and by the time they had reached Pandora's bedchamber, her aunt had played out a particularly gruesome scenario concerning possible motives, all having relevance to her favored read, *The Dangerous Duke.*

"And so you see, my dear, I was right after all," Miss McClellan concluded as she turned down the fluffy counterpane on her niece's bed. "For you do recall my warning you that it was Lady Flavia's headstrong flight into the night air that brought about her abduction; and yet, you did exactly the same thing, and got a bump on the head for your pains." With a prim pat to the bed, she indicated Pandora should have a lie down. "I am amazed that the Viscount's gallant rescue but mirrored the feats of the Dangerous Duke!"

"Does this mean I can cavort about the countryside with the certain knowledge that Lord Cardew shall leap to my aid when necessary?" Then seeing the look of horror on her aunt's face, she quickly added, "Never fear. I promise not to test the Viscount's endurance." With this, Pandora climbed into bed, and pulling the coverlet over herself, added,

"I'm too weary to even change." She made a prodigious yawn, which succeeded in sending her aunt from the room.

However, she was *not* tired, and thankfully her injuries were remarkably slight, considering her having been rendered unconscious. Gently she touched the bump on the back of her head, and discovered it was indeed still sore.

Pushing herself up in bed, she again reviewed the entire drama, which had begun with her descent upon the Viscount at the Orange Crown Inn, and had culminated with the head-bashing incident in the summer house. Perhaps it would help if she wrote everything in her diary: both the sequence of events and her reactions to them.

Thus it was that Pandora spent the afternoon industriously inscribing each event in her leather-bound journal, and it wasn't until Nora rapped on her door to announce tea that she stopped. Her fingers were ink stained and her head ached ever so slightly, but she had completed the project, and this alone cheered her immeasurably.

The sight of the Marquess taking tea and apparently holding court in the drawing room almost succeeded in casting a pall over Pandora's good mood, but forcing a smile to her lips, she entered the room and quietly took a seat next to Chloe on the gold chaise.

Lord Manakin rose with alacrity, and making a spectacular leg, said, "Miss Tremantle, I trust you are feeling better after that brutal attack you suffered in Vauxhall! I blame myself for declining to accompany your party." He came out of his courtly gesture and assumed a rigid posture, as if she were royalty.

"I am sufficiently recovered, thank you, but please resume your conversation. It is assuredly more interesting than this tale of my attack." Helping herself to a cup of tea and a small scone, she sent the Marquess what she hoped was an encouraging look, but was somewhat taken aback by the curious expression on his face as he made a study of her hands.

"You perhaps pen verse?" he queried at length, his eyes flickering back to her face. "I couldn't help but notice the ink stains, and being a sometime poet myself, I too suffer the same problem." With immaculate hands he raised a delicate Wedgwood teacup and offered a thin smile over its rim.

"Ha!" Winthrop interjected, "Not poetry! She's far too down to earth for that! But Pandy *is* cracked on her diary. Everything goes in it."

"Aha," the Marquess drawled. "Do you plan to publish it?"

"Heavens no!" Beatrix said hastily, then as an afterthought she added, "Of course, if she were to use a nom de plume like Mrs. Hawkshore does . . ." Swinging her gaze towards Pandora, she said somewhat crisply, "However, you really shouldn't come to tea with blackened fingers. Ah, but then you've been through such a shock. I had meant Nora to take tea up to you."

"Oh, no. I wouldn't have missed this gathering for the world," Pandora replied after a swallow of biscuit. Then noticing the Marquess's continued fascination with her fingers, she swiftly replaced cup to saucer and folded her hands in her lap. "What tale of intrigue did I interrupt?" she asked, wishing to draw his attention from further reference to her diary writing, for there was a greedy, questing look about his eyes that unnerved her.

"He was telling us more about the Thugs!" Chloe volunteered, then looking a bit sheepish at her outburst, murmured an apology.

"Oh, yes. The Stranglers," Pandora commented, resting back in her chair. "You know, Aunt Beatrix, I imagine you could even invite the Wofford-Sydneys to the ball were word to get out that the Marquess of Manakin was not only here, but filled with terror-stories of India!" Settling her gaze on the elegantly attired Lord Manakin she added, "Please, do continue."

Which he did well into the afternoon, and to such a convincing degree that Pandora almost began to doubt her intuitive distrust of the man. Something told her, however, that whatever the Marquess was up to, it was the Viscount who held the missing clue. If only she knew which one had the ruby.

Later that evening, as Nora was helping her mistress dress, Pandora elaborated on a scheme wherein she might not only find the jewel, but perhaps gather further information on who was really whom and why. Nora, only too happy to be privy to these adventures, offered her continued assistance in spying on the Marquess. True, she had fallen asleep on the job the other night, but on awakening had discovered that Lord Manakin had been at the books all evening.

"And so I've decided that tonight is the perfect time for me to slip out."

"Oh, but Miss," Nora said, alarmed. "What about that bump on your head? Hadn't you better wait?"

"No. It's tonight or not at all. The Viscount will be at the Waverlys', for Aunt Bea has obtained an invite for him to dinner. She is determined to buff his character to sterling finish, when he is naught but copper in disguise." Pandora sat at her boudoir that Nora might pin her thick curls atop her head. "Just work around the bump," she added on a laugh.

"I still don't see what's so perfect about tonight. It's clouding over, and like as not will rain, and—"

"*And,* with Aunt Beatrix, Chloe, and Winny also at the Waverlys' for dinner, my indisposition gives me a timely opportunity for this search. And if he does have the ruby, we don't want to give him time to dispose of it." Pandora stared blankly at her reflection, refusing to admit to herself a hope that no such evidence would be found to indict the Viscount. "And, all you have to do is keep an eye on our esteemed houseguest and his man. A job worthy of you and Jemnaz, I'm sure!"

"But what if something goes wrong?" With a swift turn of the brush Nora positioned the final curl in place. "And you looking so . . . so . . . pale!"

Pandora rose from her boudoir chair, and stepping back admired the bombazine outfit of deep blue, relieved only by a crisp white linen collar. The material fell in thick folds about her slender frame: its darkness would blend well with the night.

"It should make you feel better to know I'll be hooded, cloaked, *and* carrying my reticule," she said with a confident toss of her head.

"A lot of good that pistol did you last night!" Nora reminded her, "And it seems far more dangerous for you to be rooting about a man's private chambers than going to

Vauxhall Gardens." She set her lips in a grim line that foreboded certain disaster.

"Never fear. Remember, Lord Cardew won't be there." With a smile of self-assurance she swung her dark cloak about her shoulders, and added, "Who knows? Perhaps I shall return with the ruby!"

"But then what, Miss? Put his lordship in prison?"

Pandora paused, "I'll needs think on that," she replied, as she crossed to her chamber door from where, unbeknownst to her, the Marquess, having heard enough, crept into the shadows.

He was pleased with this turn of events, for it would provide him an opportunity to find and read Miss Tremantle's diary: he would easily handle Nora and the boy, and no one would be the wiser—least of all the meddlesome Miss Tremantle.

Chapter Five

Had the "meddlesome Miss Tremantle" known the future, she might have taken a different course, but she was determined in this matter, and certainly nothing Nora could say would have prevailed upon the impetuous young lady to reconsider.

The Marquess of Manakin, equally determined that the high card turn up in his hand, made sure that Nora's and the Indian boy's evening milk was liberally laced with a sleeping potion. This accomplished, he began a rapid search of Miss Tremantle's room until he found the diary in question.

There were the usual day in, day out observations:

Weather unbearably hot today, and most unusual for Spring. Jemnaz can recite the entire alphabet: Papa is sending another jewel!

Page after page continued in this fashion. Then his gray eyes feasted on a single sentence:

Two men have presented themselves to me as peers of the realm: at least one of them is after the jewels, of this I am certain.

Avidly he read on; and by the time he had finished, his face was an unbecoming mask of barely contained agitation. He flipped back to the entry concerning Viscount Cardew: which would be vastly amusing were it not for the finger of fear that intruded. His gaze scanned Cardew's description once again:

> *This so-called* Viscount, *who is dark of skin with a wicked-looking scar down his cheek, is not only a gambler, but alas, most probably a jewel thief!*

The drivel of confused and romantic transports that followed was of little interest to Manakin: what did capture his attention was the single line describing the Viscount: "*Dark of skin with a wicked-looking scar down his cheek.*" Could it be that the *real* Marquess of Manakin was indeed so close at hand?

Impossible! Slamming the diary on the dressing table, the man masquerading as the Marquess stared ruefully at his reflection: he too was dark complected, though vanity kept him from scarring his smooth skin for this brief impersonation. He glanced at the leather-bound diary, with its pressed and faded roses and the fancy dark script that filled the pages. He thought once more of her description of the Viscount at the Orange Crown Inn. True, it had been years since he had glimpsed the man, but if he could see him again, he would know. For the Marquess of Manakin was not a man to be easily dismissed.

Miss Tremantle, oblivious of the Marquess's activities, was fully engaged in an adventure of her own. Once again she was off to the Orange Crown, her blood racing through her veins even as she urged the gray into a gallop, which took them sailing across the ribbon of highway. Her hood had blown back, and the wind threatened to send her confined curls tumbling free. She could not have cared less; all that mattered was that she discover whether or not Cardew took the ruby—and to recover it if he had. Or so she tried to convince herself. However, Nora's remark about sending him to prison had cast a slight shadow over Pandora's script.

Cresting a hill that overlooked Kirk Cross village, she slowed the gray's pace. What if it *had* been an ordinary theft? What if the Viscount was innocent? She contemplated this as the gig descended into a thicket bereft of moonlight. The air was cool and heavy with the scent of rain. *No!* Alas, it could not have been common thievery. It had been planned, and by someone who knew she would definitely go to the summer house. What was more, the Viscount's peculiar behavior that evening clearly pointed to him.

Pandora snapped the reins as they climbed another hill. She would find the ruby, she would! For the time being, that was enough. Somehow though, the growing certainty did not elate her.

By the time she arrived in the village, her earlier enthusiasm for the venture had waned slightly. Reining in some distance from the inn, she jumped down from the gig, and tethered the gray to a post. Her hands were trembling, and her heart was pounding at her ribs like a summons at the door. She took a deep breath and started around to the back of the Orange Crown. Under the rumble of distant thunder, she ducked beneath the kitchen eaves, and holding her breath, waited for she knew not what—a stiff dose of courage perhaps! Sounds of pots and pans echoed above her head, as did an argument centered on the cooking of beef brisket. A door was heard to slam, then more squabbling.

Keep at it, Pandora thought, as she darted for the side door, which led directly to the servants' staircase. She hoped the ruckus in the kitchen would hold everyone's attention while she made her furtive entrance. This little diversion was a blessing indeed.

Clearing the downstairs' hall without mishap, Pandora began her ascent up the narrow circular staircase. It was ill lit, the rail greasy to her gloved touch, and just as she was about to clear the top step, a furry creature scampered over her slippers. She stifled a shriek and catapulted forward. This was definitely not The Quality's entrance.

Flattening herself against the wall, she listened: a supper party accompanied by singing and much laughter was in progress some distance down the hall. Their door was partially opened and flickering candlelight spilled recklessly into the hall. Unfortunately the balcony leading to the Viscount's chamber was several doors beyond. There was nothing for it but to walk the length of the hall as quickly as possible.

Her fears were unfounded: no one even noticed the cloaked figure as it slipped past them. Taking a deep breath, she pushed open the door leading to the public balcony, and quickly headed toward the Viscount's entrance. She distinctly remembered from her visit that he kept the balcony door open. But at this point, even a lock wouldn't deter her.

As she expected, the French doors were ajar and pale cotton curtains were billowing out in the gathering breeze. She paused on the threshold and allowed her eyes to grow accustomed to the darkened chamber. Fortunately enough moonlight streamed through the open door, for it would certainly not do to draw any attention to her activities by lighting a candle.

Pandora blinked, then moved slowly forward. She would begin her search in the secretary, which was hidden in an alcove opposite the four-poster bed, mounded high with linens and blankets. She tiptoed past as if someone were napping there. Then settling herself in a chair before the desk, she commenced a rapid but thorough search of each drawer and cubbyhole. Save for some blank parchment and sealing wafers, they were virtually empty. She was about to shut the last drawer when something caught her eye. Her hand shot forward and closed about a small velvet pouch. Could it be that the ruby was inside? With trembling fingers she opened the case, dreading that she might find the jewel within. But instead, she beheld a pair of dice. Dice? From the south of France, no doubt! They were ebony with pearl inlay, and cool to the touch. Visions of the Viscount rolling dice and looking every bit the gambler flashed before her eyes; but she was not so spellbound that she didn't hear the sound behind her. She whirled around, and seeing a brandy bottle about to connect with her head, dove behind her chair and was rewarded with a shower of brandy as the bottle—barely missing her head—shattered over her chairback. Then strong hands thrust her into the chair, tied a gag over her mouth, and quickly bound her hands and feet.

The heart-pounding fear that ripped through Pandora subsided somewhat at the sight of her assailant: a meticulously attired gentleman, who, having taken a chair opposite her, proceeded to adjust his neckcloth, which had decidedly gone askew in the fray. This was achieved with remarkable dexterity, considering his aged appearance, and was followed by a hasty brushing of his wide-lapeled jacket, which made him look for all the world like someone's family retainer. It was obvious that his dignity had been sorely compromised by this fracas, and the frosty scrutiny he bestowed on Miss Tremantle suggested she had just escaped from Bedlam.

Pandora stared in disbelief as the remnants of her fear evaporated. Aside from the hauteur he affected, the man had a surprisingly amiable countenance: red cheeks, a bald head, and whimsical eyes that resembled two poached eggs. However, the fidgeting manner with which he handled her pistol did give Pandora pause.

"This is all terr-ribly unseemly," he uttered in a sepulchral monotone, then looking through her as if she were not there, he added, "It simply goes to show, one cannot judge a book by its cover. I have often told his lordship that, and I do but pray he has not been taken in by you!"

Pandora blinked in surprise at his rendering of her character, although given the damning circumstances, things did not look good. *But then who was this man,* she thought, *and what on earth was* he *doing in the Viscount's chamber? And what did he mean by that reference to* his lordship? *Whose* lordship? *The Viscount? That lordship? Oh, dear! Could this be Lord Cardew's man? What had he called him?* Old *something* . . . Graves? *No* . . . Grimms? *No!* Old Grimley! *That was it. Oh, my! Then evidently his lordship* was *his lordship.* An odd sense of relief came over Pandora followed by a sickening feeling at having been caught. Still, a nagging question remained unanswered: Why would a perfectly respectable Viscount with an estate to the north of London have taken rooms in the Orange Crown?

Old Grimley, casting about for a way to fill the time, seemed about to enlighten Pandora. "His lordship shall be most distressed to learn that another attempt on his life was no doubt in the offing, and were I not certain you would scream the Inn down, I would allow you to defend yourself. Tut! Tut!" He wagged his finger at her muffled protest. "Possess yourself of patience: my master shall be returning shortly. Then we shall wring the truth out of you, for I am most curious to hear why an apparent lady of quality should wish to burgle my lord. It puzzles me beyond repair, that it does."

At Pandora's renewed struggle, Old Grimley held his hand up for silence. "However, I shall await my lordship, though I be consumed by curiosity."

The Viscount's man then proceeded to give Miss Tremantle a lecture on propriety, stressing above all that robbery, while acceptable in novels, was not to be considered among the accomplishments of a refined young lady, unlike proficiency at the harp or pianoforte. Did *Miss* understand this point? Furthermore, if Miss was in need of funds, there were surely other means. And if it was revenge against his esteemed lordship—well, good God, that would be unthinkable! Old Grimley was on the verge of expounding on this point when the door opened, and Pandora found herself staring into the startled blue eyes of Lord Cardew. He looked like the hounds of hell were chasing him, but after the initial surprise he threw his head back and laughed like one truly possessed.

"Ha! Grimley, you're worth your weight in gold. Caught a spy about my rooms, did you?" Casually he unfastened his coat, and slipping out of it, handed it to his valet, purposely avoiding the black looks Pandora sent him.

"From the smell of things I'd say you've either been nipping at the—aha!" he exclaimed on a note of discovery, and bending over, retrieved the jagged edge of the brandy bottle. His eyebrows lifted in amazement. "My, my, Miss Tremantle, not only do you have a propensity for being knocked about the head, but I do believe you have the hardest head I've ever known. Mind you, *I* did not conk you out in Vauxhall, despite what you think." Tossing the bottleneck into a rubbage receptacle, he added, "It would be decidedly bad ton to dance with a lady one minute and knock her out the next: even if she deserved it!"

Grimley stepped forward, a thoroughly confused look chasing about his face. "Do you mean, my lord, that you *do* know this young lady? Tsk, tsk. Your father would be turning in his grave, that he would. As would your mother." With a small whisk broom he crouched down and began cleaning up the remains of the bottle. "Sorry to have wasted all that brandy, your lordship."

"Yes. Pity. Twelve years old." His gaze returned to Pandora, who commenced stomping her slippered feet.

"Oh, my dear Miss Tremantle—"

"*Tremantle* is it?" Grimley said, as he dumped the broken glass into the receptacle.

"Yes, daughter of Sir Horatio Tremantle," the Viscount replied as he firmly grasped Pandora's ankles, and withdrawing a knife, cut her bonds. "Now no more kicking," he said slowly, as if instructing a recalcitrant child. Then quickly he set her hands free and undid her gag.

"*You!*" she spat the word out along with a bit of frayed cotton, then wiping her mouth, made a disagreeable face.

"I would offer you brandy, but . . ." He shrugged his shoulders with a capriciousness that further infuriated Pandora.

"Do you know that I've been tied up with . . . with your Grimley holding a pistol on me!" She rubbed her chafed wrists and sent the Viscount a look that could clearly kill.

"*Grimley?* With a pistol? 'Pon my honor!" Swinging around to his valet, he queried, "Thought you didn't like the things?"

"And so I do not, m'lord. But the young lady seems most attached to hers, and from the looks of things I thought perhaps she might *plug* you—that is, after she made off with your goods." Grimley made a bow, and said, "If you wish, I shall repair to the common room while you and Miss . . . Tremantle continue your business. But I must advise you that she is a trifle shrewish and prone to bite."

"I am not!"

"A veritable virago," the Viscount contributed.

"Ooh!"

"My sentiments precisely, your lordship. Shall I retire now?"

"Pour us a glass of port—I trust *that* is still available. Then you may have your pint downstairs. Ha! Don't worry, I shall be able to handle out little shrew."

"'*Little shrew,*' is it?" Pandora's eyes danced with a dangerous light as she rose from her chair, and, arms akimbo, advanced on Lord Cardew, who threw up his hands in mock surrender and stepped back a pace. "I shall show you who's a shrew!"

" 'Ah. Why, there's a wench!—Come on and kiss me, Kate,' " the Viscount quoted, laughing as he circled away from her.

Pandora stopped short, and gathering the shreds of her dignity, managed to say, "You are far too ridiculous, especially when . . . when . . ."

"What? When you have broken into my chamber, for heaven knows what, and are in a spit because I make a joke of it?"

"Well, it is not a joke. I came for my ruby, and—"

"I do not have your ruby: never did, and never shall. What made you think I did?"

"Well, for one thing, your behavior at Vauxhall." Swallowing her pride, she accepted a glass of port from Grimley, and with a becoming blush, reluctantly added, "Though it does appear I may have misjudged you . . . and I do apologize."

"Thank you," Cardew acknowledged. Then with a wicked grin he added, "I must say, your name becomes you."

"My father named me," she rejoined with a whip snap to her voice.

"And named you well." He studied her for a moment before adding, "Ah, how your eyes do sparkle when you're on your high ropes."

"I am *not* on my high ropes," Pandora countered, then catching the amused curl to the Viscount's lip, added somewhat sheepishly, "but what was I to think when you rushed from the dance floor at Vauxhall—that you'd suddenly seen an old friend?"

"Let's call him an old acquaintance; and unfortunately I was unable to catch up with him."

"How smoothly you improvise!" Pandora's eyes glittered slightly.

"I suppose it's the truth you're after?" Then raising an eyebrow, he said, "Do you mean to say Grimley hasn't informed you?"

"My lord!" the valet interrupted, "You swore me to secrecy!"

"Ah, so I did."

"Secrecy about attempts on your life?" Pandora prodded, feeling unaccountably chipper. "In fact, I believe Grimley fancied I was one of your assassins!"

"Naturally—when you arrived brandishing firearms."

"My lord, forgive my errant tongue. But I assure you, Miss Tremantle is not apprised of the circumstances that—oh, my!"

"Go on and have your pint, Grimley: I believe I'd best explain a few things to Miss Tremantle."

"Oh, you do, do you?" Pandora said on a rising note of interest.

"She's a hotheaded miss, your lordship," Grimley muttered as he ducked out the door.

"*Hothead, shrew, thief, murderer!* Oh what a catalogue of iniquity I'm acquiring." She took a sip of port then set the glass on a nearby table. Despite her mocking tone, Pandora was feeling strangely ill at ease, and turning from the Viscount, she moved towards the balcony, conscious of moonlight that trailed cool patterns across broad floorboards; conscious of her heartbeat; and all too conscious of him, closing in on her. With a flippance not felt, she added, "Are you sure you feel safe in the same room with me? I could have a knife up my sleeve."

"I don't think so." His hand gently touched her shoulder, then spinning her towards him, said, "Though there's probably room for *several* knives in your current costume. However, I prefer the gold gown you wore to Vauxhall Gardens: the coloring suits you better."

"It's ruined," she said abruptly, willing the tremble out of her voice, wishing Lord Cardew wouldn't stand so close. She looked up at him through her lashes, and felt her heart turn over. There was a look on his face she'd never seen before; a smile that made her feel unaccountably weak, and yes, a little frightened. "Besides, this frock is more suited for thievery, wouldn't you agree?" she added lightly.

"I'm glad you left off the murder part." He touched his cravat with reverence.

"For now," she shot back with a laugh. Pulling away from him, she headed back into the room. "Grimley has set the scene for us." She indicated the lit candelabra on the tea table, then taking a chair, looked up at the Viscount with expectancy.

"You were going to *explain things* I believe?"

Cardew, silhouetted against the moonlit night, moved towards her until the candelabra threw its amber light onto the dark planes of his face. Maintaining her outward calm, Pandora started to rise. "Well, are you? Because if not—"

"Stay seated!" He growled the command, then softly appended, "If you so please."

"Well, I do, for I am bitten with curiosity, though I daresay my questions will outnumber your replies." She pressed her lips to a line, which was a feat indeed. Flushed with conflicting emotions, she determined to remain silent, lest she say something regrettable.

"You are a clever young lady," he said after a pause. "Have you ever considered working as a Bow Street Runner? For there's a tenacity in you—an unusual trait in a female," he added with annoying casualness.

"Let us leave off discussing me," she managed crisply. "I believe you were about to divulge all?"

"Did I say *all?*" He held his wine glass to the light as if it contained his entire history. "And you believed me?"

"If you are about some game, I'll be on my way!" She started again to rise, but was frustrated in this attempt as Lord Cardew gently pushed her back.

"Now then," he began genially, "I shall tell you what I feel necessary for your own good—"

"What do you mean, *my own good?* So far all I've heard from your lying lips is—"

"Lies? Tsk, tsk. And after your heart-felt apology I thought you'd relinquished your belief that I was a blackguard out to rob the Tremantles blind. Or perhaps you find these fancies a shade romantic after all? I'm told females hold with highwaymen and the likes."

"Not this female!" Pandora started to rise a third time, but the look in the Viscount's eyes changed her mind.

"That's better," Cardew soothed, then downing his port, he abruptly sat opposite her. "You know your life's in danger, don't you?"

"That's coming straight out with it, I'd say. And shall I

refrain from casting you as villain, since you are so valiantly attempting to play the hero?" She knew her smile was a trifle smug, but at least the silly heart palpitations had ceased.

"Exactly: I'll play hero, you the damsel in distress, and that leaves the villain, doesn't it?"

"Since you're the director, I imagine you have one in mind."

"The Marquess of *Manakin.*" He said the name as if it were a loathed curse. His jaw tightened and once again his blue eyes narrowed to icy chips. Softly, he added, "I would ask you to have a care around the man: he is not to be trusted."

Pandora took a sip of her port, and after a moment said, "You knew him from India, didn't you?"

"It doesn't matter where I knew him, or even if I knew him. Just trust me!"

"Oh, and don't trust him? That's what you mean, isn't it? Even though he bears a letter of introduction from my father?"

"Damn—*dash* it! Don't ask for reasons, *or* proof." He ran a hand through his hair. "The man is dangerous, and if you must know, I'm here to—let us say—curtail his activities." The Viscount rose from his chair and strode toward the balcony.

"Oh!" Pandora uttered, somewhat taken aback; then affecting a nonchalant shrug of her shoulders, she added, "Well, if you must know, he told me just this morning that he's leaving for a few days in London. So, you needn't worry about my safety where he is concerned." Pandora watched with some satisfaction as Lord Cardew's stance visibly altered.

The Viscount turned towards her and slowly said, "That puts things in an interesting light. Even so, I would ask you to have a care."

"Very well. I shall all but fade into the walls, but—"

"I seriously doubt you capable of such a feat," Cardew said on an unexpected chuckle.

"*But,* if you wish me to trust you," persisted Pandora, "You must tell me who you are. Where do you really come from? And please no more of this foolishness about the south of France! Furthermore, you are obviously not a Bow Street Runner, so why are you after Manakin? And what of this mysterious scandal?"

"In good time."

"This is as good a time as any!" she tossed back, rising to her feet and approaching the Viscount. "And don't tell me to be seated one more time, or I shall scream!"

"I expect you would, wouldn't you?"

"I would, and will, unless you answer my questions and stop treating me like a child! Well?"

"You know, your eyes are quite exceptional when you're angry: has anyone ever told you that before?" Stepping closer to her, Cardew gently took her arm and steered her back towards the tea table.

"We would do better to finish our conversation here." His voice turned to a caress that unexpectedly jangled her insides. With a damnable smile, he indicated the chair which she had just vacated.

Pushing aside the warm and tingly feelings that threatened to surface, she snapped out, "Who *are* you?"

"A gentleman from the north of London, Justin—"

"Yes, yes, I know: Viscount Cardew. A made-up title if I ever heard one." She gave a satisfied toss to her curls.

"There you are wrong, my dear, for I am indeed who I say I am." Sending her a purposefully inscrutable smile, he withdrew a gold time piece from an equally gold waistcoat, and purred, "The rest will have to wait, my impetuous Pandora, for the hour is growing late, and unless you wish your aunt to see us returning to Chatford—"

"Us?" Pandora echoed.

"Us," Lord Cardew repeated. "Having pleaded the headache after the brandy and cigars, I left your aunt in deep gossip with the hostess; but even given possible after-dinner entertainment, I am quite sure they will be returning shortly. Of course, if you wish your reputation to be seriously compromised, with forced nuptials between us—"

"Don't be ridiculous," Pandora said, rising once again from the chair. "In any event, I am more than capable of seeing myself home: I am a crack shot with the pistol and if it's reputations you're worried about, it's far better that I leave alone." Heading for the door, she tossed over her shoulder, "You needn't see me out either. I'm using the back stairs, and that would certainly look bad for you!"

"One moment!" The Viscount crossed to her side and, snaking his hand around her cloaked arm, drew her alongside of him. "I do not allow ladies to go about unescorted."

"Oh, you don't? Well, this is one lady who is quite capable of caring for herself. I arrived under cover of darkness, and shall leave under cover of darkness. That's as plain as vanilla pudding, and unless you wish to continue our earlier disagreements, you will let me pass." She leveled her most threatening gaze on him and attempted to pull away.

"Not yet!" There was but a moment's warning before he dragged her against him and on a strangled cry brought his mouth down on hers in a crushing kiss that startled him as much as it did her. Every muscle in his body was coiled, tensed, and aching for the touch of Miss Tremantle. He felt her lips soften and yield beneath him. Abruptly he stepped back, wishing for all the world this hadn't happened, for he knew nothing would ever come of it. The sooner he finished up his business and left England, the better. Looking at Pandora, he sensed the gentle awakening his kisses had aroused. Her lips were parted and trembling, and banked fires smoldered in her emerald eyes.

"I beg your forgiveness for that breach of conduct. It shan't happen again." He made what he considered a stiff and ridiculous bow, then added, "Grimley and Chandro will escort you home. I shall retrieve them both, and *they* will accompany you down the *front* staircase. I trust that will satisfy."

Before Pandora could protest, he was gone. Her hands flew to her mouth as if their presence there might recapture the kiss. For Lord Cardew *had* kissed her! And it was nothing like the paltry attempts of Geoffrey Hyde-White! Feeling a bit dizzy, she leaned against the wall and ran a shaky hand across her forehead. So this was why ladies carried vinaigrettes. He had kissed her! The thought played a refrain in her weary brain. In the space of one evening, he had laughed at her, patronized her, lectured her, kissed her, and rebuffed her! Perhaps he *did* have bats in his upper story.

Letting out a sigh, she crossed to the tea table, and lifting her wineglass, drained its contents. No, she decided—as the shock of the kiss wore off—he was not crazy. Far from it. Nor did he fit the villainous mold she had cast for him. Worse than that. He undoubtedly considered her a helpless female, and one to whom confidences could not be revealed. In point of fact, he had explained very little! She touched her lips again and tried not to think of what delicious things that kiss did to her insides. Heavens! Ladies didn't have insides. But then ladies didn't go about unprotected at night either. But of that kiss; no doubt this was part of his usual style: to cajole, patronize, and make love to the women in his life, then just as quickly turn that frosty look on them and speak of proper conduct. Proper conduct indeed!

Wouldn't she just see about that. So, the Viscount feared for her life; even warned her to watch out for the Marquess, as if Pandora had no sense. And though her cheeks still burned and her lips tingled, she would not think of that. No, instead she would consider how to best this Viscount. So, he wanted some evidence against the Marquess: well, she would find it first! After all, Lord Manakin was a guest at Chatford, so it shouldn't be too difficult to locate something incriminating on him. That would surely show the Viscount Cardew that Pandora Tremantle was not just an empty-headed bit of fluff.

Chapter Six

Grimley insisted on driving Pandora home in the Viscount's closed carriage, while Chandro, who was ever eager for this adventure, hopped onto the seat of her gig, cracked the reins, and sang out a series of Hindi commands which prompted the gray to burst into a spirited canter. Any hopes Pandora had entertained of prying secrets out of Old Grimley were neatly dashed by the family retainer, who obviously had been schooled well by his master. Upon assisting her into the carriage he quite solemnly announced that she would be saving her breath if she refrained from attempting to interrogate him.

Having managed to remove the Viscount from the forefront of her thoughts, Pandora spent the balance of the journey home contemplating Grimley's sudden appearance. Obviously he had come from the Viscount's estate, which if truth be told lay somewhere north of London. Undoubtedly Lord Cardew had needed something, or perhaps his man had information.

As if things weren't confusing enough, Pandora arrived home in the midst of chaos moments after Beatrix, Chloe, and Winthrop had alighted from their carriage. Chandro, having been apprehended by the head groomsman, was shrieking in Hindi and flailing his skinny arms and legs in an attempt to free himself from Parks's hold on him. Beatrix, in a dramatic pose with her hand over her bosom, seemed in the throes of a Grand Swoon, and Chloe and Winny stood torn between tending to her and the Indian boy.

Pandora, not waiting for Grimley, wrenched the carriage door open, and headed straight to Chandro's defense. Parks, used to Miss Tremantle's willful ways, reluctantly set the babbling dark-skinned boy down, and with a derisive sniff, motioned for the gawking stable boys to set about their numerous tasks.

Beatrix swept forward, taking care to stop short of the Indian boy, who, face down in front of Pandora, had commenced to mutter in his native tongue.

"What is the meaning of all this?" Miss McClellan demanded in operatic tones. "And what was the Viscount's tiger doing in *our* gig?"

"Chandro was bringing it back for me," Pandora replied, drawing the frightened boy to his feet.

"Oh, I but shudder at the explanation!" Pressing her lace handkerchief to her nostrils, Beatrix cast an apprehensive glance at Grimley, who stood a respectful distance from the scene. "And who, pray tell, is that?" she drawled.

Taking the initiative, the Viscount's man stepped forward, "Grimley's the name, ma'am. I have been his lordship's valet since he was in leading strings."

"His lordship?" Beatrix repeated.

"Viscount Cardew!" Winthrop said on a jovial note. At the retainer's modest nod of his head, he added, "Come all the way from Lord Cardew's estates, eh?"

"Precisely, sir." Old Grimley's chest swelled slightly at this acknowledgment.

"What I wish to know then," Beatrix said peevishly, "is why are you here with my niece, instead of the Viscount? And why in heaven's name was Chand . . . Chando, or whatever his name is, bringing back *our* gig?" She took a fretting breath then slowly exhaled as reality dawned. "Oh, my stars! *Pandora! You didn't!*"

"Obviously she did," Winthrop said, giving his sister a wink.

"Did what?" blurted out Chloe, unable to restrain her curiosity any longer.

"Went calling, one might say," Pandora replied on a laugh, then giving Chandro a reassuring hug, added, "You and Grimley had better be returning to the Orange Crown."

"Yes, I go, memsahib." His eyes gleamed like warm chocolate. "Chandro! Hindu!"

"Oh dear, oh dear, oh dear!" Beatrix muttered. "Another heathen!"

"Hindu!" the boy repeated gleefully, then shaking hands with Pandora, he slowly enunciated, "Good night, Miss Tremantel." Turning to Beatrix, he presented such an endearing smile along with his palm, that she actually shook hands with the boy. "Good night, sleep tight," he advised the thoroughly disarmed Miss McClellan before his joining Grimley at the reins of the Viscount's carriage.

"I fear I must fortify myself with something strong before you commence your presentation!" Beatrix murmured as Lord Cardew's vehicle carried Grimley and Chandro into the night. Then with the air of one destined to constant upheavals, she led the way up the marble steps of Chatford Abbey.

Winthrop, in keeping with his sterling image, declined the sherry, which their aunt declared was a necessary restorative for her.

"For I fear the very worst, and must brace myself." She sank back against the gold settee and after fluttering her eyelashes appropriately, said, "Proceed, Pandora."

"Yes, do!" Chloe urged from her position next to Winthrop on a rose-colored loveseat.

"To begin with, my reputation is quite intact, for no one saw me either entering or leaving the Orange Crown." At her aunt's renewed groans, she quickly added, "And nothing of consequence occurred in the Viscount's company: what I mean to say is that although we were alone, he did not compromise me."

"Oh, upon my word! Worse and worse!" Beatrix groaned. She had abandoned the sherry for her vinaigrette, and was even now prodigiously sniffing it.

"Would you prefer that he had ravished me?" Pandora said unblinking. Her aunt merely choked at this, as if the vapors were imminent.

"I say, Sis! Sounds to me as if you're a bit cracked on the chap," Winthrop observed, making a great ceremony of taking snuff.

"Nothing of the sort!" Pandora snapped.

"Oh, my child," Beatrix said, managing a rapid recovery. "Nothing could please me more, *but,* to throw yourself on the Viscount in such an unseemly manner! What must the beleaguered man think?"

"I did not throw myself on him!"

"Oh, I think it is most romantic," Chloe uttered, her little hands clasped in ecstasy. "And I am sure you were most discreet in your rendezvous."

"Chloe!" Beatrix cried. "Do contain yourself. This is a matter most serious—and remember that one does not have discreet rendezvous, especially at places like the Orange Crown Inn." Swinging her gaze back to Pandora, she added, "The most we can hope for is that the Viscount will forget this unfortunate interlude. Though heaven knows his servants will probably chatter it all over the country by morning."

"Nothing of the sort," Pandora said testily. "Chandro doesn't speak English, and Grimley is the faithful family retainer. I seriously doubt that butter would melt in his mouth. And as for Lord Cardew, you needn't worry, for there's nothing to forget—well, almost nothing."

"Aha! Now the shocking truth comes out. Chloe, I believe you should retire." Beatrix had straightened considerably, and a most engaging look swept her countenance.

"What I have to report will not burn our cousin's ears: for you see, Aunt Beatrix, I had broken into the Viscount's chamber—"

"Broken in?" A horrified gasp punctuated this exclamation.

"Yes! I had broken in to find the ruby pendant which I believed the Viscount had stolen—"

"Pandora!"

"And in the process, was apprehended by Grimley, who mistook me for a thief." She smiled sweetly, and in the stunned silence, added, "He near broke a bottle of twelve-year-old brandy on my head, then proceeded to tie me to a chair while we awaited the Viscount's return."

"Tied you to a chair?"

"Well, if I hadn't thought the Viscount a thief—"

"Oh! To accuse Lord Cardew of stealing the ruby pendant!" Beatrix clutched the vinaigrette anew, and at Pandora's affirmative nod, she slumped against the settee. "Ruined! Ruined!"

"That was a bit steep, Sis," Winthrop muttered with a raised eyebrow.

"And yet he sent you back with an escort," Chloe reminded everyone.

"That is because he is A Gentleman," Beatrix moaned. "And one we probably shan't see again!"

"I am certain we shall," Pandora assured everyone in a calm, flat voice.

"Oh, my girl, you have taken things too far this time," her aunt said dramatically. "For it is the death knell you've rung on this little romantic concerto!"

"Please, Auntie—"

"You have torn the budding flower from the vine and crushed it in the dirt! Oh, foolish girl!"

"Rubbish!" Pandora cried, rising from her chair, "We are not ruined! I've rung no death knells, nor flung any flowers to the ground." Pandora paused before the sideboard and considered a glass of sherry, for it had been a trying day, but with a shrug of her shoulders she decided she'd had enough spirits for one night. Instead she picked up a candlestick with a lighted taper and said, "I simply wanted to do a little investigating, and although it was somewhat curtailed, I am indeed satisfied that Lord Cardew did not steal the ruby."

"Merciful heavens!" Beatrix said. "He was your savior at Vauxhall Gardens! How could you imagine him capable of such a thing?"

"It's of no consequence now. I expect it was stolen by a common thief. Alas, I shall miss it." She let out an appropriate sigh and headed for the door, her mind abuzz with other possibilities concerning the ruby pendant's whereabouts.

"Pandora!" her aunt called, "You must not breathe a word of this to anyone: and *if* Lord Cardew *should* show for tea tomorrow, you will make no reference to the incident; for to do so would be quite unthinkable. Oh, but this is a most unfortunate concatenation of circumstances!"

"Oh, for pity's sake, Aunt Bea, do not fret so! I shall be as mum as an oyster." As she turned and made her way up the stairs Pandora heard Chloe's renewed transports of delight, Winthrop's hale laughter, and Beatrix's moans.

She had nearly forgotten that Lord Cardew was coming to tea on the morrow: she wished she could forget him completely! But how, when his kiss was as intoxicating as wine? It was sweet and heady, and to her chagrin Pandora could not forget it.

Upon entering her bedchamber she crossed to her boudoir glass, and holding the candle close, studied her lips for a moment. They were the same rosy, full lips she had been in possession of that afternoon. Not a trace of the kiss remained: the tingle was invisible, but the feel of his mouth as it had pressed against hers was more than just a memory. Absently she brushed her lips with the back of her hand. *Foolish girl,* her aunt had called her. True, true. She wouldn't think on that just now. Setting the candle down she prepared for bed, all the while trying to plan her next move. Nothing brilliant came to mind, but that was hardly surprising considering what she had been through in the past two days. Thank heavens Old Grimley had missed with the brandy bottle!

Pandora had snuffed out the candle and was drifting off to sleep when she suddenly realized that Nora hadn't been by, as was her usual custom. Well, it was late. The girl had probably grown tired of waiting up for her. On a deep yawn, Pandora assured herself there wasn't anything of significance to report anyway; and besides, she would be seeing Nora before breakfast and would be apprised of the Marquess's actions then.

The following morning, however, brought several unfortunate incidents: Nora did manage to appear with Miss Tremantle's chocolate, but looked so drawn and pale that her mistress instructed her to retire immediately and that *she* would attend to *her!* The abigail fussed about the unseemliness of this role reversal, but finally admitted that she was *not* herself, and hadn't been since last night, when—alas—she had fallen asleep and not kept her peepers on the villain. Pandora set her fears to rest, and after putting her abigail back to bed, brought her tea and thin gruel. Learning from Nora that Jemnaz was in a similar condition, she hastened to the boy's chamber and was greeted by a plaintive hello and a valiant grin. He too was nourished on gruel and tea, and told to rest. If Pandora's patients were not improved by afternoon, she would call in a doctor.

Thankfully such drastic measures were not necessary, for by noon the peculiar malady had righted itself, and while the rest of the household buzzed with activity preparatory to the Viscount's arrival for tea, Nora and Jemnaz returned to the library and continued unpacking Sir Horatio's books.

Beatrix, having drawn Pandora into the garden, where she was clipping some daffodils with a rather lethal pair of shears, was about to lecture her niece on propriety when Hawkins appeared. He bore a silver salver and presented the message thereon to Miss McClellan. As was appropriate, he waited in case there should be a reply.

After perusing the message, Beatrix managed to mutter, "Very good," in a voice that clearly indicated that it was *not* good at all. She grasped a wrought-iron chair and slowly sank into it. The shears dropped to the ground, and after fetching a sigh her rosebud mouth flattened to a trembling line suggestive of imminent hysteria. After the butler backed off, she crumpled the missive to her breast.

"It is as I thought," she moaned, thrusting the note at Pandora, "Lord Cardew, unable to endure your contumacious behavior, has cried off and shall not come to tea: no, not this afternoon, nor any in the future. Oh, when I think that had you not played the hussy he might have asked for you!"

"Do calm down, Auntie. Look, he says quite plainly that urgent business has called him away unexpectedly."

"Naturally! It would be a mark of dreadful breeding were he to pen the awful truth." Contemplating her shears she retrieved them as if they were instrumental in her immediate demise. "There is but one course open: we must press to London immediately, and pray that the Viscount will be sufficiently recovered in time for Chloe's ball."

"Heavens, Aunt Beatrix, don't you understand that I am not interested in making a nuptial knot with Cardew!" Pandora cast her eyes to a cluster of daffodils, praying the sudden flush to her cheeks wasn't too evident.

"If your papa had been here all these years instead of thrashing about those foreign places, I daresay you might have turned out to be normal! Why, you act as one whose stuffing is falling out, I do declare you do! *Two* eligibles at your feet and all you can do is pursue a course of folly! *Folly!*" she repeated, pressing the ever-present hankie to her brow.

"I shall try to deport myself with restraint in the future," Pandora promised. She was at once thankful that Lord Cardew, for whatever reason, had declined tea, and yet wished this conversation would cease, for it was another unseasonably warm day. Her gaze wandered to the white pagoda which overlooked a bubbling stream and a glorious bed of early spring flowers.

Beatrix, having lapsed into a brief respite from her drama, due no doubt to both the heat and the unfortunate turn of their conversation, rallied herself enough to say, "At least try to remember yourself while we're in London!"

"I shall," Pandora replied obediently, as she tucked an errant curl in place.

"Oh, and I do wish you would remember to wear your bonnet! You know how terribly you burn, not to mention those wretched freckles, and the season is just starting!" her aunt exclaimed. "And *should* the Viscount—" Abruptly she cut herself off, and sotto voce, added, "Try not to be too much of a goose: for the other plum approaches!" With a wave of shears, she indicated the Marquess, who was heading down the flagstone path towards them. He was arrayed in a moderately sensible waistcoat, buff pantaloons, and Hessians that gleamed with reflected sun, but his quizzing glass and several fobs and ornate neckcloth—which surely took the better part of the morning to assemble—lifted him above the ordinary, as undoubtedly was intended.

"Lord Manakin," Beatrix breathed in a welcoming tone. "I trust you are all prepared for your venture?"

Making a spectacular leg, he said, "Yes. All is at the ready, though I shall miss your bright company." His glance strayed towards Pandora, "And yours, Miss Tremantle."

"Oh, but Lord Manakin," Beatrix interjected, now fully recovered from the Viscount's note, "we too are going to London. And I am possessed of a wonderful notion. You could do us a great favor by stopping off at our town house and informing the servants we shall be arriving two days hence."

"I should be delighted to assist you in this matter." The words rolled off the gentleman's tongue in much too charming a manner, Pandora decided. Indeed, there was very little to recommend the Marquess, though to witness her aunt's transports one would assume him to be of the first stare.

"Splendid!" Beatrix ejaculated. "Why, if your affairs keep you in London longer than anticipated, you simply must stay at our house in Grosvenor Square."

"Enchanted with the invitation." After a peremptory bow, he said, "Seeing that you are fast in conversation, I would have a stroll about your lovely garden before tea." His eyebrows traveled skyward as he added, "I understand the gentleman who rescued Miss Tremantle at Vauxhall is coming to tea, and I do look forward to making his acquaintance. Until then: your servant, ladies!" With a smart click of his heels he pivoted about and headed towards a terrace of sculpted yew trees.

"Well!" Pandora said with relish, "I note you refrained from informing him that the Viscount would *not* be partaking of tea and crumpets with us!"

"How gleefully you say that," Beatrix retorted. "If you must know, I simply did not wish to distress Lord Manakin unduly, for I believe he is of a delicate constitution: all those years in India!"

"Delicate?" Pandora sputtered.

"Yes, and had you paid the least attention to him, you would have noticed how meticulously he eats everything on his plate. I have no doubt he is starving for decent food. I do wonder what he ate in India," she mused as an afterthought.

"Ground glass wouldn't surprise me," she replied, her eyes twinkling devilishly.

"Pandora, you shall turn into a waspish spinster if you don't take a care! As it is, I am amazed that these two eligibles, which fate has so kindly dropped at your feet, are giving you the time of day." With a sniff, her aunt gathered the daffodils and rose to her feet. "We shall have tea as planned, and these flowers will make a cheery centerpiece." She wagged them under Pandora's nose as if the yellow blooms would compensate for the Viscount's absence. "For after all, we still have a Marquess to entertain! And I do hope you will wear your mauve silk. Pity you had your ruby stolen." This last was tossed over Miss McClellan's shoulder as if her niece had hired the thief.

Pandora was left standing on the garden path, slightly openmouthed, not at Beatrix's idle chatter, but rather in amazement at the idea that presented itself with all the subtlety of an afternoon thunderstorm: why hadn't it occurred to her before? Ha! Yes indeed, she would wear mauve silk to tea; perhaps she would don several ostrich plumes to her fiery curls as well! For if the assumption, which she was about to investigate, was correct, not only would the Marquess be apprehended as the villain he was, but the Viscount would get a taste of Miss Tremantle's mettle. *Helpless female!* Poppycock!

Pandora wasted no time in reaching the Marquess's chamber: Nora and Jemnaz were posted as lookouts should he return from his constitutional in the gardens. Then as carefully and quickly as possible, she went through not only his dresser drawers and secretary, but the baggage by the door as well. Going to London on business, was he? What sort of business, she wondered, as she pulled out a hefty sack from the portmanteau. Sinking her hands into its depths, she withdrew a rough-cut stone that resembled a jagged piece of ice. Recklessly she crossed to the secretary and spilled the contents onto the drop leaf. There were at least a dozen sparkling gemstones: rubies, emeralds, sapphires, and diamonds. Sunlight splashed across them, filling the room with rainbows. Pandora felt her breath catch in her throat and her palms grow moist with sudden nervousness. A rap at the door made her almost jump in the air, but scooping the jewels back into the satchel, she unceremoniously thrust them back in the portmanteau. She had completed her search just in time: his lordship had returned, and as Nora said, there would be the devil to pay if he ever found out she had been about his chamber.

"Well, he shan't find out," Pandora assured her abigail, who with Jemnaz had followed her back to her room. "And believe you me, I intend to find that ruby!"

"Oh, Missy Sahib, the man is very smart. Beware! If he hit you on the head once to get it, think how mad he will be if you take it away!"

"Miss Pandora is just talking, Jemnaz," Nora said on a hopeful note, "for though we do not like the Marquess, we are not certain that he stole the pendant." Crossing to her mistress's armoire, she added, "You must leave us now, for I'm to prepare Miss Pandora for tea."

"Jemnaz, wait," Pandora said. "I have a small favor to ask of you."

"It is already done, Miss Sahib!" he pronounced on a bow that practically took him to the floor. Then looking shyly up at her, added, "Do you wish me to put the sword through the bad man's ribs?"

"No, nothing so drastic!" she said on a laugh. "But could you have Maiden's Prayer saddled and waiting for me outside the stables as soon as the Marquess leaves for London?"

"Oh, Miss Pandora, whatever are you planning now?" Nora asked, her voice filled with dread.

"On recovering my ruby," she replied with a gamine smile. "Now, let's see. Aunt Bea said I should wear the mauve silk to tea: she has high hopes of my enticing our villain!" Cocking her head to one side, Pandora joked, "Shall I wear ostrich plumes in my hair, or would that be unseemly?"

"The only thing unseemly is the little intrigue you seem set on. For I do not see his lordship handing you the ruby even if he had it. And all the ostrich plumes in the world won't help." Nora pulled out the mauve silk and was smoothing the skirt when Pandora quite innocently added, "Oh, I shall wear something quite different for my encounter with the Marquess: breeches, waistcoat, a respectable cravat, headgear, *and a mask!*"

"A mask?" Nora and Jemnaz chorused in horror.

"Of course. What self-respecting highwayman would dream of going abroad without his mask?"

Chapter Seven

Even as Pandora was preparing her masquerade for the *Marquess,* the gentleman known as Viscount Cardew was firing out a volley of instructions to his man Grimley, who stood aghast at the manner in which Lord Cardew was tossing things pell-mell into a small satchel.

"Your lordship, I do implore that you allow me to do that task properly: you are making a muddle of it. Begging your pardon, of course."

"Of course," the Viscount agreed absently, as he fastened the leather thong on the satchel. "Done. Now then, you know your part in the plan: Even though *our Marquess* is leaving for London, I have hired two *gentlemen* to keep watch over Miss Tremantle, starting tomorrow. One of them will report each day to you; and should anything go amiss, you and they know to find me at the Jolly Squire."

"Rest easy, my lord. When I delivered your message this afternoon, I made the acquaintance of Miss Tremantle's abigail, and she has promised also to keep me informed as to her mistress's activities."

"Ha! Has an abigail, does she? You'd never know it the way she flies about the country. Good work, Grimley." Crossing to the beveled dressing glass, his lordship achieved, with several flips of the wrist, an outstanding cravat, adjusted his shirt points, and with practiced ease slipped into his own coat.

"You know, my lord, that I am ever at your service, and have been since you were in leading strings, though it does baffle me how you insist on doing my job!" His eyebrows rose a trifle at the set of his master's driving coat, indicating he was far superior at dressing his lordship.

"Surely you don't miss the old days, Grimley?"

"At least back then you knew what a valet was for, my lord." Stepping forward with a clothes brush, he commenced to whack the Viscount's coat with a vigor suggestive of knocking some sense into the gentleman. "I do believe that Indian climate has made you forget your station."

"In some ways you are right," Cardew agreed, indicating with a wave of his hand that his man might cease brushing his coat. "Though not in the way you imagine."

"Well, if going about pretending to be Viscount Cardew—"

"But I *am* Viscount Cardew!" his lordship reminded Grimley.

"Yes, but have you forgotten the Marquess of Manakin?"

"You speak of me or the pretender?" the Viscount queried on a laugh, only to quickly add, "You know full well I intend on unmasking the man, but since there's no crime in masquerading as someone else, I must perforce catch him at his craft, which is the main reason I wish to reach London before he does. Since I am not apprised of his true name, I shall catch the fellow on the run, so to speak. It's quite obliging of him to reveal himself so openly." Picking up his baggage, he called for Chandro, then heading for the door added, "Take that stricken look off your face, my man: I'm out to find myself a jewel!"

"My lord, with all due respect, I need remind you the Bow Street Runners set London on its ear, if you'll remember, and were unable to find Lady Lorena Dowling's ruby or her murderer, and that was eight years ago!"

"Yes, but that very same ruby has now surfaced and been stolen again, this time from Miss Tremantle. We shall not haggle the point; I remember the setting well. It is the jewel I gave Lady Lorena, and it is most peculiar that my impostor presented the ruby to Miss Tremantle." A delicious smile of triumph swept his countenance.

"Then why not stay here, instead of chasing after shadows in London?"

"I would not call the masquerading Manakin a shadow, and I feel certain this sudden trip to London has something to do with the ruby, probably among other jewels, for I've no doubt his stay at Chatford is connected to the Snow Leopard treasure." With an affable smile he turned to the grinning Indian boy. "Well, Chandro, you may have grown up in Bombay, but no man has lived until he's seen London!" He patted the boy's slim shoulders, and Chandro responded by looking up at his lordship as if he were Krishna himself.

"Chandro goes to Lun-dun," he sang out with glee, as he tugged on *the real Marquess's* coattails.

"My lord," his valet began, "*if* the impostor at Chatford Abbey was responsible for Lady Lorena's death, you may be dealing with a ruthless murderer."

"Mur-der-er," Chandro recited by rote, as if it were in cozy company with such words as *Hindu* and *Lun-dun.*

"Murderer," Grimley repeated, much to Chandro's delight, who continued to whisper this tricky word. "And although it is not my place to remind your lordship, I do so nevertheless: Lady Lorena was only a step above a Cyprian, and were you to have married her your Mama would have gone to her grave that much sooner! I shall further add, at risk to my position, that Lady Lorena not only played you false, but undoubtedly brought about her own most unfortunate end by her association with—"

"The Duke of Diamonds," interrupted Cardew. "And were it not for his peculiar habit of leaving the ace of diamonds at the scene of all his robberies, I would have most likely been sentenced to hang for the murder of my betrothed." The Viscount paused before adding, "Rest assured, I have always been aware of my deceased fiancée's 'flaws,' and have never carried a torch for the lady. I go, not to avenge the lovely late Lorena, but rather my once good name."

"Well, then," Grimley uttered in a more moderate tone, "I wish your lordship and young Chandro a fruitful journey."

"Thank you, my man! And since you seem set upon playing the valet, when this imbroglio is cleared up and the jewels recovered, perhaps you and I shall take our leave of England for a time."

"Any place but India, my lord."

"The south of France is quite pleasant," Cardew said with a hint of a smile, as an image of Miss Tremantle, resplendent in her golden gown and with laughter in her emerald eyes, fogged his vision momentarily. The smile vanished: there was no future in that dream. He might avenge his once good name, but he could never retrieve it. Although he had been cleared of the murder charge, society had not forgotten the scandal of his alliance. His years in India might have continued indefinitely, but for the Snow Leopard Jewels. To return now only to find his title born by an impostor, perhaps the very man responsible for the lovely Lorena's untimely end, was an irony which would have amused his lordship, were the villain less dangerous. A man so obsessed with jewels that he had strangled a woman for a ruby, a few baubles: a villain once known as the Duke of Diamonds, the notorious London jewel thief whose unquenchable thirst for gems had led him to India in pursuit of the fabled Snow Leopard cache. Had the lure of yet more jewels brought him full circle? Or as Chandro would say, back to his *Karma?* Had he, in truth, surfaced again as the "Marquess," or was this impostor after other game?

Shaking these thoughts off, the Viscount strode toward the door. "We'd best be off," he called over his shoulder. "Keep a careful watch on our Miss Tremantle!"

"Our Miss Tre-mantel?" Chandro asked, his question echoing down the halls of the Orange Crown Inn.

Nora had set to trembling and clutching at her skirts as her mistress hoisted herself upon Maiden's Prayer, who was whinnying softly at this nocturnal treat. "I don't like it above half what you're about to do: it is dangerous in the extreme, and were Miss Beatrix to find out, it should be a very sticky wicket!"

"I shall return within the hour, *with* the ruby, and the Marquess none the wiser." Pandora secured the dueling pistols, which she had neatly stuck in a holster. "Do I not look the part of a dangerous rogue?"

"Miss Sahib, not without your mask! And you must talk

like a very bad man." Jemnaz's voice plunged an octave as he thrust his chest out and affected an appropriate swagger.

Putting on the black mask, she said, "I hope this is the fashion for highwaymen this season. I know it's very popular at balls and fêtes. Ha! *'Your jewelry or your life!'* " she managed to growl before subsiding into nervous laughter.

"Oh, Miss, I do wish you would reconsider this folly," her abigail pleaded in watery tones.

"Heavens, Nora, you are beginning to sound just like Aunt Bea. I'm only going to—"

"To hold up his lordship's carriage!" Nora interrupted, "And for a ruby that might not even be there! Oh, and just think of what your aunt will do if she finds out!"

"She won't."

"But, what if Lord Manakin wrestles your brother's dueling pistols from you?"

"Let the villain try! Well, wish me luck," Pandora said urging the horse forward, then touching the rim of the hat that hid her curls from view, she trotted down the moonlight-spangled path rehearsing her speech.

Although Pandora had ridden this road at night before, she had certainly not done so in a highwayman's raiment. Nevertheless, as riding astride was nothing new to her, she managed to keep up a right good canter on the high-spirited Maiden's Prayer.

The moon, which had been nearly full a few nights earlier, now dipped in and out of the clouds like a gleaming soup-spoon in thick porridge. Pandora prayed it would cast her in shadow at the moment of truth. And if she had figured correctly, she should catch up with his lordship's carriage before he turned onto the coach road to London.

Gathering confidence that her seat was secure, Pandora urged Maiden's Prayer into an even faster canter, verging on a gallop. As treetops whizzed overhead, and the cool night breeze slapped against her, she fancied a carriage some distance down the road, and with excitement realized she was rapidly gaining on it. Would he recognize her beneath Winthrop's cast-off buckskins and her mask? Of a sudden her heart took up the hoofbeat pattern of the hard-packed road and she felt an exhilarated excitement course through her as if she were slightly tipsy.

Careening alongside the carriage, she noted it to be dark, and if there was a family crest, it was nigh impossible to see. Pulling one of the dueling pistols out, she brandished it with all the imagined fierceness of a true brigand.

"Halt!" she cried recklessly, throwing herself into the role of one of Mrs. Hawkshore's fictional highwaymen, and waving the firearm as if it were a sword, she motioned that the occupant of the carriage should reveal himself, stand and deliver.

No one appeared, but the driver, swinging about in an attempt to disarm her, so alarmed Pandora that she near toppled from her horse. A flash and a deafening report was followed by a sharp oath as the driver clutched his arm, a look of fury stamped on his face. With a horrified gasp, Pandora realized she had accidentally shot him, and that there would be no ruby from this gentleman, for he was none other than Lord Cardew, with Chandro peeping over his shoulder!

No sooner had Pandora thrust the pistol home, than Maiden's Prayer bolted down the road at such a gallop that it was some minutes before she managed to check the horse and bring her under control. Wheeling about, Pandora started back. Dear heavens, she had wounded the Viscount! What a dreadful, terrible thing to do. She had never done anything like this before; thank goodness it was only a flesh wound, and that Chandro was there to tend to him. She drew tight on the reins as her initial panic subsided: returning would only make matters worse. No, she would have to proceed with her plan, for it would be awful to have wounded Lord Cardew for nothing!

Turning about, and without risking a glance behind, Pandora urged the horse to top the nearest fence, and together they fairly flew across the meadow. Still, the picture of the Viscount gripping his arm haunted her. At least Chandro could handle the ribbons well enough to steer a course back to the Orange Crown. But what if she *had* killed him? Taking a ragged breath, she reminded herself she hadn't; nor need she worry he would pursue her over field and stream. Even so, it was some time before she slackened her pace: her heart was racing, and her face felt flushed, though the night was cool.

At length she managed to regain her composure, determined more than ever to waylay the Marquess. But where was he on that long stretch of road? In front of the Viscount or behind him? If she kept on her current course, she would reach Gate Crossing, which bordered the Wofford-Sydney property and led to the London road. There she would lay in wait, hidden by the curve of the road, until the Marquess came into view.

A terrible thought occurred to Pandora as she reached Gate Crossing: what if she were to entangle with the Viscount yet again? No! It was not to be considered. Even as she was possessed of this troublesome possibility, she heard the approach of horses' hooves. This time she managed to quiet her tumultuous heart somewhat, and withdrawing the other pistol, advanced forward as the coach swung into view. Yes! It was the Marquess's vehicle: she was certain.

"Halt!" Pandora cried in a voice she barely recognized—for surely it squeaked with the fear that drenched her. "Halt, I say!" And brandishing her weapon, she was amazed as the driver—needing no further urging, pulled the carriage to a shuddering halt, threw his pistol into the swirling cloud of dust, and quickly began to empty his pockets.

"Keep it!" Pandora said gruffly, managing to throw herself into the role of highwayman. Thankfully it wasn't Tribbs at the reins, and God willing she wouldn't have to tangle with him. "I'll clap me peepers on the bloke in your box, though." Then directing her attention to the occupant within, rasped, "Empty your treasure chests, and keep a muzzle on your mouth, for I've no need to hear a hard luck story."

Slowly the carriage door creaked open and a lone pistol was tossed to the ground. White-topped boots came into view, then biscuit-colored breeches, and finally the man himself, looking more enraged than Pandora could ever have imagined. His valet, it appeared, hovered in the background. As the Marquess reached for his quizzing glass to inspect her, Pandora snapped out, "Leave off that business. We'll not meet again, mate. Coins, bills, and jewels, if'n you please. Right here in this sack!"

"You'll not get away with this," the Marquess ground out as he reluctantly produced the desired articles, his eyes barely leaving hers, and so filled with such fury that a cold chill crept up Pandora's spine. When he fumbled with a leather case, her heart nearly stopped. It was the last item he placed in her sack, and from the way he paused, she was certain it had to be the ruby. She swallowed hard against any other possibility, and pulling the sack into her lap, touched pistol to hat, and with a flick of the reins, galloped home.

"Well, I did it," Pandora cried, as she divested herself of cap, pistols, and riding coat, then giving Nora and Jemnaz a quick hug, she added, "That is, I think I did—though there were a few rough spots . . ." She paused momentarily, then plunging her hand into the leather case, withdrew a banded folio of papers. Tossing them to one side, she searched the case again, this time producing a velvet box.

"The ruby!" Nora and Jemnaz chorused.

"The ruby," Pandora replied with relief, withdrawing the jewel and holding it aloft to catch the light. Then placing it carefully back in its case, she ruefully added, "Things didn't turn out exactly as I'd imagined."

"Did you pop the bad man?" Jemnaz asked, his eyes aglitter with the drama.

"No, I rather think I 'popped' the good man."

"The *good* man?" Nora and Jemnaz echoed.

"Well, it was an accident," she muttered, almost wishing she hadn't said anything, but nevertheless indicated they should accommodate themselves for the telling, which she accomplished in fits and starts while pacing in front of the fireplace. By the time she had completed the tale, her captive audience of two was glued to its seats.

Jemnaz broke the silence. "You are a most amazing lady, Missy Sahib, to have unwitted this Viscount. But never fear, he will recover fast."

Nora, too stunned for immediate words, merely regarded the pistol with a distinct shudder, then finally pronounced, "Nasty things these are, though I don't think they've been fired before tonight."

In an attempt to shrug off a wave of guilt, Pandora flippantly replied, "How appropriate that I should christen Winny's new Manton dueling pistols by wounding the man I had thought fleecing him!" Her brows made twin furrows between her eyes. "I shall clean both pistols straight away, then return them to the arms chest before he misses them. You needn't wait up for me, Nora."

"Such a day it has been." The abigail rolled her eyes effectively, and pausing at the door, added, "Whatever will the two lordships do this evening?"

"Knowing the Viscount's obstinacy, he'd press on to hell if he had an engagement with the devil."

"Oh, Miss, the words you use!" Nora said.

"And the Marquess, having been thoroughly burgled, would lose face and feel like a beaten school boy if he returned. Besides, I intentionally overlooked the jewels in his portmanteau, so he is probably congratulating himself on his cleverness in concealing them." Pandora brightened considerably at this image. "Oh, how I would love to be a mouse in his carriage and see what calls him to London!"

"I'll not listen to any more of your schemes, Miss Pandora! Come, Jemnaz." She gave her mistress what was clearly intended to be a look of warning, then putting an arm around the Indian child, scurried out the door.

Yes, Pandora thought as she changed into her dressing gown, *I should love to be a mouse in his carriage!* Ah, but she had the ruby, and except for shooting the Viscount . . . Her thoughts returned to the dreadful accident. If only he hadn't reached for her pistol, it wouldn't have happened. But it *did* happen: suddenly the full horror of what she'd done struck her most forcibly. It would seem they were destined to doomed encounters as if capricious fate were playing a game with them. If only he hadn't been on the road! With a sigh, she stopped pacing, and sank into her boudoir chair. *But why* was *he on the road, and* where *was he going at that late hour?*

Enough! She must stop this round-robin thinking or she would go mad. Thus pushing aside these ruminations, Pandora retrieved the ruby, and after studying it for a moment, replaced it in its velvet case. Then idly she turned her attention to the sheaf of papers that the Marquess had relinquished. On first glimpse they appeared to be legal documents with various seals and impressive signatures, but when she saw that one of the letters bore her father's signature, she gave it her full attention, carefully reading the correspondence. But why was it addressed to Mr. Rice of the Bow Street Runners? Why indeed, unless the man who had presented himself as the Marquess of Manakin *was* Mr. Rice, and had been hired by her father, as this letter suggested.

> . . . Again my thanks for keeping a watch on Chatford Abbey. I will rest easier knowing my house and family are under your protection.
>
> Yrs,
> Horatio Tremantle
> Bombay, India

With trembling hands Pandora hastily lay the letter on the table before her, much as an expectant gambler might spread his hand. All the correspondence was addressed to Mr. Rice, and referred to various Bow Street matters. But it was her father's letter that stood out like an ace among the others: that he had hired a Runner was apparent, but were things in such a state that Mr. Rice felt compelled to pose as Lord Manakin? *And,* if he really were a Runner, how did he get the ruby? For someone *did* knock her out for that jewel. And it had ended up in Manakin's possession. That much she knew. But if the Marquess were a Runner, wouldn't he have said something? Pandora shuffled through the rest of the letters in an attempt to make sense of this newest development, if that were possible. But it was late, she was tired, *and* she was very confused.

If Manakin were *a Runner,* then perhaps he took the jewel off the man who had knocked her over the head. But who? *Cardew?* Surely not. No, not Cardew. Her fingers touched her lips as did the remembered whisper of a kiss.

Just *who* was Edmund Rice? Pandora glanced once more to the letters before her as if some overlooked clue might present itself. She had been so sure that Manakin was the villain of the piece. Nothing else made sense. But how then did he come by those papers? The same way he apparently came by the jewel? Took them off a Runner her father had hired? *Runner? Marquess? Thief?* Oh, what a muddle! In a single sweep she gathered the correspondence and thrust it back in its case. No matter what, she would follow through with her plan. If the Marquess was the guilty party, her game would call his hand. With this certainty and pistols in hand, she headed down to the gun room.

The following morning was a whirlwind of activity as Miss McClellan rose to her métier in orchestrating the caravan that would whisk them the short distance to London. Although she had decided on an even earlier departure than originally intended, not a detail was to be overlooked: even though there was an adequate staff at Grosvenor Square, it would be augmented by several of Chatford's servants. One would have thought they were getting set for a lengthy journey instead of a brief shopping jaunt.

Despite these hectic preparations, Miss Tremantle awoke the next morning as bright as the sunshine that poured in her window. This mood, however, was suddenly brought up short as she recalled the disastrous encounter with the Viscount. Nonetheless, it would certainly not do to sink into guilt and remorse. So pushing these feelings to one side Pandora, determined to find out how Cardew was faring, penned him a brief missive. It would be sent in care of Grimley, who would, she hoped, find the Viscount. Not wishing to divulge her guilt, and feeling a sudden wave of unaccountable recklessness, she taunted him with the following:

My Lord Cardew:

The ruby is now in my possession! And I am having it appraised!

Yrs faithfully,
Miss Pandora Tremantle
<u>Grosvenor Square, London</u>

She underscored *Grosvenor Square,* hoping that curiosity *and* an ambulatory condition would impel him to pay call and see the ruby for himself. Perhaps then he would take her seriously. Of course he must never learn that she had been his assailant.

The expedition to London consisted of three well-sprung carriages that progressed at a lumbering pace: with Parks at the reins, and Jemnaz at his side, the lead carriage bore the Tremantle crest on its doors and the family within. The second vehicle transported Nora, Pattybone, and several giggling belowstairs maids. The third carriage was filled with bandboxes and empty trunks which on the return would be bursting with not only costumes for the ball, but a rainbow of silks and satins for other occasions, and an equally impressive representation for Winthrop.

Unbeknownst to this little entourage, a fourth vehicle, a rather nondescript gig, followed in its wake: at the ribbons were two *gentlemen,* as unlike as two peas in a pod, cast together as watchdogs for Miss Tremantle. They considered themselves honorable chaps, and as such would do justice by their contract with the nob who hired them; although there was certainly no mention of chasing about the countryside after the lady! Recompense would naturally be made, though heaven only knew the outcome of this particular twist in their assignment.

Upon reaching their destination, the squat fellow, appropriately called Dumpling, turned in the gig to his partner, with the equally descriptive name of Bone, and said, "There ain't a doubt about it: these folks be heeled in gold. Just look at them!" He stared quite agog as the Tremantle carriages were being unloaded in front of their stately mansion on Grosvenor Square.

"Aye," Bone agreed. "And we's to keep our blinkers out for unsavories, for that's what we was fetched for."

"But," Dumpling countered, "Lunnon's full of 'em. How's we to know which one to plug?"

"We ain't *plugging* any! I got the brain, and you—being champeen fighter, or so you say—be the muscle."

Dumpling nodded. "And we's both come up a peg. For Grimley said we's to take up lodging at the Jolly Squire and catch up with his lor'ship there. Why tonight we be set up like Quality, swillin' fine wine, 'n'—"

"No such thing! I be the one to meet with the Viscount. You will keep watch on Miss Tremantle."

"A body's got to sleep! 'Sides, I be the one for the Jolly Squire."

"It will be me; and there's the end of that!" At Dumpling's deflated look, Bone added, "For it's you what's got the brawn to protect the lady. Mind you keep to the shadows, and don't go plugging no strangers!"

While Bone and Dumpling fussed about their task, their employer, the Viscount, was listening to Chandro babble forth a stream of Hindi as he changed his lordship's bandage. Nothing seemed to phase this true jewel, who had not only delivered them to the Jolly Squire the night before, but having just returned from his first assignment, was a cauldron of vital information.

"And now, sahib," the boy said proudly as he knotted the linen bandage on the Viscount's arm, "I shall draw you a map of where the man they call the Marquess stays." Perching himself on the edge of a rough-hewn oak chair, and propping his elbows on a rather scarred all-purpose table, the boy earnestly took up quill, and after dipping it into the standish, commenced to sketch an elaborate map. At the appropriate juncture, Chandro marked an X.

"This Marquess must have a lot of money," the boy said, looking up from his artistic rendering, "for the house is very grand, and two stone lions guard the entrance. You were smart to know the man's carriage would pass this way."

"And you, my lad, were fast in following him on that pony of yours, else we'd not have this fine map to show for your efforts." The Viscount leaned back, a thoroughly pleased expression on his countenance. "So, our *Marquess* either lives on or is visiting Green Street, in what I should imagine are fairly fancy digs. Do you think you and your pony can find it again?"

Chandro nodded his head enthusiastically. "Without the map! Shiva and I—" He paused, then quickly added, "I have named our new pony after the god! That way we have protection. Well, he and I make a good team, probably because we are both skinny and dark. We got *this* close to the Marquess." He held his thumb and index finger an inch apart. "And I saw him hit his driver. He was in a mean mood. But he doesn't scare me, and I bet you want me to tag after him tonight, right?" His eyes glittered with the adventure.

"Not tonight. I'll tend to that, but on the morrow, while I'm about some other business, I would like you to follow him like the shadow you are. Note every place he goes, and then we will see what needs to be done." The Viscount closed his eyes briefly and leaned back against the pillows. He was clad in dark breeches and the remains of what was once an exquisitely tailored shirt, the loss of whose left sleeve having rendered it beyond redemption. The fresh bandage had yet to show blood, which was a good sign—not that any doctor had pronounced it thus, for in this rough-and-tumble inn, his lordship was lucky to have had it tended to at all. Still, he and the boy would make do, though it was a cramped and airless room, and the sight of peeling paint and dingy windows was not exactly heartening.

"Sahib not feeling so good?" Chandro asked, taking up a position next to the cot on which the Viscount reclined.

"A bit uncomfortable," he replied on a laugh.

"Pistol. Bang! Make hole," the boy chirped in English, "Right, Sahib?"

"No, Chandro. Just a flesh wound, not a hole."

Lapsing back into his mother tongue, the child rapidly said, "I'll go and fetch dinner and some ale for you." He grinned. "And for me too!" Then as an afterthought he added, "You are a very brave man: so many people try to pop you off: Thugs, highwaymen. Tonight I shall say special prayer to Shiva *and* Kali."

"Kali?" the Viscount asked, amused at this vengeful twist.

"Yes. To destroy those who would harm you. We send them back their Karma." With a beguiling grin, the small fellow darted out the door, leaving his lordship to consider those words.

Ah, but he would miss the little chap: his tiger, valet, and now spy. However, eventually he would have to keep his promise to Sir Horatio, that he would deliver him safe and sound to Chatford Abbey.

The Viscount shifted his position on the mound of pillows Chandro had fashioned for him, and feeling a twinge of pain, roundly cursed the sprig of a green highwayman that nearly shot off his limb. A humbling experience that. Ah, well. He'd experienced worse. Far worse, he mused, remembering the natives hired to make his killing appear a Thug sacrifice, when Cardew knew only too well the grip of a true Thug; knew also the rapacious greed that drove the mysterious Duke of Diamonds: again he thought of the strangled Lorena, the ace of diamonds playing card, and how the newspapers had reported that the verdict had truly rested on "the turn of the card." Thus the Viscount went free, *but* so had the villain.

His thoughts were interrupted as Chandro came whistling into the room, laden with an enormous tray. "This food is not like the Orange Crown's, and theirs was bad enough." Staggering towards the room's only table, he plopped the tray on the edge while he pushed the map and inkpot to one side, then with a little grunt, he slid their supper onto the table. "If you like, I shall bring it to you in bed."

"The devil you will!" the Viscount said, rising. "I am neither on my deathbed, nor in my dotage, and shall sup sitting up! Good Gad, what's that?" He stood, appalled at the oddly shapen piece of meat Chandro had just uncovered.

"Sahib, I shall have my usual vegetables," the boy said, pushing the entrée as far from him as possible. Then taking a chair, he politely added, "I believe it is part of a dead cow."

"Umm." The Viscount eyed it speculatively. "I too shall pass; however, this ham hock looks respectable, and the pickled salmon I assure you is harmless."

The child, happily munching on a boiled cabbage leaf, began innocently chattering about the nice Miss Tre-mantel, and was she *really* Sir Horatio's daughter? His lordship replied that yes, it would appear so. Wishing to shelve this somewhat painful topic, which the Viscount had miraculously managed *not* to think about, he attempted to change the subject, but the boy, determined to forecast the future, relentlessly pushed on.

"Sir Horatio said that maybe you would marry his daughter." Popping a small potato into his mouth, Chandro managed to ask, "Will you?"

His lordship choked on a rather insipid ale. "I doubt Sir Horatio ever said anything of the kind, and the answer is no."

"That's too bad, because Miss Tre-mantel is so tall she might not ever find a husband. And her father said that soon she would be on the shelf." Chandro blinked two very dark eyes, and blithely continued. "Does that mean that no man will buy her?"

"In England we do not *buy* our wives. And I seriously doubt anything would ever keep Miss Tremantle on any shelf. She is far too outspoken and unpredictable for such an existence."

"Ah, that is good. Just like you, sahib." Having apparently had his say, Chandro began vigorously mashing a pile of pale green peas, leaving the Viscount in considerable agitation.

Taking refuge in the ale once again, his lordship fought back the feelings he did indeed hold for the spirited lady. Yes, by the saints, she did have mettle! No mincing, fainting damsel she. Her eyes were as green and brilliant as any emerald he'd ever seen, and when she was on her high ropes, nothing could compare with those eyes. Nor with the feel of her in his arms: long-limbed, slender, and so delicious that it had been almost impossible to release her. Then there were her lips, soft, yielding, and sweetly scented. He felt his entire body tighten at the memory.

Damn the kiss! He slapped the tankard down so hard that ale sloshed over the rim. Chandro looked up, thoroughly startled, but then with an inscrutable grin, said, "Miss Tremantel is amazing."

"Amazing? Yes, I suppose if one considers the constant scrapes she assuredly gets herself into."

"She is beautiful too!" Chandro said scooping a forkful of green mash into his mouth.

"Granted. Point taken. But we are about other business." His lordship looked fleetingly at the pickled salmon: it had been the specialty at Vauxhall Gardens *that night.* So, Sir Horatio had mentioned his nuptial dreams to the lad too. Damn and double damn!

"*Beautiful!*" This time Chandro said the word in English, as if this feat would further capture his lordship's interest. Then in Hindi he quickly added, "But since you are not going to keep your word to Sir Horatio and marry her, we should probably stop talking about the beautiful, tall lady who will go to the shelf where no one will buy her."

"I did not give my word to her father!" the Viscount said, starting. "Besides, I have nothing to offer her but a good purse and a bad name!"

A pounding on the door interrupted this moment of high drama. Chandro scooted forward and swung wide the door on one of the guards the Viscount had hired to watch over Miss Tremantle. It was then his lordship felt a sudden sinking feeling as if something very dear to him had just been irrevocably snatched away.

Chapter Eight

That this was not the case was immediately made apparent, and his lordship, vastly relieved that Miss Tremantle had not come to harm, instructed Bone to keep constant watch over her, and should a certain gentleman, whose description Bone and Dumpling knew, be seen anywhere near her person, they would take whatever steps were necessary to ensure her safety.

"Even if it means *popping* the cove?"

"Preferably not, but if necessary, yes, *pop* away."

This bit of advice seemed to warm the cockles of the man's heart, who upon departing was heard to murmur something about curling up the villain's toenails.

Leaving the Indian boy to rest up after his day's work, the Viscount hailed a hackney, and after instructing the driver to let him out at Green Street, slipped into the darkened carriage. The night was thick with fog, and not a star or a moonbeam could be seen. Still, the narrow streets were choked with all manner of conveyances as they jostled for their share of the road.

Pushing the window curtain to one side, his lordship stared into the blanket of night that wrapped about the carriage like a soft cocoon. Like the night, the Viscount was dressed in black, relieved solely by a simple linen cravat. He also carried a rather remarkable walking stick, which had been custom-made in India: its dark wood was crowned with a carved-ivory elephant head, innocent looking, but unsheathed it became the handle of a long and deadly dagger, which had more than once saved his lordship's life.

When they had reached Green Street, the driver asked if he might wait for the gentleman, and gave a shrug to his shoulders when he was told no, that the gentleman would prefer to take the air. The driver mumbled something about the lack of fit air to be had that night, and with a click to his reins, vanished into the skeins of swirling mist.

Turning about, the Viscount started down the street. The paving beneath his feet and the houses, flush with the sidewalk, were visible enough. When Chandro had drawn his map and avidly described the villain's lodgings as being a red brick house of grand proportions guarded by stone lions, his lordship seemed to recall the house. The Viscount, having a town house himself on Half Moon Street, had been well acquainted with the Mayfair district of eight years ago.

Lord Cardew's boot heels clicked and echoed in the fog-enshrouded street. It was empty to the eye, but sounds of laughter and other footsteps were muffled in the night. He stopped abruptly before two squat lions, whose pug faces gave them a decidedly Oriental flavor. Had they been positioned much farther onto the sidewalk the Viscount would have tripped over them. Casting a glance over the classical facade he noted that it was crowned by two pediments and possessed of square dormer windows and a clock tower. Impressive indeed. Even more gratifying, however, was the fact that the place was occupied, as was indicated by the flickering lights which slipped through curtained panes to pierce the fog.

A sound within alerted him, and stepping beyond the amber glow that flooded the sidewalk as the front door opened, his lordship perceived the figure of a gentleman, caped, gloved, and thoroughly prepared for an evening's extravaganza. This intelligence was confirmed as the gentleman briskly strode to the curb just as his carriage approached. An underling all but spread a cape for the exquisitely arrayed person to tread upon. Steps were pulled down, and the gentleman was assisted into the vehicle. All of this was viewed through a haze of fog, but the Viscount noted that *he*—whoever *he* was—considered himself to be in the high kick of fashion, for beneath the vermilion-lined opera cape flashed an equally vermilion waistcoat and a cravat that resembled the icing on a wedding cake. There was a flash of boot and more cape as the gentleman situated himself in the carriage. By this time several servants had appeared, though they seemed a bit superfluous. However, when the butler called out, "Sir Rupert, Sir Rupert! Your quizzing glass!" and rushed forward with this indispensable item, the Viscount smiled in spite of himself.

Sir Rupert Montescue. Of course! He had inherited the title of baronet, *and* a propensity for a lifestyle of excesses. He was known in all the gaming hells, purportedly played a good hand, and was famous for his outlandish bets. The man would bet on anything.

As his horse and carriage rumbled over the cobblestones and was devoured by the night, Cardew whistled softly in amazement at just how much he could remember about Montescue. Although born of a good name, his excessive lifestyle kept him out of Society. He preferred the prize fights and the men's clubs to the dances at Almack's, and was never seen at any of the various balls and parties given for young ladies. The Viscount stared at the silent stone lions for a moment before heading towards Grosvenor Square: oh but the tales they could impart.

Sir Rupert Montescue—*the Duke of Diamonds?* It seemed unlikely that this exquisite was quick and clever enough to have burgled half of London. He could easily picture a liaison between him and the lovely Lorena, but ruthless murder over a few baubles? That would certainly take Society by surprise! The Viscount recalled hearing of an estate somewhere between London and Bath, and when Montescue wasn't there, he tooled about Europe, or so the gossips said. To such a one, India was undoubtedly a stone's throw, and the Snow Leopard Jewels would of course lure any jewel addict. Nevertheless, Cardew had difficulty reconciling these two identities.

Cardew paused before turning onto Grosvenor Square, as an elegant carriage rattled past on slick cobblestones: laughter floated on the air, only to be carried away on a wisp of fog. His lordship, tapping a steady beat with his cane, resumed his evening constitutional. So this is where the Tremantles resided when in London. Sir Horatio had compared himself to their stone mansion, declaring they were both old, drafty, and full of stories. They had supped that night in Bombay over a particularly pungent curry while lackeys fanned them, and a skinny lad named Chandro had taken delight in regaling the Viscount with the legend of the Snow Leopard Jewels. That was also the night he had learned that the Duke of Diamonds had taken up residence in Bombay.

His lordship's pace slackened a bit as he neared the Tremantle house: as Sir Rupert's was identified by stone lions, so the Tremantle establishment was marked by a coat of arms emblazoned above an impressively broad front door, a door which would easily receive several people abreast. There were candles ablaze in the downstairs windows, and judging from the hour, the occupants of the house were probably dining. He was tempted to blunder in on the instant and give Pandora further warning: but realizing the social inappropriateness of such tactics, he merely presented his card to the butler and left word he would pay a call on her the following afternoon.

Before searching out a hackney to transport him back to the Jolly Squire, his lordship made note that Miss Tremantle's personal guard had posted himself across the street. Satisfied that the situation was moderately well in hand, the Viscount hailed the first carriage for hire that passed, and sinking against the cushions, took inventory, and made plans accordingly. Considering all things, he would later repair to his house on Half Moon Street, that he might be nearby in case there was trouble—or so he tried to convince himself.

By nature, the Viscount was not a man to overlook anything, and had he been, his years in India would have surely eradicated that flaw. However, he had not counted on such close association with the unpredictable Pandora Tremantle, nor was he apprised of the fact that she was now in possession of the vital clue: the ruby pendant. A not-so-insignificant fact, which would cause him considerable consternation.

Pandora's slender fingers longed to race across the pianoforte's keys in an attempt to conclude with the lugubrious piece: Chloe, on the other hand, totally enthralled, lingered over every note, looking charming in her pale saffron frock with its frilly lace. Her hands were clasped in front of the rapid rise and fall of her breast, and as she neared the completion of the love song, she gave a toss of her yellow curls and effected an exquisite trill, which brought Winthrop out of his chair in a burst of applause worthy of the opera house.

Miss McClellan, who had been fitfully dozing on a gold-covered sofa, came wide awake, and reaching for her salts, murmured, "Is something amiss?" The lady, decked in gold, made an unfortunate blend with the sofa, and thus appeared to have enlarged considerably since their arrival in London. Pulling herself upright, she repeated the query in ringing tones.

"Our Chloe has just sung her heart out!" Winthrop cried, crossing to the pianoforte.

"Sung her heart out? Winny, that is such a vulgar expression: I am but thankful there is no one of significance here. Heavens, the trip did exhaust me."

Whatever else might have followed this pronouncement was effectively curtailed by the discreet knock on the saloon door, followed by the butler's appearance. He started for Miss Tremantle, who was still seated at the pianoforte, but at Beatrix's imperious "I shall see to this, Hawkins!" he changed directions, and presented the silver salver to Miss McClellan. She snatched the card up, then with a raised eyebrow, said, "The Viscount Cardew? Here?"

"No ma'am. His lordship said he would pay an afternoon call on Miss Tremantle." With a bow, he made a crisp exit.

"Oh, my! The Viscount trailing you to London—and after I thought all was lost! Why, this is the most fortuitous turn of events!" she ejaculated as her niece hastened to sit beside her. "Look!" Beatrix commanded, thrusting the ecru-colored card at her.

As her aunt gushed forth ecstatically, Pandora turned the card over in her hand as if it were a trump. So, Lord Cardew, on the mend, *would* be paying a call. Oh, and what a treat it would be to watch his reaction when she unveiled the ruby.

"Well, child? What have you to say?" Beatrix demanded on a thrilling note.

"Oh, famous it is!" Chloe said, sitting eagerly across from

her aunt and cousin. "Do you not agree, Winny?" she added, sending him a coquettish look from beneath thick lashes.

"Capital fellow, the Viscount!"

"Why, I am persuaded to proceed with a tea for him. Naturally, we shall retire after the repast; for I am sure he means to have *significant words* with you, and—"

"Unchaperoned?" Pandora asked, blithely interrupting.

"Oh, fiddle! It shall not be spread about town. Besides, having had your first season, *and* your second, it will not be unseemly. Winny, come, help me up!" she commanded, her bejeweled fingers fluttering in midair. This accomplished, Beatrix swept toward the double doors that led onto the main hall, and executing a remarkable pivot, made to inspect both Pandora and the pink saloon. "You must wear your mulberry satin with the gold ribands, and have Nora do *something* with your hair." She made an impatient gesture with her hands, then screwing her features into a look of profound distaste added, "I but wish we had ordered those new draperies earlier: the sunlight has faded these to a most insipid rose—though I expect he will be impressed with our ceiling!" She indicated the painted spectacle of gods and cherubs that cavorted amongst puffy clouds and brilliant blue skies. When originally executed, the orgy of deities had caused quite a stir, though gradually, like the rose curtains, it too had faded, though it was looked at rather fondly by all those fortunate enough to gaze upon it.

"I am certain Lord Cardew will find himself right at home amongst the Olympians!" Pandora said with a sniff, not revealing her delight that the man was coming at *her* behest.

"I beg of you, Pandy, do not put the Viscount in a taking with your talk!" Beatrix commenced to moderately pace the length of a brilliantly colored Oriental rug, her gold skirts swirling and swishing with each step she took. Pausing beneath an airy portrait of a demure ancestress in a powdered wig, she heaved a breath and added, "It is obvious our Viscount has seen fit to forgive and forget your little attempt to burgle him of a jewel he did not have; and I think it is a magnificent gesture of goodwill. I but pray you will act accordingly."

"Aunt Beatrix," Winthrop inserted, "I should think perhaps she piqued his fancy *with* her impetuous behavior."

"Winny, don't, please, encourage Pandora's carryings on," Beatrix replied. "Nevertheless, I do applaud your vision of Pandora and the Viscount. Oh, heavens, that shall make her his *viscountess!*"

"I have no desire to be his, or anyone else's *viscountess!*" Then affecting a dainty yawn, which she was far from feeling, she slowly rose and announced the trip had fatigued her too. Pausing at the doors leading to the hall, Pandora promised her aunt that she would wear the mulberry silk, and that she would refrain from barbarous conduct. As a finishing touch, she added that perhaps she would sleep in tomorrow morning. Beatrix said they should all rest up for the afternoon's tea, and that the trip to the modiste's could be made the following day.

No sooner had Pandora cleared her chamber, then she dove with great relish into her portmanteau and retrieved the velvet case which held the ruby. It was still affixed to the black choker, and that was exactly the way she would wear it tomorrow. She would needs keep it out of sight until the Viscount arrived, then she would unfurl her shawl, thus revealing the jewel. It would make his lordship's mighty head spin! Ah, and wouldn't it look grand with the mulberry silk, which was just a shade darker than the jewel.

By the time Nora appeared to prepare her mistress for bed, Pandora had already changed into her white linen night shift and was seated at her rosewood secretary, engaged in writing.

"Oh, Miss, you'll be needing more light than that!" the abigail exclaimed, plunking her own candle down. "That is, unless you want to lose your eyesight." Crossing to the massive four-poster bed that dominated the room with its pale blue hangings, she pulled back the matching spread and puffed up the pillows.

"Finished!" Pandora announced, replacing the quill in its standish.

"From that wicked look about your face, I'll bet you're up to some mischief!"

"I am simply planning out several possible plots to ensnare the Marquess," Pandora replied as she padded barefoot across the room, "And have written them all down: if the first doesn't work, we shall move on to the second, and so forth." Gaily she waved the sheet of paper in front of her abigail's eyes. "Oh, I know such organization is not my usual style," she said, stepping up into the bed. "However, it will I hope avert the sort of lamentable accident which befell Lord Cardew on the London road." She scanned the scrawled list, then with a satisfied sigh, folded the sheet in two and slipped it beneath her pillow. "You shall be apprised of my every move, never fear! Oh, I *am* beginning to feel sleepy." Sinking into bed, she smiled contentedly, then on a stifled yawn added, "I suppose you have heard that Lord Cardew is coming for tea tomorrow."

"Why no!" Nora said, her eyes growing round as owls, "I have been with Jemnaz these past hours. Coming to tea, you say?"

"Yes, Viscount Cardew is having tea with us," Pandora repeated. "You know, Nora, I do believe he thinks I have straw for brains, though I must admit after shooting him in the arm, it gives even me pause."

"No such thing, Miss! Besides, it was an accident."

"Yes, yes." Pandora thought on this for a moment before adding, "Though I doubt he would see it that way. As it is, I think he considers women mere objects of amusement."

"Perhaps he was wounded in love," Nora ventured.

"The only place he was wounded was in his arm," Pandora replied grimly. "And aside from that, I doubt any female could wound the estimable Viscount. I suspect he is so taken with his own opinions that if one of Cupid's arrows should stray in his direction, his thick hide would neatly deflect it." She closed her eyes as if sleep was fast approaching, then snapping them open, said, "I do not mean to imply he is in the same boat as the Marquess. Ah, but don't let me keep you from your sleep, for tomorrow morning I'd like you and Jemnaz to accompany me to the jewelers, where I intend to have the ruby appraised. *But,*" she added in hushed tones, "we must keep this information from the others, for naturally they would wonder how I regained the stone, and I do not believe any of them are capable of withstanding the truth, even Winny." She nodded to her abigail, and feeling as if she had done a fair day's work, bid her good night.

Nora, however, did not budge. "Miss Pandora, I sense you have a pot of mischief you're keen to stir; for I've seen that look about your face before." Then gesturing to the note beneath Miss Tremantle's pillow, she added, "You might as well tell me what you've got planned, so I will be prepared when the mayhem happens tomorrow."

"Oh, tomorrow's venture will be mild indeed," Pandora managed on another yawn. "When Lord Cardew and I are left alone, which Auntie assures me is her intent, I shall show him the ruby."

"You are mad! Oh, beggin' your pardon. But Miss, this will cause no end of trouble, for he'll know you stole it back from the Marquess!"

"Heavens, that should relieve him. At least now he knows that I cannot possibly continue to suspect him of the foul deed. Besides, I already wrote him that I had recovered it." Pulling the sheets about her chin, Pandora snuggled even deeper in the bed. "This is to be his Great Lesson."

"I don't think he'll take too kindly to that."

"At our last encounter, the Viscount was, by turns, rude, patronizing, and . . . and . . ." She could hardly say *amorous* to Nora. Instead, she hastily added, "Arrogant. He treated me as if I was some missish female!" Reaching out to touch her abigail's hand, she added on a gentler note, "You needn't fear: he's not going to bite off my head. After all, the ruby *is* mine. Actually, his coming around should cheer you immensely; for now you will see for yourself that I did not wound him seriously."

"Perhaps not in the arm," Nora said as she picked up the candle. Softly she added, "Good night, Miss Pandora." Then turning, she quietly passed from the room, leaving it in darkness.

Perhaps not in the arm! Dear Lord, with Aunt Bea this sort of behavior was to be expected: she lived and breathed to see her nieces marry noblemen, but Nora? Pandora let out a sigh, and turning on her side toward the windows that opened on to Grosvenor Square, watched as fingers of fog pressed against the glass panes. She heard the Watch declare from the street below that it was ten o'clock and that all was well.

The Viscount had come through all that fog, she thought sleepily, and had left his card. Such a quick response to her note. Perhaps he didn't believe she had the ruby. *My, but wasn't he in for a surprise!* she thought. A little thrill went through her at the thought of their confrontation on the morrow; for he would be quite angry and put out with her, which would give Miss Tremantle immense satisfaction.

Pandora arose the following morning to a vista of gray shot with slivers of light that heralded the dawn: it would be one of London's bleak spring days. Nevertheless, she sprang from the bed and set to dressing herself in a cheerful yellow walking frock, and after arranging her curls on top of her head, placed an upstanding poke bonnet over them. It would definitely suit for her visit to the jewelers.

She was putting the ruby into her reticule when Nora entered with her morning chocolate and a plate of fresh buns. After thanking her abigail, Pandora took a few sips of the hot drink while she scribbled additional notes on her list. Then popping part of a bun in her mouth, she impatiently gestured with the other half towards the bedchamber door, and mumbled that they'd best be on their way.

"Without a proper breakfast?" Nora asked in a tone suggesting a breech of proper conduct.

"It's imperative the others not learn of my mission." Seeing her abigail's disapproval at Pandora forgoing nourishment, she stuck the rest of the bun in her mouth, and chewing furiously, headed for the door.

Given the early hour, there was little traffic about, and so Miss Tremantle, her abigail, and Jemnaz arrived at Rubsley and Malk Jewelers at ten o'clock sharp. Pandora had chosen this particular shop because several years ago she had read about it in connection with a much publicized murder mystery involving a priceless sapphire necklace. An odd recommendation for a jeweler, but so be it. The mystery appealed to her.

"You know, miss, it might have been more correct if Parks had driven us," Nora said as they hopped down from the gig, leaving an enthusiastic Jemnaz to take the reins.

"Yes, and Aunt Beatrix would have heard all about it on the instant. No, it is much better this way," Pandora replied as they entered the shop. "And you can rest assured this won't take but a few minutes. For I am possessed of curiosity concerning this jewel, which must be satisfied!" Turning toward the approaching proprietor, she rapidly addressed the assessment she required, but as she handed the ruby over to Mr. Malk, her curiosity was piqued even further by the strange light that settled in his tawny eyes. He was a short, trim man, modestly dressed in a buff-colored coat, waistcoat, and breeches. His one bit of flamboyance was a diamond ring on his little finger. That he had to crane his neck to speak to Miss Tremantle seemed not to signify in the least.

"May I ask how you came by this jewel?" He held it up to the light with a certain reverence as he spoke.

"It was a gift." Pandora answered without hesitation. "It *is* a ruby, isn't it?"

"Oh, yes," he assured her, laying it carefully on a square of black velvet.

"But how can you be positive? What I mean to say is, do you not have to look at it under a special light?" She gestured toward the numerous glass display cases which housed a rainbow of jewels. "Surely all of these require close inspection."

"Normally, yes. But this is no ordinary ruby." His glance went from the jewel that lay between them to her eyes for what seemed to Pandora a rather intense scrutiny. One which made her feel a trifle uncomfortable.

"Well, thank you so much for your time." Pandora reached for the jewel, but his voice stopped her.

"You say it was a gift, but you didn't mention the giver."

"Oh! The Marquess of Manakin brought it to me from—"

"Ah, I feel much better," the man said on what was obviously a sigh of relief. Then leaning toward Pandora, he added, "You see it was the Marquess who commissioned me to fashion this very ruby as a present for his fiancée. Ah, but then I am sure you know all about *that* unfortunate story!" Swiftly, as if the jewel might talk, Mr. Malk placed it back in its velvet case. "However, I am so pleased to see he recovered the jewel, *and* found another lovely neck on which to display it." After a pause, he pulled on his earlobe, "I don't suppose they ever found him."

"Found whom?" Pandora asked, feeling most confounded by this new intelligence.

"Why, Lady Lorena's murderer. For after his lordship was acquitted—"

"The Marquess? Acquitted of what?"

"Why, of strangling his fiancée, Lady Lorena Dowling!"

Chapter Nine

Miss Tremantle did not faint, nor come anywhere near it, despite the fluttering attendance foisted upon her when she put her hand to her brow, and repeated with some stupefaction, "*Strangled* his fiancée?"

"Yes, most disagreeable," Mr. Malk squeaked out, as he motioned for an apprentice to bring brandy, "although of course he was cleared of all charges." The visit was further confused by Mr. Malk's persistent assumption that Miss Tremantle was, in fact, the new fiancée. That he had so grossly let fall the eight-year-old scandal was obviously a faux pas. His profuse apologies were quickly accepted, but not the brandy. Pandora wanted only to get out of the shop.

Let him believe anything he liked, up to and including that she was affianced to the Marquess, which was looked upon by Miss Tremantle as a fate equal to death. Nora, bless her, managed to keep an admirable grip on things, but once they were back in the gig with Jemnaz tooling the gray towards Grosvenor Square, the abigail threw herself into justifiable laments.

"Oh, Miss, I knew we should not have gone! And to think that toady little man has your name!"

"He wasn't that toady," Pandora countered on a nervous laugh. "And we can only hope that this story doesn't get about town."

"Bosh! A body might as well ask for the sun not to rise. Some people are just natural gossips! And Mr. Malk has all the marks of one. Why, he'll have you and the Marquess married before the month is out!"

"You and the Marquess?" Jemnaz echoed. Tightening on the reins, he narrowly missed a vegetable stall. "Married?" He flashed his brilliant smile, thoroughly enjoying his role as driver. "So," he added, "this must be very funny English joke."

"It won't be so funny if the Marquess has words with that Mr. Malk," Nora said on a practical note. "For you know his lordship is in London, and undoubtedly hopping mad that the ruby is no longer in his possession."

"Yes," Pandora sighed. "And if one is to believe *you,* by tomorrow all of London will know he has returned from India, is freshly betrothed, *and,*" she added ominously, "that the betrothee is sporting the very ruby for which Lady Lorena was strangled."

"*Betrothee?*" Jemnaz repeated, puzzled as to how he had missed this rich addition to his ever expanding vocabulary.

By the time they reached home breakfast was under way, and as Pandora slipped upstairs she heard the Viscount's name mentioned several times.

The Viscount! Pandora thought with a delicious sense of their pending encounter. She quickly changed into an apricot-colored chintz frock, then after glancing at her list, realized—somewhat lamentably—that it would needs be altered. Settling herself at her secretary, she dipped pen in ink and quickly scratched a thick line through Item Number One, wherein she had planned to flaunt the ruby jewel in front of the Marquess at an appropriate time. She had considered the masked ball, but everything would be in such confusion that she relegated that idea to the bottom of the list. No, Pandora would have to find some other way to test the Marquess. He might, after all, truly be Mr. Rice of Bow Street. But if he were Manakin, why would he have strangled his own fiancée for a ruby he had given her in the first place? A bit redundant, but then he had achieved the duplicate results with her at Vauxhall: first he gives the lady he fancies the jewel—though heaven forbid he should ever fancy her—then he either strangles her or knocks her on the head, and steals it back. Peculiar.

The familiar smell of grilled kidneys assailed her nostrils as Pandora entered the breakfast room: immediately she wished to absent herself, but Beatrix, determined at all costs to further instruct her niece in the necessity of sterling behavior when the Viscount arrived, waved her forward with one hand, and summoned a servant bearing oatmeal porridge with the other.

"There!" she said triumphantly, as the oatmeal was set before Pandora, "I told them on no account were you to face a plate of kidneys! For I would not have you feeling queasy with the Viscount coming to tea."

"We don't know for sure if he wishes tea," Pandora said, dipping her spoon into the warm cereal.

"My dear child," Beatrix began patiently, "The man could request gin and pickled veal's knuckles, and I would oblige him. I do declare I would! And if you have any sense, you will present a picture of serenity and grace." With a flamboyant gesture, she indicated Chloe, who sat dutifully to her other side, contentedly consuming a small biscuit. "In the days your cousin has been with us, she has learned to modify her impulsive tendencies. You would be wise to take a lesson from her."

"Oh, Auntie," Chloe protested, "it is much easier for me to be restrained. I daresay I am plain vanilla and Pandora is . . . is—"

"Too saucy a dish! And it is a thing most miraculous that the Viscount still has an interest for her. Oh, when I think of how you would have burgled back the ruby had it been in his possession!" Miss McClellan made a face, and amended all this by adding, "Pandora, you have me so rattled, I hardly know what I am about."

"You were about to eat that kidney," Pandora pointed out as she poured herself some tea.

"Ah, here comes Winny!" Beatrix said, ignoring Pandora's remark. "How fortunate we all are that he brought Lord Cardew into our lives!"

Pandora applied herself to her oatmeal, barely able to contain the riot of jubilant feelings that arose from her fantasy of the Viscount's reaction to the ruby. Oh, but she would surely scream if she had to listen to another moment of his beatification! At least Aunt Bea had left off praising the Marquess, seeming able to enshrine only one lordship at a time.

Excusing herself from the table, Pandora made a hasty retreat back to her room, where she would not be disturbed. Not that Chloe and Winny would bother her—they were too far advanced in the malady of love to notice anything but the color of each other's eyes. But Auntie, like a great sea vessel, was not easily checked once her course was set.

Crossing to her secretary once again, Pandora withdrew her list, and quickly scanned the various plans. At Item Number Seven she did chuckle, and striking a line through it, she moved on to the next, which had a more rational turn to it. Still, the distinct flavor of Mrs. Hawkshore's romantic style shined through. Perhaps, Pandora mused, she should consider penning a romance: *The Mad Marquess*?

The balance of the afternoon sped by as Miss Tremantle gave free rein to her vivid imagination, and by the time Nora arrived to prepare her for the Viscount's call, she was in high spirits.

"Miss McClellan is having palpitations," Nora informed her as she helped her into the mulberry confection.

"It is to be expected," Pandora said through layers of silk. As her head emerged she added, "These transports are actually quite good for her health."

"Yes, but Miss, if she knew of your plan with the ruby and all, she might transport to the next world."

"I doubt it is ready for her!" Pandora laughed, adjusting the bodice of the high-waisted gown. Then, seating herself at the glass, she checked her mirrored image.

"I thought you were set on giving his lordship a comeuppance."

"I am," Pandora blithely responded, turning her profile first one way, then the other. "A pity patches went out of favor."

"Oh, Miss, they have been out for ever so long; and I can't think why you would want to wear one anyway." Nora hovered over her mistress, silver-backed brush at the ready as she considered Pandora's tangle of red curls.

"You are quite right! The ruby should be sufficient in arresting the Viscount's attention." She smiled wickedly in the glass, and added, "Please do something glorious with my mane! For I wish to leave a lasting impression on this Viscount."

"I expect you will, Miss," Nora said, as she commenced arranging Miss Pandora's coiffure.

The results of her labors, which produced a halo of fiery curls about Pandora's face, along with the exceptional mulberry silk gown, were well received indeed by his lordship, the Viscount Cardew. He shot to his exquisitely booted feet upon her entrance to the pink saloon, and executed a remarkable leg: however, the troubled look in his eyes was definitely at variance with this bit of formality. His usual raiment of dark coat and breeches was relieved by an embroidered waistcoat of deep burgundy and an elaborately folded neckcloth that signified him to be the very top of the trees.

After presenting his apologies to Miss McClellan for having been called away the very day of her tea, he then flattered the lady with a host of questions, which to Pandora's ears had the ring of a Bow Street Runner interview: Had she noticed anything peculiar happening about their environs? Did they lock and bolt their doors each night? And so on. Beatrix, utterly beside herself, made trembling gestures as she alternately answered his queries and pressed ham biscuits on him. The way she kept his teacup filled to the brim, one would have thought him a rare plant in need of frequent waterings.

The afternoon tea, interminable to Pandora, plummeted to uncharted depths, as Beatrix, launching into her own catechism, directed his lordship's attention to the waters in Bath. From thence she expounded on their fakery, and how her poor sister Statira refused to budge from the place.

At last, Beatrix rose to her feet—which was amazing considering the number of ham biscuits she had eaten—and announced that she, Chloe, and Winthrop had matters to attend to. If the Viscount should require further sustenance, Pandora should ring the bell. In a crinkle of lilac taffeta, and followed by Chloe and Winthrop, she made a regal exit, leaving a somewhat startled Viscount in her wake.

It was some moments before his lordship spoke, and from the strange look that played about the corners of his mouth, Pandora wondered exactly what his approach would be. She had to admit that she *was* thankful that his arm had not given him any visible trouble, though she certainly could not inquire as to its condition.

"I am to congratulate you, Miss Tremantle," he said, lounging against the chairback and staring at her from half-shuttered eyes. "For not only have you put your life in jeopardy, but you have magnificently bungled things." He might have been speaking of the weather, given the inflection he affected, but those blue eyes were as hard as ice.

"*Bungled?*" Pandora shot out the word as if it were ammunition. "I am quite sure I do not know what you mean by *bungled.*" She would liked to have tossed off a glass of strong sherry at that moment, but instead took a dignified sip of lukewarm tea. Of a sudden she felt her cheeks grow unbearably hot, and wished it were not so. Oh, but to have that Viscount think he was the cause of what appeared a blush! "Perhaps you refer to my correspondence with you?" she finally asked in what she hoped was a calm and collected manner.

"It is inscribed in my memory. I received it shortly before setting out this morning."

"But I thought you received it yesterday."

"It is inconsequential when it arrived," he said in a weary voice. "However, if you must know, I had planned on paying a call anyway; for my first intention was to inform you of the fact that the Marquess, of whom I had previously warned you, was in London. Indeed, my sole reason for declining Miss McClellan's invite to tea was to investigate this man's background, for I have reason to believe him to be a most dangerous person. And now that you've stolen back that blasted ruby, there's no telling what manner of revenge he'll execute." The Viscount ran a harried hand through his hair, thoroughly rumpling whatever effect he had hoped to achieve.

"There's no way he'll ever find out I did it," Pandora countered, hardly noticing the serving girls who scurried in to replenish their refreshments.

"You *are* a green girl!" the Viscount roared on an incredulous laugh. "Chatford is not exactly on the beaten path. Who the devil else would have taken it? When he finds the jewel gone, he will immediately conclude you reclaimed it. And I tell you the man is not above murder."

"And I say he will not because I—" Snapping her mouth shut, she reached for a cucumber sandwich and resolutely stuffed it in her mouth. Oh, when would she learn to think before she spoke?

"You what?" the Viscount asked, leaning forward in his chair, "What exactly *did* you do? Rob him on the King's Highway?" He gave another bark of laughter, but at Pandora's gasp and sudden white face, the intelligence of his remark struck him most forcibly.

"Why . . . why it was *you!*" Pandora chanced a look at him, and noticed that probably for the first time in his life, the Viscount appeared bereft of his senses. "It was *you,*" he repeated as the further enormity of it brought life back to his face and a sudden blaze of anger to his eyes. "Good God! *You* shot me!"

"Yes," Pandora managed to choke out in an exceedingly little voice. "But I assure you I thought you were the Marquess—at first that is—"

"You mistook me for *him?*" Lord Cardew's voice cracked at this pronouncement.

"Well, not after I saw you; but alas, then it was too late, for you were intent on wresting my brother's pistol from me, and so I . . . I . . ."

"You winged me, Miss Tremantle!" The Viscount, whose temper was ever quick to subside, added in a thoroughly amazed voice, "How could you contrive to be such a ninny?"

She bit down on her lower lip, futilely wondering how it happened that she was receiving the very dish she would have had him choke on. This was *not* the way the afternoon was supposed to proceed. With a toss of her head, she managed to regain some of her aplomb, as she recklessly announced, "I was sufficiently sure you had sustained only a minor wound."

"Thank God for your lamentably poor aim." Seeing her bristle at this barb gave him deep pleasure, for he added, "Where *did* you receive your instruction on firearms? Some romance novel? For the way you came upon my carriage was the mark of an amateur: a hopelessly inept highwayman! A blur on the profession." He watched her grope for a reply: gone was the pale, shocked countenance, and instead he beheld a face fanned with flaming color, and green eyes sparked with anger.

"I have never robbed a carriage before! Though I do apologize for shooting your arm. It was horrid of me, and I assure you, you are the first person I've ever taken a pistol to."

"I suppose I should be honored," he said dryly.

"Perhaps you should," she retorted in kind. "For I may pursue this line of work and become quite famous, for I do have knowledge of firearms!"

"Yes, I seem to recall you sported one at Vauxhall, *and* when you visited me at the Orange Crown. Need I remind you the consequences of *those* excursions?" He lifted a tiny sandwich from the platter, and after a moment's contemplation, consumed it. His pistol-happy companion was looking slightly chagrined, for her pretty mouth was pressed into a tight line, suggesting she might burst into a tempest at any moment. Instead, however, she smiled sweetly and murmured, "I do believe you are out of humor not because I shot you, but because I succeeded in getting the ruby."

This would not serve. No, nor would his lingering with Miss Tremantle, for despite her unpredictable and outrageous behavior he still felt an absurd but considerable attraction to her. One which he preferred not to consider. He wiped his mouth with the linen napkin, then tossed it to the table and rose abruptly to his feet. "Well, where is this ruby you got off the Marquess?"

"About my neck," she replied archly, still nursing a touch of petulance. Then slowly she uncoiled a silk scarf whose artful drape had concealed it.

"Indeed," he mused, noting the ruby choker about her slender neck, and a great deal more besides. His gaze swept over her bare shoulders and onto the bodice of her wine-colored frock. There was a bit of gold riband edging the neckline, and just above it her bosom rose and fell quite rapidly. Normally he wasn't a man to notice *what* a lady wore, but on Miss Tremantle's handsome figure, one could not help but noticing.

"Did you manage to inflict a wound on Manakin, too?"

he asked. "Or did the fellow chuck it over to you when you issued your *stand and deliver* speech?"

"At least he didn't try to grapple the pistol away from me the way you did!" she answered saucily, and giving a toss to her red curls—which she was wont to do when under stress—she stood up and added, "Well, you might congratulate me on retrieving the jewel."

"Conceit is unattractive in a lady," he said, aware of the growing effect she was having on him. In two strides he could have her in his arms. Instead, he turned towards the windows that let onto the square, and quietly said, "As I told you earlier, you have placed yourself in jeopardy."

"You forget," she countered, crossing over to where he stood, "he doesn't know I have the ruby."

"If he is who I suspect him to be, he is a very dangerous man." The Viscount's eyes met hers, and for an insane moment he didn't care what the deuce happened to the ruby *or* Sir Rupert. He did know that he very much cared what happened to Miss Tremantle. And yet the girl refused to take any of this seriously. What would it take for her to listen to him? The truth? Everything about his past? Lady Lorena? No! Not that. Instead, he inquired of her what precisely she intended to do with the ruby, since she had bungled his chances of catching the villain with the jewel. He purposefully used that word, *bungled,* for he knew it nettled her, and if she stayed agitated enough, there would be little chance of his sweeping her into his arms again. That must be avoided at all costs.

"Well," she replied in clipped tones, "had you told me of your little plan, I might not have 'bungled' it! Nor would I have shot you in the arm! As it is, I am in possession of the jewel, and can hardly give it back now." Her brow furrowed with precisely the agitation the Viscount desired.

"I am assuming Manakin will be returning to Chatford?" he asked in as offhanded a way as possible.

"Yes. In fact, I'd been considering laying a trap for him myself, but—"

"Do not be a little fool!"

"Watch how you speak to me!" she countered as her chin jutted forward and a dangerous glint settled in her eyes. "I shall do exactly what I please. Besides, I have gathered certain facts about our Marquess."

"What facts?"

"It was in confidence—I am not at liberty to say!"

"What the devil! Tell me!" The Viscount, barely able to contain himself, spoke through gritted teeth.

"I am not beholden to you, Lord Cardew! And quite frankly, it is none of your business."

"It *is* my business," he said on a rising note of anger, then hardly aware of the gesture, he grabbed her by the shoulders and pulled her towards him.

"Let me go!"

His hands dropped to his sides as if she were fashioned of hot coals. "I am concerned for your welfare, that's all."

"Well, you have a most peculiar way of showing it," she rejoined. "As it is, you should be pleased I happened upon this bit of news, for it has led me to alter my plan."

"Your plan?" The Viscount could but wonder at the workings of her mind.

"Originally I had intended on flaunting the ruby before the Marquess—"

"Good God! On no account are you to do such an absurd and dangerous thing!" The urge to shake Miss Tremantle was almost overwhelming.

"Please, Lord Cardew, you need not order me about. I just told you that—"

"You have been telling me a stream of things all afternoon, most of which have been exceedingly difficult for me to fathom." The Viscount ran his hand through his hair; then in a controlled voice, said, "Miss Tremantle, believe me when I say you might indeed be putting your life in immediate danger were you to go forward with that hare-brained scheme."

"Well!" She straightened visibly. "It was not a hare-brained scheme! I think you're simply annoyed that I, a mere female, could conceive of it."

"That has nothing to do with it!" He eyed her speculatively, wondering exactly how much he should divulge. "I have my reasons for what I say."

"So do I! After all, I have gathered intelligence on him, and would certainly not—"

"Please stop rattling on about what you are not willing to reveal!"

"Stuff! I will say that his past marks him as a most disagreeable man." She idly trailed her finger on the edge of the tea table as she slowly circled it: her eyes downcast as if in contemplation of the finger sandwiches.

"Disagreeable?" He laughed, and resting his hands on the table, leaned towards her. "You call murder *disagreeable?*"

"You are trying to scare me."

"Yes!" Damn, he would tell her about India, though not, he decided, his true identity. Whatever she'd heard about the *Marquess of Manakin,* was undoubtedly about himself: she had found the gossip—as she put it—*disagreeable,* and so undoubtedly would find the real Marquess equally repugnant. It was just as well, he thought with a sudden savageness he was loath to claim.

"Yes," he repeated, backing off from the table to get a better look at Miss Tremantle. Defiance sparked in her eyes, as if nothing had ever scared her before. "Yes, I fully intend to scare those idiotic plans straight out of your head."

"That you cannot do! In fact, I am of a mind to execute them anyway. For I think you are full of stories."

"Perhaps. But you, my dear, read too many novels!" His hand shot out, snatched the ruby from her throat and neatly pocketed it before she knew what he was about.

"You . . . you go too far!" She lunged forward in an attempt to retrieve the jewel, but he gripped both of her wrists and drew her towards him.

"Maybe I do," he laughed lightly.

"Give me back my ruby!"

"It is *my* ruby," he said, backing up a pace and dangling it before her.

"Not now!" she triumphed, snatching it back.

Cardew whistled softly in amazement: *damn, she was fast!* "Shall we say it was my ruby, but if you wish to believe otherwise, let's just say I attempted to rob you for your own good."

"Oh? A noble act, I suppose? Thank you for your chivalry in wishing to protect me."

"I tried. However, it would appear you haven't been listening to my little stories."

"As I said before, you are full of stories."

"Then listen to this one," he said softly, advancing on Miss Tremantle until he was close enough to touch her. "I lied to you about the south of France." Cardew watched for some reaction, but she merely blinked back, matching stare for stare. Omitting significant details, he continued, "I was traveling in India for pleasure, believe it or not, and while in Bombay struck up an acquaintance with your father. The old school connection and all that, you know. Seems he went to Cambridge, too."

"I know," Pandora said, maintaining an unreadable face.

"Allow me to make short shrift of an involved tale: Prior to my meeting your father, he had discovered the whereabouts of the Snow Leopard Jewels. When he confided his discovery to your *Marquess,* he did not know that he was sharing his secret with the man I feel certain is the infamous jewel thief known in London as the Duke of Diamonds. Your father was subsequently attacked, knocked unconscious and—" He paused at Pandora's gasp. "Sir Horatio is all right. Like you, he incurred a blow to the head."

"Are you saying—"

"Precisely. I have good reason to suspect that Manakin is one and the same as the notorious Duke of Diamonds. And if you think your Marquess above murder, you should know that eight years ago he brutally strangled Lady Lorena for *her* jewels, which are not nearly as valuable as the Snow Leopard cache. It was this same unnatural inclination that sent the villain to India, where he planned to relieve your father of the treasure. However, to his dismay, Sir Horatio had already sent the jewels on to you at Chatford Abbey. Thus Manakin, having gained your father's trust, came straight here."

"You are mistaken. My father sent no jewels. Furthermore, I have reason to believe that the Marquess is not Manakin, but someone else posing as him. In point of fact, a Bow Street Runner," she added triumphantly. "Besides, how do you know for sure Manakin is the one who attacked my father?"

The Viscount regarded her with lifted brows for a moment, then responded. "In the first place, it is highly improbable that a Runner would hit you over the head and snatch your ruby, m'dear. In any event, the Duke of Diamonds, who robbed Lady Lorena Dowling of her famous jewels, including—by the way—the ruby subsequently presented to you, always left his calling card—an ace of diamonds—at the scene of each crime. One such card was found by your father after he was attacked." He paused to let this sink in.

"Lord Cardew," Pandora began, cocking her head to one side, "That does not prove the Duke of Diamonds is Lord Manakin, who I know for a fact was acquitted of the murder of Lady Lorena." Pandora paused before adding, "I think it's time you tell me what really happened eight years ago, and no more filleted tales, as if I might choke on a bone of truth like some hapless damsel with an empty upper story."

"Heaven forbid the thought, Miss Tremantle! If anything, you have extra stuffing in that chamber." He crossed his arms in front of him and regarded her with what she considered to be a most annoying look.

"*Extra stuffing!*" Challenging the intensity of his gaze with one of her own, she said, "Answer me this: how do I know this story about the Duke of Diamonds isn't another of your fabrications?"

"I believe you sampled his style in Vauxhall Gardens. Besides, what would I have to gain from such a prevarication?"

"The Snow Leopard Jewels!" she replied in a thoroughly vexed voice. "Besides, no playing card was left when *I* was knocked out!"

"Thoughtless of the fellow," Cardew answered. "However, I don't think he wished his presence known."

"You seem to have answers for everything: tell me then, how is it Manakin came by that letter of introduction from my father? And why was there no mention of you in it? Or for that matter, of the attack on his person?" She threw him a victorious glance, then idly picked up a cucumber sandwich and consumed it with relish.

"Your father, assuming the man to be honorable, gave him the letter quite freely. Later, when I learned of the attack on Sir Horatio and the mysterious ace of diamonds, I knew that the villain, frustrated in his quest for the jewels, would proceed to England after all. Upon presenting a query to your father, I discovered he had indeed told your Marquess that the jewels had been sent home." The Viscount held his hand up to stem Miss Tremantle's protestations. "Whether or not the jewels have yet arrived is another matter. The important thing is that the Marquess has indicted himself by stealing the ruby from you—which, alas, you have taken back. The point being, my dear Miss Tremantle, that we have not one shred of proof against the man. And I beg of you, no more talk of flaunting the ruby, or he might do more than hit you upon your very pretty head." He reached out and touched one of her fiery curls, then abruptly let it drop.

"You have not answered all my questions!" she said, all too aware of the little spots of color her cheeks now possessed. He was standing far too close for comfort. Still, she tilted her chin in high defiance of anything he might say *or* do!

He laughed: the man threw his head back and laughed at her! "I should hope not. For if I answered all your questions, I should be here through the supping hour, which would be presumptuous and highly irregular. Do you not agree, Miss Tremantle?"

"I say you are a smooth talker, Lord Cardew!" *Too smooth,* she thought, noting the snap to his blue eyes. "And if I thought the truth might be wrung from you, I'd quite fly in the face of convention, and sit up all night listening to you: for we Tremantles are shockingly out of the ordinary. Having made the acquaintance of my father, *surely* you know that!" She paused to ascertain his reaction, and seeing none, added, "But then how am I to know you are telling the truth about meeting him in the first place?"

"Because, my dear Miss Tremantle, *I* have the 'true jewel' your father sent!" He paused but a moment, then after making a spectacular leg, departed from the pink saloon, leaving Pandora, for once, bereft of speech.

Chapter
Ten

The true jewel! Chandro? But of course! Pandora practically overturned a chair in her haste to catch up with him, and might have but for Miss McClellan's sudden appearance as she burst through the door in a manner suggestive of an imminent attack of the vapors.

"Auntie!"

"Oh, my girl, my girl, whatever have you done to put Lord Cardew in such a peculiar humor?"

"Nothing!" Pandora lied, wishing to be done with this interrogation that she might pursue the Viscount and determine the meaning behind his remark.

"Well! He just made his farewells to me, and there was an exceedingly possessed look about his countenance. You have managed quite neatly to give him pause. And this time I do not think he will return for more of your . . . your hoydenish behavior! And just when I was thinking something might come of it."

"My manners were impeccable: we spoke of . . ." Pandora paused, her fingers idly touching the ruby at her throat. "Of jewels." Abruptly her hand closed about the ruby, and turning slightly, she managed to slip it off without her aunt noticing the gesture. "Would you perhaps like a cucumber sandwich?" she inquired, moving towards the tea table, and hence the door.

"Heavens no! For when I think of how you are flying in the face of Providence, I can not even imagine the smallest of morsels passing through these lips." She sighed heavily, and in a rustle of lilac skirts, sank onto the gold couch and added, "I suppose it is my fault for nourishing thoughts of you as viscountess. But please, do not fault me for wishing only the best." She wrestled with a valiant smile, and in a somewhat resigned voice, added, " 'Tis a pity, you know. Two nieces, and not a title to be had—for though I am delighted Chloe is dealing handsomely with Winny, I would have had her linked with the Earl of Davish, and I had hoped Winny would vie for Lady Charlotte. And for you—"

"If you say *Cardew* or *Manakin,* I shall not be responsible for my actions!" Tongues of fire leapt from her eyes as she headed for the door.

"Well, then there is Lord Oglethorpe. He seemed pleased with you last season," Beatrix said as she pulled her recumbent figure to a more suitable position for viewing the cucumber sandwiches.

Pandora whirled around. "But I was *not* pleased with him; and I cannot imagine what perversity drove you to mention his name. He was decrepit and miserly then and is assuredly more so now, if indeed he has not shuffled off this mortal coil!"

"He is still among the living," Beatrix said with a sniff. "And from all accounts, doing quite admirably. *And* you would be—"

"Lady Oglethorpe: a thought which would send me into dreaded spasms, were I of that nature."

"Very well, I shall leave off Lord Oglethorpe. But tell me, do, what passed between you and the Viscount?"

"A volley of venom!" said Pandora in a lighter vein. "And I do declare, Auntie, that should delight you, for the gentleman seems to thrive on it!"

"As long as he comes to the ball," Beatrix said absently, as her attention wandered to the sandwich platter.

"I shouldn't imagine it would matter one way or the other whether he came. It's to be a masked ball, and no one knows him in any case." Her attempted departure was halted once again by Beatrix.

"Oh, but it does! The Marquess is ever so looking forward to meeting Lord Cardew. He has said so on several occasions."

"Ah, yes. I had forgotten." Pandora paused, her hand on the brass door fixture, then slowly she added, "We mustn't do anything to overturn our Marquess's desires, must we?"

"Pandora, I do not like it above half when you get that look on your face. It always means trouble." Then with a weary shrug she propelled herself forward, the little rounded sandwiches rapidly vying for her full attention.

"*Trouble?* What possible trouble could I incur in the confines of Grosvenor Square? Unless, of course, you consider our visit to the modiste's establishment to be on a par with a gaming hell."

Beatrix, now intent upon the tea tray, looked up briefly, and said, "Tsk, tsk. I have no wonder Lord Cardew looked so harassed upon his departure." She daintily lifted a crescent-shaped delicacy to her mouth, and after rapidly consuming it, she said thoughtfully, "I do hope you've given consideration to your costume for the masked ball. If not, I think you would make a lovely Juliet."

"Have you told the Viscount he's to be Romeo?" With a very satisfied smile, Pandora swept from the room, suddenly overtaken with an ingenious idea for her disguise at the ball. And, yes, she *would* wear the ruby! That was not all she would do that fated night. Both she and the ruby would be bait, and fashioned in such a way as to truly undo the Marquess of Manakin.

She hurried upstairs to inscribe this latest plan. Excitement mounted with each stroke of the pen as she envisioned her plot unfurling, and the Marquess caught like a fly in a spider web. Then there was the Viscount to take into consideration. That she should be the one to trap the villain instead of him gave her a thrill of triumph such as she rarely experienced. Indeed, just who did the Viscount think he was?

There was but one loose end that caused her no end of curiosity—namely, the Viscount's remark concerning the *true jewel.* Obviously it was the boy Chandro. But she sensed there was a deal more to the story than that. In fact, she was now convinced that the Marquess was indeed the villain, and she shuddered to think of poor Mr. Rice, the Bow Street Runner whose papers the Marquess possessed.

* * *

The following morning's visit to the modiste's was quite a gay undertaking, and especially so for Pandora, who reveled in the conviction that her costume would be the undoing of the Marquess. No question, the jewel and her costume would lure Manakin right where she wanted him. She felt a wicked pleasure in picturing the Viscount's reaction to the drama she had planned.

By the time fittings had been accomplished for the three ladies, Beatrix declared she was feeling quite the thing, and what a clever outfit Pandora had decided upon, and how grand it was that Madame had the odd pieces of fabric to fashion both the gown and the headgear. Indeed, perhaps this festive costume was a sign that Pandora was wishing to comport herself in the spirit of things. Beatrix could but pray such was the case. Chloe, however, had chosen the traditional and more sedate shepherdess disguise for herself.

"You should always wear pink, my love," Beatrix informed Chloe as they traveled by closed carriage back to Grosvenor Square. She then fell into a discourse on colors: what was and was not acceptable, though she did have to admit that at a masked ball, almost anything could pass. For this sumptuous event, she had chosen to portray herself as an Iris. Naturally the gown would be an addition to her wardrobe of purple satins. Her headpiece was a creation of stiff taffeta that protruded from atop her auburn curls to resemble the flower. Madame promised that these creations would be ready by the end of the week.

Winthrop, meanwhile, knowing full well what his disguise would be, thus not needing his tailor's services, decided to tool his phaeton through Hyde Park. A singularly delightful foray for a cool spring morning, and one wherein he could exchange pleasantries with a variety of friends, most of whom would be at the ball the following week. Having given up cards and spirits in virtually the blinking of an eye, he found that this little exercise, with his gray at the head of his high-perch phaeton, gave him greater pleasure than previously, especially in the park, where all manner of equipages vied for the path: barouches, curricles, and of course a smattering of Winthrop's favored, the phaeton. In the hands of a novice, he declared, they were death on wheels, and he had seen more than one overturned vehicle to attest to this grim fact. However, Mr. Tremantle considered himself to be quite the whip with all manner of carriages, and so did not give himself over to such troubled thoughts.

Having completed a circuit through the park, he was trotting toward the gate when he spotted the Marquess just entering the park. He hailed his lordship, but the curricle had sped past, and it would be most unseemly to chase the man down. At this same moment Lord Whimley, a friend of Mr. Tremantle's, having seen him wave towards the Marquess, approached him on horseback, and engaged him in some minutes of gossip, wherein at length he pressed to know how he and Sir Rupert Montescue were acquainted. Winthrop, falling prey to the family tendency to rattle out great quantities of information, assured his friend that the gentleman was none other than the famous Marquess of Manakin, who was houseguest at Chatford Abbey, and whom he would meet at the masked ball. Oh, no, his friend contradicted him, that was Sir Rupert Montescue fresh from some foreign adventure.

Thus the two gentlemen engaged in a mild disagreement over the gentleman's identity, and would have undoubtedly kept at it, had not a torrential rainstorm come upon them, sending both men charging out the gate in a splatter of mud, but not before Winthrop's friend called out, "Come to Boodle's tonight and see for yourself!"

Mr. Tremantle arrived back at Grosvenor Square thoroughly drenched and shivering, but despite all this he was filled with a curiosity that refused to be put to bed. *Dashed if that wasn't Lord Manakin,* he thought; after all, the Marquess was houseguest at Chatford, he ought to know the gentleman's identity. Deciding to give this matter further consideration, however, Winthrop ordered hot water to be brought to his chamber that he might bathe away the chill. He had two courses open to him: he could either go to Boodle's and confirm the Marquess's identity, though he would have to do so on the quiet, or Pandora would surely think he had reverted to his gaming ways; or he could wait until the masked ball and present the Marquess to his friend, who seemed so certain this fellow was Sir Rupert.

By the time the bathwater had grown cool, Winthrop had

reached a decision. He would go! After all, he was a member of Boodle's, and besides, Lord Whimley would expect him.

Were Winthrop of a more circumspect nature, he might well have chosen some third alternative to ascertain the questionable identity. But given the Tremantle streak of rashness coupled with the need to prove himself right to Lord Whimley, he announced quite boldly at supper that evening that he had gentleman's business to attend to, and that no one should on any account wait up for him. The dewy look this pronouncement evoked from his darling Chloe quite overshadowed any protestations his aunt might have thrust upon him. Pandora managed to quell her avid curiosity until they had quit the table. However, he had not cleared the foyer before she rounded on him, a look of determination clearly written on her face.

"Winny, what idiocy are you about to pursue?" she demanded, detaining him by the sleeve of his exquisitely tailored coat.

"It is *not* idiocy," he replied stiffly, shaking her hand off his person. "I have an errand of some considerable merit to tend to. It is to be expected when in London. *You* certainly tear off and do as *you* please!" He added this last in a triumphant manner that he hoped would put to rest any further queries.

"That is different! I am three years older than you, and not given to your crackbrained impetuosity."

"Ha! You, who are unable to open your mouth without making a muddle of things, are lecturing *me?* Bother!"

"Oh, Winny! You are green about the ears," she said in exasperation. "And I am but concerned for your well-being. We are in London, you know."

"I am *not* green about the ears!" he uttered, thoroughly flushed in the face at such a suggestion. "I daresay if I were, Chloe would—" He closed his mouth with an abruptness that suggested crowbars would be needed to open it again.

"Oh, pray do not look so stricken. We are all aware that you are besotted with each other, which is all fine and good—"

"It is?" he said, unlocking his jaw, and regrettably allowing it to hang midair.

"Of course. And though Auntie would have preferred you to dangle after Lady Charlotte, I care not a fig. But of this mysterious evening's escapade, I am going with you!"

"You most certainly are not!" Winthrop said with renewed vigor on a shocked note. "You forget yourself!" Sheer astonishment stamped his face and with his jaw clenched back in place, he spun on his heel and strode down the steps to his awaiting carriage. Parks was at the reins, and as soon as Winthrop had leapt inside, he cracked the whip, and they took off, vanishing into the lightly gathering fog, leaving Pandora in a fair state at the curb's edge.

The Watch had called twelve bells before Winthrop's return, and whatever Pandora, who was waiting up for him, had expected, it was certainly not the slumped and staggering figure of her obviously inebriated brother. Were it not for Parks, who navigated Winthrop towards the gold sofa, he might well have crashed into the marble bust of Venus; as it was, he merely collided into a small table, sending the articles on it rattling to the floor.

"Oh, heavens! Get him onto the sofa before he wakes the house up!" Pandora held a candlestick aloft, and looked with disapproval as Parks eased the now groaning Mr. Tremantle onto the sofa.

"Mr. Winthrop seems not to be himself," the coachman remarked, then raising a discreet eyebrow in Miss Tremantle's direction, added, "Will that be all? Or shall I assist him to his chamber?"

"No, but if you could bring a basin of water and some cloths, I'll just—"

"What *is* all this racket? Oh, my stars!"

Pandora turned to see Beatrix, nightcapped, clutching her robe, and looking quite a fright.

"Bring the cloths, then that will be all, Parks," Pandora said. Then to Beatrix she added, "You'd best go back to bed; I'll see that Winny is—"

"We shall tend to this matter together," her aunt said as she swirled into the room, only to be followed by a sleepy-eyed Chloe, who, however, came wide awake upon seeing the recumbent Winthrop.

"Winny!" Rushing past Beatrix, and forgetting all propriety, she sat promptly beside the young man and began to chafe his wrists, then looking to Pandora, asked, "What has happened?"

"He's simply foxed, is all, and shall undoubtedly sleep it off."

"Foxed?" Chloe echoed, and would have said more, but for her beloved's moan of genuine pain.

"Sir . . . Rupert?" Winthrop attempted to sit forward, but collapsing back, muttered the name again and inquired quite pathetically where he might be.

"In disgrace, I should expect!" Beatrix informed him as she sank into a nearby chair.

"He has been to Boodle's," Pandora said wearily, "though *why* remains a secret."

"I *had* to go; why, it was practically a matter of honor," Winthrop said defensively. "And while I was awaiting Whimley—for you see we'd made a bet in the park—I received word that I was expected in one of the upstairs chambers—"

"You've been betting again?" Beatrix asked querulously.

"It was only a small bet—made in all innocence," Winthrop countered as he pulled himself to a sitting position, then with a renewed groan, dropped back, clutching his head.

"This will help," Pandora said, accepting the basin and cloths from Parks, then wringing out a cloth with unnecessary vigor, added, "Chloe, perhaps if you play angel of mercy, Winny will tell us about his bet, *and* the fine bottle of brandy he and Whimley seemed to have enjoyed."

"Oh, back with the spirits again!" Beatrix intoned.

"It was a good year," Winthrop protested feebly from his supine position.

"I am sure it was forced down your throat," Pandora said. "However, earlier you said you were about a gentleman's business.

"I was!" Removing the cloth from his brow, and sitting forward once again, Winthrop managed to regale them on how he had been lured into betting on Lord Manakin's identity.

"Do you mean to say that you never even saw Whimley

at the club?" Confusion reigned supreme on Beatrix's face as she grappled with the facts.

"No. For it was Lord Manakin himself who invited me to have the brandy; he thought it a great joke that he should be mistaken for a Sir Rupert."

"Oh, then it was Manakin . . ." Pandora let the words trail off.

"The Marquess saw you in this condition?" Beatrix practically choked.

"Well, naturally, but I do not think he took offense, for—"

"Oh, great Caesar's ghost! To make a falling down spectacle of yourself! It will be all over town by morning." Beatrix took a wheezing breath, only to add, "We shall be ruined."

"Oh, Auntie, you do exaggerate," Pandora said on a laugh. "Besides, I've already ruined our reputations with my behavior towards the Viscount."

"I am praying he will not spread it about, my girl. Oh, but for Winny to disgrace himself at the feet of our guest, and then be carried out of his club, is more than I can bear."

"Only a few glasses of brandy," Winthrop mumbled, slapping a cloth on his brow and resting back once again.

"You simply are not a drinking man," Chloe assured him, briefly touching his arm, "and if we are indeed to be ruined, then word must be sent out that Mr. Tremantle was . . . drugged!"

"Nonsense," Beatrix contradicted. "However, we can pray that the Marquess will put out that you were taken ill, though of course he knows the horrid truth. I further trust he will let the incident fall from his memory." She held herself as one deeply injured, then on a sigh added, "First Pandora with the Viscount, and now you with the Marquess! At least Chloe has not shamed the family, which is a veritable mercy." Her glance alighted on Miss Deeds, then with a shake of her head, Beatrix tilted towards the door. Over her shoulder she said, "We shall repair back to Chatford Abbey as soon as our costumes are ready!"

Pandora withdrew shortly thereafter, leaving Chloe to nurse Winthrop's headache and undoubtedly to bolster his pride. It was a pity he had endured such shabby treatment at Manakin's hands, for Pandora was now quite ready to believe her brother *had* been drugged. And if this were true, then possibly there was also some merit to this Sir Rupert mixup. If only she were a man, she could check the matter out at Boodle's; however, she was not about to don another disguise toward this end.

The following morning was bleak: heavy clouds hung over the city presaging a steady drizzle before noon. The scene at the breakfast table was equally somber, and the ever-present grilled kidneys did nothing to alleviate Miss McClellan's mood of gloom and doom. Chloe made several attempts at gaiety, then she too succumbed to the all-pervading ennui. Winthrop was still about his chamber, no doubt nursing the headache, and Pandora—quite absorbed in determining her next move—presented an appropriate demeanor, considering their imminent topple from polite society.

Shortly after breakfast, Beatrix, in an attempt to lose herself in Mrs. Hawkshore's latest romance, took to the sofa in the pink saloon. No sooner had she opened the novel, however, than the butler appeared bearing a calling card.

"We have a visitor?" she said, clearly overjoyed that they were, in fact, *not* social outcasts. Lifting the card up, she uttered, "Oh, my! Show the Marquess in, immediately! Oh, and have the others come down." Thrusting her novel to one side Beatrix smoothed her dark blue skirts, wishing she had worn the purple or burgundy gown instead.

Lord Manakin coming to pay a call! Oh, but this could only bode the highest of fortunes!

Chapter Eleven

Pandora, who had been about to enter the saloon when the butler brought this news, stood stock-still, marveling at this propitious arrival. Perhaps some light would be shed on Winny's misfortune, for even now the subject of her inquiry was approaching her.

"Ah, Miss Tremantle!" the Marquess exclaimed, pausing to execute an admirable leg.

"Lord Manakin." She tilted her head to one side and smiled graciously. "How kind of you to pay us a call. I know my aunt must be eagerly awaiting you." She pivoted about and preceded him into the saloon. The flurry of formalities was repeated as Beatrix welcomed the Marquess, and begged him to accommodate himself. She would have undoubtedly kept up a steady stream of chatter had not Chloe and Winthrop appeared. The latter was somber faced and arrayed in a wine-colored morning coat and matching waistcoat. These articles of clothing would have stood him in good stead but for the hastily knotted cravat, which seemed to indicate he might have been contemplating hanging himself instead of receiving callers. Chloe, however, never one to remain blue-deviled for long, was dressed in a sweet yellow muslin frock that brought out the gold in her hair and the sparkle in her eyes. To her further credit, Chloe did not seem overly impressed with his lordship this time, Pandora observed; nor did she gush forth her usual sentiments. Instead, she wished him a good morning and settled herself beside Pandora on the peach-colored sofa. Winthrop, in a decidedly modest and proper tone, asked after Lord Manakin's health and made sincere apology for his unseemly conduct the night before.

"Nonsense!" the Marquess replied, as Winthrop concluded his speech of contrition. "I came here to set you straight on that very matter."

An appreciable sigh escaped Miss McClellan, who after the briefest of pauses thanked his lordship for coming by, then commenced to rattle out all her direst fears concerning the possible gossip which Winthrop's debauchery would undoubtedly incur.

"My dear lady," Lord Manakin began, in what could only be described as a purr, "as a youth I, too, passed out at Boodle's, and while it is buzzed about for a fortnight, it is soon forgotten. But of the brandy we drank: I had a single glass, and even so upon retiring I was unreasonably out of sorts, and had the most dreadful headache upon arising. So, I put the blame on an inferior bottle, and have spread this story about." He paused before adding, "I felt you should know of this, especially considering your sensitivity, Miss McClellan."

"Oh, you are in every way a gentleman!" She sent Pandora an I-told-you-so look, then said, "You have put my mind to rest. I am only sorry that you, too, were indisposed."

"It was a trifling inconvenience compared to Mr. Tremantle's experience." With a flash of white teeth he smiled.

The balance of the visit was spent in amiable chitchat, but again, Pandora noticed Chloe hung back and responded only when directly addressed. It would seem there was a touch more to this child than had first met the eye.

Of one thing Pandora was fairly certain: the Marquess *had* drugged Winny, for his tales of spoilt brandy smacked of fabrication. But why? Whatever had Winny done to the man? Could it be he *was* Sir Rupert? Nonsense! Having previously concluded that Manakin was *not* Mr. Rice, the Bow Street Runner, she could not accept yet another masquerade. Besides, why would one peer of the realm wish to pass himself off as another? For a fleeting moment Pandora wondered what the Viscount would make of this latest development.

* * *

The Viscount Cardew was at that moment being fully informed of the Marquess' whereabouts, as Chandro, practically leaping about, chattered out his tale in rapid Hindi.

"Easy, easy!" the Viscount said on a laugh as he turned towards his writing desk. He withdrew a sheet of paper from a lower drawer and said, "I feel it is time to send Miss Tremantle a note."

"*Our* Miss Tre-mantel?" Chandro asked in a ripple of excitement as he peered over his master's shoulder.

"You rapscallion! When did you learn to read English?" His lordship dipped his pen into the standish and commenced writing in a hasty, scratchy scrawl.

"I practice right now! 'Dear Miss Tre-mantel,' " he said in English, " 'I am sorry you are on the shelf, but I do not keep my word—' " Chandro leapt to one side as Lord Cardew tossed a small book at him.

"Beautiful lady on the shelf!" Chandro taunted from his crouched position behind an ornately carved whatnot, then seeing that the Viscount had returned to his letter writing, he crept forward, and reclaiming his position, asked softly, "What *do* you write to our lady?"

"She may be *your* lady, but I think she would be most displeased to think of herself as *my* lady. But then, I'm afraid you don't understand, my lad."

He made an attempt to resume his writing, but Chandro tugged on his sleeve, and said, "She should be very pleased to be your lady. Does she know how close your house is to hers?"

"No, and please don't tell her!"

"But she would like this big house," the boy protested as he arched his neck to view the Viscount's study, a vaulted chamber in dark wood with glassed-in bookcases. Idly he stepped toward a globe of the world, and after spinning it several times, announced that there were too many wicked people in it, and that he especially wished he could do more to save the beautiful lady.

"You're doing a great deal, Chandro," his lordship observed as he sanded the note. "And I would ask that you post yourself outside Miss Tremantle's house, and as soon as the

Marquess departs, you give this to her. If she desires to respond, then you will wait."

"Yes, sahib!" The boy's dark eyes glittered with the thrill of adventure as he held out his hand for the note.

"Be off now! And no more questions!"

Chandro snatched the folded paper as if he were starving and it were a delicious treat indeed, made an obeisance to the Viscount, and scampered out the door.

From his position by the tall, curtained windows, Cardew watched his little emissary dash down St. James in the direction of Grosvenor Square. Why he had bothered with the note, he couldn't even say, for he knew full well she would not acquiesce to his request. In truth, it was the flimsiest of reasons to write to her. *Dash it!* he thought; he couldn't get the bothersome female out of his mind. She had accosted him, attempted to burgle him, and shot him, all within the space of a few days. Not that he had been any paragon. Still—

Oh, damn and double damn! What *was* wrong with him? Why did he keep thinking on Miss Tremantle? He spun around and commenced to pace the room, conscious of a strong desire to see the infernal chit again. The cool, slightly superior facade he had displayed at their last parting was rapidly crumbling, leaving the Viscount at the mercy of emotions quite foreign to him. That he should thus remain in their grip was intolerable. The realization, no longer deniable, that he harbored tender feelings for the lady distracted him only more. It was an absurdity that was not to be considered! Nothing could come of it, as well he had counseled himself; and yet, he could hardly allow her to engage in whatever mad schemes she was cooking up to entrap the 'Marquess.' He loosened his cravat, muttering curses as he paced about.

If only he hadn't made that agreement with Sir Horatio. But at the time he had felt sorry for the old man, and in his fondness for him had agreed to deliver Chandro. He had not placed much store in Sir Horatio's tale of the Snow Leopard Jewels—that was, until the gentleman was knocked unconscious for them—but now it was quite clear that Sir Rupert, posing as the Marquess of Manakin, knew them to be somewhere at Chatford Abbey, and Cardew was certain Miss Tremantle did not know their whereabouts.

Miss Tremantle! Cardew distractedly ran a hand through his hair, then sinking into the comfort of an old leather arm chair, he contemplated a dusty corner of his library, and tried to push aside the promise Sir Horatio had urged on him; a promise which Chandro *had* heard. The Viscount stared blankly at a heap of old books and papers that sat precariously on the edge of an occasional table, and realized he would need to hire more servants to keep the place up. But dashed, he was *not* going to live here! *Could not* live here, not as long as his name was shadowed with the scandal of Lady Lorena.

His glance swept over yet another eyesore: the white marble hearth littered with ancient ashes. What had possessed him to return home, when he could just as easily have remained at The Jolly Squire? *To be near her,* he realized with a start. Miss Pandora Tremantle. Yes, Sir Horatio *had* tried to extract a gentleman's word that he might consider his daughter. He had described her accurately and lovingly when he said that she was too tall for many men, and too headstrong for most: but how on earth Chandro had understood and remembered the English phrase, *on the shelf,* Cardew would never know!

Haunting words, those.

The Viscount had not, however, pledged himself to the man's daughter. In fact, he had even gone so far as to recite the entire drama that had propelled him out of England. Sir Horatio found it *interesting,* but as he had tried to assure Cardew, the Tremantles were an odd lot, and didn't give a hang for convention. His lordship had remained adamant: he would take the boy to Chatford, then be on his way; depending on the state of affairs, he actually *had* given thought to the south of France. There was one thing, however, that had *never* occurred to him, and that was falling in love with the irrepressible, impetuous Pandora. Leaning forward, elbows riveted to knees, he plowed both hands through his now thoroughly disheveled hair.

It was this scene, embellished with a brandy bottle on the table next to him, that greeted Miss Tremantle upon her brisk entrance into *sahib*'s study.

"Well!" she uttered, at a loss for saying anything more intelligible. Chandro and Jemnaz, directly behind her, whispered excitedly in their mother tongue.

"What the devil!" His lordship was on his feet in the instant and moving towards the lady who so plagued his thoughts.

"I am not the devil," she began, rapidly recovering from her own small shock. "Though it is clear you perceive me in that light." Her voice was crisp, and full of authority. Unfortunately this was a magnificently constructed front, which the least wind, she feared, would demolish.

"Pandora! Forgive me! This is most irregular." He stood before her, clearly bedeviled, and apparently slightly foxed. His neckcloth was askew, his coat discarded, and his waistcoat ill kept.

"I came," she began in a miserably high voice, which she immediately lowered, "I came in response to your missive." She thrust it forward as if it carried the plague, and when he refused to accept it, she slapped it down next to the brandy bottle. An unfortunate quantity of dust arose from this act, which precipitated several sneezes and a handkerchief offer from the depths of the Viscount's waistcoat.

"No thank you," she managed somewhat stiffly between the second and third sneeze. Behind her she was aware of the continued Hindi chatter and occasional giggles. The Viscount must have been aware of her thoughts, for he issued an order to Chandro, who babbled something back, then reluctantly led Jemnaz to another equally dusty chamber.

"I came to tell you that . . . although I appreciate your solicitude in warning me to steer clear of the Marquess of Manakin, I will be able to fend for myself the night of the ball."

"You came to tell me that when you could just as easily have written it?" Of a sudden Pandora noticed he had sobered up to a remarkable degree, *and* he'd assumed that intolerable stance he affected so well. He moved closer to her, and to her surprise there was not a trace of brandy about him. She backed up in some confusion: he moved forward, and Miss Tremantle felt her foundation shift ever so slightly.

"You walked over here to tell me *that?*" he repeated, then throwing his head back, laughed in a most bewildering way.

"Yes!" she insisted, then with a brittle laugh of her own, added, "and I wanted to make sure you didn't get any valiant ideas into your head about saving me. I am quite able to take care of myself, despite the mishap in Vauxhall Gardens."

"And the fiasco in my room at the Orange Crown?" he added on a light note. "You *do* remember that night, do you not?" As his hand reached out and touched the side of her face, she felt a shivering lightness pass through her. That same hand curled around the nape of her neck, and drew her towards him: slowly, very slowly until their breaths mingled, and until she knew he must be able to hear her heart beat. She made no move to escape the confines of this prison, for she wanted the feel of his lips upon hers, the tenderness of his kiss.

And then it happened: he kissed her, and he didn't stop kissing her until she thought she might faint from lack of air, for she had almost forgotten how to breathe, to speak, to think even. The only thing she needed saving from was herself. She wanted to say something, but words would not come, only a maddening flush to her cheeks, which was not at all like her.

"Oh God!" he said in a voice she hardly recognized. Thrusting her from him as if she were death itself, he stared at her with a look that baffled her.

It was at this inappropriate moment that Chandro and Jemnaz, bitten with curiosity, reappeared, but immediately fell silent upon seeing the Viscount's black countenance. Pandora, thoroughly shaken, took this opportunity to make a hasty retreat. Barely able to look at Lord Cardew, she mumbled a civil good afternoon, and clasping Jemnaz's hand, fled his lordship's company, quite unaware of the anguish and frustration that assailed this gentleman.

It was a brisk walk home, and one filled with such enlightenment that she hardly noticed the drizzle of rain. By the time they had mounted the steps to the Grosvenor Square house, Pandora felt almost in need of Aunt Beatrix's hartshorn and water. Instead, she bade Jemnaz have a hearty luncheon with Nora, then retired to her bedchamber to collect her tumultuous thoughts.

Setting her bonnet to one side, she plopped in front of the

glass and stared at her reflection: the same eyes, lips, nose—everything was the same. She had vaguely thought that perhaps falling in love would have changed them. Oh! She pressed her hands to her cheeks, and propping her elbows on her dressing table, looked for further signs. There were none. As her little finger traced the edge of her lips, she was suddenly aware of feeling overly warm. Abruptly she rose, and crossing to the window, opened it and breathed deeply. The rain had stopped, and the air was fresh and cool on her cheeks. It was then she was aware of a small tear that threatened to trickle down her face. She brushed it away, and with a sigh, crossed towards her secretary, and sat some minutes before reaching for her quill.

In love with Lord Cardew, she murmured to herself, stunned at the realization. Not just in love, but *hopelessly* afflicted! And to what end? An unexpected sob erupted from her, and throwing herself across the table she gave in to this surprisingly satisfying emotion. She remained thus for some time, and when at last she did raise her head, she felt some minor relief. After applying her handkerchief to her reddened nose and eyes, she attempted to set this revelation aside, as one might a depressing novel. She had best consider how to ensnare the Marquess of Manakin, for that was something she felt more than capable of doing. Matters of the heart had ever eluded her, so she would *not* think on the Viscount. He had used her shabbily, as he undoubtedly did all women. Pandora chewed on this morsel for a few moments before putting quill to ink, then quickly she jotted down a few notes. The charade she had planned for Chloe's ball would teach him a lesson. And after all, hadn't that been her intent from the start? His trifling with her only fanned the flames.

But why had *Lord Cardew* set his sights on the Marquess? His certainty that the Marquess was the notorious Duke of Diamonds was hardly justification for his relentless pursuit of the man. No, there had to be something more which Pandora had overlooked.

This part of the puzzle, absorbing Miss Tremantle for the better part of an hour, had the blessed effect of distracting her from the recent affliction to her heart. When the one missing piece suddenly snapped into place, it did so with an obviousness that astonished Pandora.

"Of course!" she cried, "The Viscount *is* the Marquess!" Everything had pointed to it, she had simply been too goose-capped to notice. The strongest clue was Chandro, the 'true jewel'! Only the real Marquess would have been privy to her father's private reference to the orphan children. That was why the impostor was confused at her father's message of a jewel, and why he had suddenly produced his valued ruby, with every intention of later stealing it back. For it was he, the Duke of Diamonds, who had strangled the lovely Lady Lorena for it, and tried to implicate her betrothed, the real Marquess, in the deed.

Pandora took a deep breath as the mystery rapidly unraveled. All of the pieces were falling in place. No wonder the Viscount's pursuit had seemed so driven. His pronounced interest in the ruby was to avenge his betrothed's murder, and to that end he would do anything! That was why he wished to catch the Marquess with the ruby: not only was it his jewel to begin with, but it was all the proof he needed to send the impostor to the gallows.

Pushing away from the secretary, Pandora rose and crossed to her dressing table. She retrieved the ruby from its hiding place and stared at it for a moment. By all rights she should return it to Lord Cardew, for it *was* his. However, she would wear it one last time, and *then* present it to him along with the villain and her compliments!

The solving of Lord Cardew's identity should have elated her, but somehow it had the opposite effect. She found herself wondering about the glamorous Lady Lorena. What had she been like, to have inspired such passion? While Pandora felt the Viscount's devotion to his lady was admirable, especially in his relentless pursuit of the assassin, she did not approve of his odd behavior, and in particular towards herself. The certain knowledge that she was merely a diversion was worse than depressing, it was humiliating! Oh, but he would see her mettle!

Another piece of the puzzle fell neatly into place during luncheon, when Beatrix, out of the blue, said, "*Now* I remember hearing of Sir Rupert!" She paused, her spoon hovering over the Madeira syllabub. "A noted gamester! Though several years ago he seemed to absent himself from England. Ah, that's no doubt why I didn't remember him at first." Eagerly she dipped into the dessert.

"Question is: did the chap look like our Marquess?" Winthrop asked.

"Oh, I've never seen him," Beatrix replied between spoonfuls of syllabub. "As I recall he never moved in polite circles, preferring, shall we say, a faster crowd. But if your friend confused their identities, they are probably of a like mold." This last was delivered in a stentorian voice meant to awaken the dead: obviously Beatrix felt her niece's silence up until now was a dangerous sign.

"Definitely!" Pandora replied, gratifying her aunt, who commenced to conjecture on this *Sir Rupert.*

Pandora reflected on Winthrop's encounter at Boodle's. *Of course!* This mix-up of identities was a farrago of nonsense. Sir Rupert, or whoever, posing as the Marquess, to get the Snow Leopard Jewels; the true Marquess posing as the Viscount in order to entrap him; and the real Viscount Cardew undoubtedly somewhere masquerading as goodness knows whom!

Taking a taste of the creamy syllabub, she felt a little thrill go through her at having finally divined the mystery. Now all that remained was the denouement, which, if everything went as she envisioned, would occur the night of the ball. And why not, pray tell? Anything short of victory did not bear thinking on!

Chapter Twelve

Had Miss McClellan not been so enthralled with her plans for the ball, she might have wondered why Pandora's two "eligible swains" had not paid further calls at Grosvenor Square. This was quite to her niece's liking, who had spent the balance of the past two days either amiably entertaining her various London friends, or sequestered in the library, refining her plans. By the time Madame Chabrière's costumes arrived, Pandora was in the highest of spirits. A gay morning was spent as the ladies tried on their gowns, and by the time luncheon was served, Beatrix, thoroughly delighted with Pandora's charming manner, declared the girl had quite changed her stripes, and perhaps there was hope that she would consider one of her gentlemen.

Later that afternoon, prior to their departure for Chatford Abbey, Beatrix drew her niece aside, and confided that she was somewhat distracted by little Chloe's recent behavior. Oh, not that Miss Deeds *ever* did anything to bring censure upon her pretty golden head, but in her own quiet way she was showing signs of being a bit of a hoyden! And after the perfect picture she had presented. This came as news to Miss Tremantle, who privately applauded this spark of spirit in her cousin. Beatrix, then sinking further into these fears, confessed she was partly responsible.

"Oh, yes, my girl!" she whispered hurriedly. "For it was I who introduced Chloe to Mrs. Hawkshore's latest novel—you know the one, where the villain spirits the heroine's ninny sister off to Gretna Green?"

"Ah, *The Defiant Duchess,*" Pandora replied, biting back a smile. "But surely you don't think Chloe and Winthrop are of that inclination?"

"I do not know *what* to believe! Except that I am responsible for the girl's welfare, and Statira would likely go into a decline were the child to do something foolish! I daresay, as it is, there will be the very devil to pay, for her Mama had the highest hopes for the Applegate heir." She dabbed her forehead with a lace hankie and looked furtively about the small parlor for signs of the girl. "And I will further tell you, for all her sweetness and light, she will undoubtedly grow into a headstrong miss!"

"Chloe?" Pandora sputtered on this, then putting an arm around her aunt's shoulders, added, "Come, let us not give it another thought, for I fear you are overwrought."

"But *Gretna Green!*" she uttered in horrific tones.

As they cleared the half-landing, Pandora whispered, "Winny would *never* countenance anything so shabby."

Miss McClellan's fears on this topic, however, were reinforced during their carriage ride back to Chatford Abbey, as Chloe, in the grips of yet another of Mrs. Hawkshore's romantic tomes, clasped it to her bosom, and announced that above all things she would like to go to Gretna Green! This unfortunate statement caused Miss McClellan to start violently, only to sink back onto the cushions.

"My salts, my salts!" she muttered, thrusting her reticule at Pandora, who immediately found and produced the desired restorative.

Realizing the inappropriateness of her comment, Chloe patted her aunt's hand gently and amended her declaration, "I did not mean to upset you. It is just that I have taken it into my head to do some traveling about, and since everyone appears to go to Gretna Green, it seemed a place I might enjoy."

"My child," Beatrix managed in a constrained voice, "no one of consequence ever goes there: you will notice that Mrs. Hawkshore makes sure of that!"

"That was why I had fancied it," Chloe pointed out. "And when I mentioned it to Winny, he seemed to think it a capital idea too. Oh, but don't trouble yourself, Auntie. I shall set him straight on the matter." Looking out the carriage window, she gaily waved at Winthrop, who had chosen to ride alongside them.

"Oh, I shall go distracted!" Beatrix cried, her salts at the ready this time.

"Nonsense!" Pandora countered in a tone intended to snap her aunt out of the impending vapors. "Chloe is simply caught up in a story. Isn't that right, Cousin?"

"Oh, yes! Mama doesn't have books like this in Bath. I feel as if an entire world has opened up for me."

"It is not part of our world," Beatrix said with surprising vigor. "And I am shocked at Winthrop for humoring you in this unfortunate myth. But then it's a miracle he and Pandora have not long since gone to ruin, what with their father absenting himself on these wild goose chases." She closed her eyes, and rested back on the cushions once again.

The remainder of the journey to Chatford might have passed in relative quietude. The overwrought Miss McClellan fell into slumber, Chloe returned to her romance, and Pandora resumed her plotting. All this would have continued were it not for a sudden commotion outside the carriage.

"Oh, great heavens, we are set upon!" screeched Miss McClellan, coming fully awake and tumbling forward as their carriage came to a careening halt in a cloud of dust. Reticules, small bandboxes, and a variety of goods crashed to the floor, and were it not for Pandora, her aunt would undoubtedly have ended up amongst those articles. Chloe, who had held fast to *The Craven Count,* let out a shriek as Winthrop, leaning down from his horse, yanked open the carriage door.

"I caught the miscreants!" he declared nobly, pointing toward a gig that teetered on the brink of a gully. "I had seen them about Grosvenor Square, and today, when they followed us out of London, I decided to find out the reason!"

At this point everyone began talking at once: Beatrix's "Oh my's!" intermingled with Chloe's "Oh, Winny!" and Pandora's questions. Finally Pandora, giving up her line of query, descended from the carriage. Beatrix reached for her, muttering about desperate criminals, only to collapse once more against the pillows.

Jemnaz, with a blinding smile on his dark face, held a pistol on the two men in the gig, and at Pandora's approach, said jubilantly, "More villains! I see them before too. They are like shadows, these new admirers of yours, but not so splendidly gowned as your Viscount."

"Sis, I would not speak to these unsavories. And that we not lose time, I intend on taking them with us to Chatford, then sending Parks for some Runners to gather them up."

"We be innocent," the short fat one declared from his position on the gig's seat.

"Save your breath, villain!" If Winthrop had had a sword, he would have undoubtedly unsheathed it.

At this point Beatrix, emboldened by heaven knows what, and assisted by the wide-eyed Chloe, arrived on the scene, though for once in her life she was too stunned to utter a single sound.

"We ain't villains," the tall skinny one said, clutching his rumpled hat and twisting it every which way.

"Aye, and we ain't plugged no-body!" his partner added, "Though according to the—" He stopped short, and ducking his head, said, "According to the rumor, there be plenty of coves to plug in Lunnon." The fat one then scratched his head as if he was trying to recall the last cove they *had* plugged.

"Don't be jabbering like that!" the skinny one said. "You wants to be a-scareding Miss Tremantle?"

"Oh!" Beatrix intoned, as the gift of speech was once again bestowed on her, "they are bandying your name about! I never! They are definitely criminals: desperate ones. Such language!" She was so thoroughly horrified that all recourse to salts and the like vanished. "Oh, and just look at the public spectacle we are making!" With a wave of her hanky Beatrix indicated their caravan of coaches that had pulled across the road, and the gawking servants that leaned out the windows.

"We wasn't making no spectacle."

"Oh, such language!" Miss McClellan repeated.

"We speaks the same as you'm," said the one that Pandora thought looked like mashed potatoes. "Onry difference is we got special words you don't."

"Enough!" Winthrop shouted, reining in his horse. "Jemnaz will ride with you! He is from India where life is cheap, and shall have no compunction about shooting you, should you try anything!"

"Oh, Winny, what *do* you intend on doing?" Beatrix queried, torn between fear and outrage.

"They shall go back to Chatford Abbey!"

"But that is most unseemly; whatever shall the servants say?"

"Auntie, that is the least of our troubles," Pandora replied, then shading her eyes from the noonday sun, looked at these unlikely villains, who of a sudden seemed quite amenable to the enforced journey.

"That be fine by us," the one who resembled a bone said. "For that's where we was a-following you to, anyways."

"I *knew* you were following us! Well, if you were expecting warm milk and a bedtime story, you shall be sadly let down," Winthrop said, miffed by their unvillainish behavior.

"Oh, no doubt, but 'twill be better than sitting up half the night gawking at your door," the little fat one said, a ridiculous smile on his round face.

At Winthrop's "It shall be the dungeon for the likes of you," both men looked quite concerned.

Pandora, feeling a sudden urge to laugh, reached up for his bridle and quietly said, "We don't have a dungeon, and you know it! Can't you see these men are relatively harmless? Let me talk to them."

"You can do that in the dungeon!" He nodded to Jemnaz that they might leave, then to his sister, he added, "Be so good as to round up Aunt Beatrix and Cousin Chloe: this sun is quite hot." Turning his horse about, he rode ahead at a spanking trot. Undoubtedly he was aware of Chloe's rapt adoration of his heroism.

Had there been any question in anyone's mind on this point, Miss Deeds quickly laid it to rest, and spent the rest of the thankfully brief journey extolling Winny's golden attributes. Mrs. Hawkshore's novel was pressed to her breast, and her eyes were dewy with the burgeoning emotion of love.

The most startling event of the afternoon, however, yet awaited them upon their return: Statira Deeds had arrived from Bath the day before, and was burdened down with news of the utmost significance. She requested Chloe's immediate presence, unencumbered by other members of the family. Dauntlessly Miss Deeds floated into the gold saloon: nothing could mar her perfect afternoon. After she had seen her Mama, they would all have a bit of tea, and Winny would report on the villains, whom even now he was locking up in the cellar.

Pandora was upstairs in her bedchamber unpacking the clever costume Madame Chabrière had fashioned for her when the first scream pierced the air. She froze for an instant, imagining all manner of things, but flew into the hall, as did Beatrix. Another scream was heard as Pandora raced down the stairs, her aunt directly behind her. Before they reached the first floor, Winthrop had charged up from the cellar, prepared to defend the distressed damsel, who appeared as if on cue, her eyes red-rimmed and a little hankie pressed to her mouth against future outbursts. One look at Winthrop and a flood of tears streamed down her round cheeks. Immediately he closed the space between them and crushed her to him. Pandora, having just cleared the stairs, had an excellent view of the drama: as the lovebirds clung to each other, Mrs. Deeds, looking grief-stricken in a gown of black bombazine, tottered in the arched doorway of the gold saloon. Chloe was now sobbing freely onto Winthrop's coat, and he was taking it all in the manly way. Indeed, Pandora couldn't remember her brother ever being so mature.

"Oh, Beatrix!" Statira choked over this greeting, then motioning toward the entwined couple, made another strangled noise, and backed into the saloon.

"Get a hold of yourself, do!" Beatrix admonished, suddenly assuming a mantle of authority. Then sweeping past the lovers, as if they were an ill-placed sculpture, she rounded on her younger sister, who had melted into a dark puddle on the gold sofa.

"Whatever happened?" Pandora said in a hushed tone to Chloe, who had lifted her tear-stained face.

"Oh, the most horrible!" she replied, her lips quivering. "My life is ruined!"

This brought a moan from her swain, who gritting his teeth, said fiercely, "Not as long as I draw breath shall anyone touch a hair on your head!" As if to prove this point, he stroked her yellow curls most tenderly.

"Stalwart," Pandora said. "But don't you think we should repair to the saloon and sort this all out?"

"There is nothing to sort out," Chloe replied. Then blowing her nose into a hanky, she smiled weakly and said, "But if you wish to hear what my mother has done, I will endure it again."

"I shall be at your side," Winthrop murmured, as together they passed into the saloon. At the sight of them, Mrs. Deeds let out a pitiable groan.

"What madness is all of this?" Pandora demanded, rounding the sofa and looking directly at her Aunt Statira.

"I shall go mad!" the woman replied, in near hysteria. Her several chins wobbled, and little red spots bloomed on her cheeks: Pandora was reminded of a well-fed chicken.

"I should never have made this trip, especially in my delicate health. However, something of the most grievous forced me to chance the hazards. If not for my own sake, then for my darling Chloe!" She dabbed effectively at her close-set eyes before resuming her tale of woe.

"I am bankrupt!" she announced, clutching her neck in a most effective manner. Then, pleased with the gasps this elicited, added magniloquently, "But the day is saved! For Lord Larkin Pettigrew—you know the fabulously wealthy Pettigrews of Bath—has come to our rescue, and offered for Chloe, even though she has not a farthing to her name, and most likely will develop one of the numerous ailments that plague our family, thus being a millstone around his neck. Still—" her voice rose to fend off Pandora's hasty retort, "still, he is willing to marry my little one, *and* pay all my debts—which have been so monstrous—and settle a nice sum on me! Is this not Providence most divine?"

"It is Providence most *hideous!*" Pandora cried, in utter horror. "Millstone around that old goat's neck! Why, he shall be gone to grass before Chloe could even possibly be an encumbrance. *And* since Chloe has yet to have had a sick day in her life, I seriously doubt she shall make a career of it once married."

"But he will care for her," protested Mrs. Deeds, grappling

for her vinaigrette, "and though I had hoped for Sir Applegate, this is even better."

"Stuff!" Pandora retorted, not giving her stunned brother, who had been wearing the mantle of hero so valiantly, a chance to make a rejoinder. In a similar fashion, Beatrix sat with her mouth partially open at the verbal arrows this conversation provoked.

"You are a heartless girl to call it *stuff!* And I notice you have remained a spinster." Her lips twisted with a venomous satisfaction.

"By choice!" Pandora retorted.

"Anyway, it is settled! I have told Lord Larkin I would put his suit at Chloe's feet, and—"

"And if she has any sense she'll kick it all the way to Hades!" In her fury, Pandora commenced pacing, that she might resist the impulse to throttle the idiotic woman.

"But he is paying my debts as well, and is willing to see that I am well cared for in my advancing years." She sniffed bravely, as if her dotage was lying in wait around the corner.

"I will not marry that miserly old goat!" Chloe said with unexpected firmness. "I shall go to a nunnery!"

"But my dear, you aren't even Roman Catholic," Beatrix remarked quite practically.

"I shall convert! Or if they won't have me, the Thames will!" Her small hands were clasped in supplication.

"Neither shall claim you!" Winthrop said in a booming voice. "For though I am not a terribly rich man, I have sufficient funds to care for you." Then heedless of the audience, he turned to Chloe, and implored, "Will you marry me, my dearest one?"

Even as she replied that she would, her mother announced she was *definitely* going mad, would soon be a raving lunatic, and then they would be sorry!

"Monstrous debts, just monstrous!" she was heard to exclaim as her maid assisted her to her chamber. She would dine there for the balance of the week, though she might be cajoled to attend Chloe's ball. But she would *never* give her blessing on Chloe and Winthrop's wedding plans!

"I would say we practically have a full house," Pandora remarked that night at dinner. "Aunt Statira in the blue chamber, and our villains in the cellar. By the way, Winny," she said casually, as she speared a sweetmeat, "Have you seen to their comforts?"

"Naturally. They are fully accommodated, and from their manner, you'd think I'd set 'em up in a private room at Boodle's!" Winthrop looked slightly bewildered at this admission, then cutting into his pickled salmon, added, "I have posted Jemnaz outside their door, and—"

"I pray you have not put them in the wine cellar," Beatrix said, fretting over three peas that refused to go onto her fork.

"Do you think me mad, Auntie? They are in the fruit cellar."

"Well, you can't keep them there forever," Pandora pointed out, "And after dinner I intend on questioning them—"

"Oh, no, no!" Beatrix sputtered into her wine. "You must not on any account do that! They could be ruthless cutthroats!"

"Stuff. They've done us no harm. You know, there are laws against keeping people in one's cellar against their will. I daresay we could be the ones locked up for this act."

"But if they're happy in the cellar," Chloe said, defending her beloved's actions, "then what harm is done?"

Pandora would have undoubtedly expounded on that, had not Hawkins appeared, looking thoroughly undone, to announce that the Viscount Cardew awaited Miss Tremantle in the gold saloon on a matter of the utmost urgency.

"I shall come at once!" Pandora said, tossing her linen napkin in a heap beside her unfinished dinner.

"Oh!" Beatrix cried, cherishing a renewed hope. "By all means. At once! Romance is, after all, in the air!" The fact that her sister Statira had cursed the flame of love between Winthrop and Chloe was beside the point. After all, in Mrs. Hawkshore's novels, everything *always* was nicely rounded out. She must write to the author for her secret. Ah, but the Viscount, here at Chatford Abbey; undoubtedly he was prepared to forget Pandora's previous behavior.

In this, Miss McClellan was mistaken. Indeed, the gentleman still bore the signs of travel upon him: his person was in disarray, his riding costume was splashed with mud, and his brow was black as thunder. He was pacing the room, slapping his riding crop against his leg when Miss Tremantle appeared.

"So," he said in a tone he barely recognized. He paused in his pacing, and flexing the whip in his gloved hands added, "Where are my men?"

That Miss Tremantle had the good grace to start at this query showed sense on her part. "*Your men?*" Her voice, as lovely as he had remembered it, sounded appropriately mystified.

"Yes. The two men I idiotically hired to watch over *you!*" His jaw tightened, and he felt a fool for the position his two hirelings had put him in.

"Oh. One of the gentlemen wouldn't be short and fat, would he?"

"An accurate description," Cardew managed on a more civil note. "And the other is quite the opposite. Tell me, Miss Tremantle, does havoc *always* trail after you?" He bit back a look of satisfaction at the incriminating color that swept her face, then cordially he added, "Please lead me to them."

"Very well. Follow me," she said, turning abruptly.

Cardew noted the manner in which she tossed her red curls—curls so soft to the touch. He checked himself on this thought, and sardonically said, "Undoubtedly they are trussed up."

"In our dungeon," she shot back. Her quickened step afforded him great pleasure in the view of her slim ankle as she led him toward the nether regions. That the woman bedeviled him could not be denied, nor could the feelings he held for her. Damn, he would be glad when this whole business was concluded!

"As you will see," Miss Tremantle said, presenting the Marquess with a taper, and taking one up herself, "We have yet to put the thumbscrews on our prisoners."

"I am obliged, ma'am," he returned, taking unexpected pleasure in what he had assumed would be another scene with the tempestuous Miss Tremantle.

Thus, she led him down a tortuous winding staircase, making idle chitchat about their vats of boiling oil and racks, then just as they cleared the last step she tardily admonished him to watch his head. A cracking sound and a rejoining oath filled the cavernous chamber.

At their approach, Jemnaz jumped to attention, and said the sahibs were wanting playing cards. Pandora said they were to be freed, and stepped aside as the boy performed this office. The prisoners were just finishing up generous portions of salmon and other delicacies and greeted his lordship as if they had not been inconvenienced in the least. As a matter of fact, if they were to be watching over the young miss, this was as good a place as any. His lordship said that no, he felt the Tremantles had been imposed on enough for one evening.

"I would, however, want them present at the costume ball. They could come as themselves, you know." Lord Cardew made this remark as they ascended to the upper floor.

"Whatever for?" Miss Tremantle asked. At his slightly raised eyebrow, she acquiesced, "Very well, your men are welcome. But please, know that I have plans of my own."

"Don't be an idiot!" he said savagely. "Flaunt that ruby, and it's the last time you'll wear it." He smiled through gritted teeth as Miss McClellan, clearly in her element, bore down upon him and Pandora.

"Oh, Lord Cardew!" sang out Beatrix, hands clasped to her bosom. "How fortuitous that you should—" Her words fell away abruptly, as loss of speech again afflicted her. The smallest of gasps escaped her lips, but was covered admirably with, "I see you travel with your . . . servants! La, how splendid." She made a fluttery gesture toward Bone and Dumpling, who grinned back quite amiably. Then turning her attention back to the Viscount, she reminded him that the masked ball was a mere four days away. Her coquettish attempts to discover his costume went to no avail, and after a slight pause, wherein Pandora feared her aunt might press him to be houseguest, she bid him safe journey back to the Orange Crown. Obviously she considered his *servants* to be of questionable origins, and would just as soon not house them at Chatford.

No sooner had the great bolt slid across the oak portal behind them, then Beatrix, executing a dramatic pose, uttered, "How did those ruffians come to be in the Viscount's hire?" Her eyes narrowed then flitted from Winthrop to Pandora, as if *they* were the responsible culprits. "Well?" she demanded, "Don't you realize we could have been murdered in our beds? Murdered—"

"Nonsense," Pandora began. "If Winny had left well enough alone—"

"I?" Winthrop straightened visibly. *"Had* they been villains, you'd have sung a different tune!"

"Oh, but you were very courageous, nonetheless," Chloe offered.

"I did what I felt necessary," Winthrop replied, bestowing a smile on his beloved. "However, I feel the need for a constitutional," he added as he strode towards the door. "I have much to think on."

To Pandora it was patently clear he felt wronged and wished to meditate on some way he might redeem his image as The Man of the Manor. She was tempted to say something about pride going before the fall, but let the matter rest, not realizing that Winthrop's ways would be the cause of yet more chaos.

Chapter Thirteen

The sun rose innocently enough on the day of the masked ball. The sky was a brilliant blue, and only a dusting of clouds was on the horizon. Miss McClellan declared it presaged great fortune for all those lucky enough to attend the fête. The dear lady was in a veritable twitter the entire morning, checking and rechecking every last detail, so that by midafternoon she was in such a state of exhaustion that she took to her chamber for a nap, and recommended everyone else follow suit.

Thus it was that Chatford Abbey, decked out in all its glory, fell into slumbers: every inch of the stately Jacobean manse had been scrubbed and polished until reflections could be seen everywhere. Beatrix, with the help of Pandora, Chloe, and Nora, had arranged colorful bowls of flowers and placed them in the great hall, the ballroom, and the gold saloon. Half the morning was spent fashioning a flower chain which was intricately twined about the carved oak banister of the main staircase. Capriciously, Pandora had stuck several jonquils, which later drooped rather pathetically, in the armored figures at the top of the stairs.

Then of course, there were the edibles, the making of which took Cook and her staff several days. The unmistakable aroma of baking, which always reminded Pandora of her childhood, filled the house, as little finger cakes, turnovers, and other sweets were made. There would be fountains of iced champagne in the great ballroom, and even in the garden. Chloe was delighted to learn that paper lanterns would line the many paths that curled through the labyrinth of boxwoods. Nothing had been overlooked in preparing for Miss Deeds's ball. It was no wonder therefore that everyone was in need of that afternoon nap which would prove so fateful—everyone save one: the *Marquess!*

Thus it was as they slumbered innocently away, Sir Rupert repaired to the library to resume his search. After all, who would think it amiss if *Lord Manakin* spent a quiet afternoon at his favorite pursuit, browsing among dusty tomes. But then no one knew that his research in London had confirmed something he'd first learned in India: The Snow Leopard Jewels lay beneath the tooled binding of a set of Islamic books. Rubies, emeralds, diamonds, and sapphires formed a pattern on each book cover, which held clues to some mystic legend.

From his perch he spied the corner of one last box of books under the window seat. The twine had been cut and the wrapping pulled aside, but as yet it had not been unpacked. Carefully Sir Rupert climbed down the ladder, ever mindful not to mar his close-fitting pantaloons nor put a scratch on his highly polished boots. Libraries were such dusty places, not at all to his liking. But then several things had not been to his liking: his prized ruby had been snatched, he appeared to have been thrust back into the marriage mart, and finally, despite inquiries, he had been unable to track down the Viscount at the Orange Crown Inn. Was this Viscount the real Marquess of Manakin or not? Be damned if he were! For hadn't Sir Rupert been assured by the assassins he had hired that they had strangled the Marquess, making it look like a Thuggee killing? But if that were not the case, he would have to find him. And this time he would make an end of the man who, had the fates been different, would have swung from the gibbet for Lady Lorena's murder. Sir Rupert paused at the foot of the ladder as the memory of that night eight years ago rose up like a specter to haunt him: his hands about the lovely Lorena's neck, choking the life out of her, and for what? *A fortune in jewels!* A witness to his hasty departure that stormy night had sworn it was Lady Lorena's betrothed who had strangled her. In time, the real Marquess had managed to clear his name, though his reputation was shredded, and thus he had abandoned himself to the wilds of India.

That Sir Rupert, for very different reasons, had sought out that teeming subcontinent was a curious twist of fate indeed. Once again it was treasure, this time the Snow Leopard Jewels, that lured him on. And nothing—*nothing*—would stop him from finding them.

Pushing all thoughts of his past to one side, Rupert pulled up a chair beside the box of books and quickly withdrew the top volume for inspection. Immediately he noted its heft and thick binding, though it was a small volume with gold-edged pages. With a growing sense of excitement he ran his fingers over the cover: the hairs on the back of his neck rose in the thrill of discovery. He drove one of his fingernails beneath the binding and slowly managed to peel it away, thus revealing the treasure he had so desperately been seeking. A six-pointed star winked back at him, its brilliance dimmed by centuries of leather binding. But there it was, the first of several: all different, all exquisite, all priceless—and all for him! He couldn't tear his eyes away from the treasure, yet, like a spoiled child surrounded by too many presents, he wanted to tear open everything immediately. Still, his gaze lingered on this ancient star that had been fashioned from diamonds and sapphires. Silver tracework edged the design which lay on a deep blue binding.

Sir Rupert's reverie was cut short by the sound of a muffled sneeze which came from across the room. Instantly he was on his feet, a pistol at the ready, and before Jemnaz could succeed in escaping, he had clapped a hand across his mouth, and with the butt end of his pistol rendered him senseless. *Damn!* he thought. He had not bargained on this intrusion. He would have to hide the boy in his room until after the ball. After that it was immaterial what was to be done with the child; however, Rupert would have to dispose of him later. But he couldn't very well snuff out the boy's light and plant him under a rose bush. If only he had brought Tribbs with him. But what of it? He cared not, for he would use the balance of the evening to prepare for an early departure the following morning. As for the ball, he would most certainly make an appearance, then take his leave after everyone had gone to bed. Pity he'd have to leave without the ruby. Nevertheless he had found what he had come for, and nothing else mattered.

Sir Rupert paused to determine whether he could go safely through the great hall, then hoisting Jemnaz over his shoulder he quickly crossed to the stairs and made his way to his chamber. Once there, he drugged and bound the child, then deposited him in a hamper. This accomplished, he secured the jeweled books in his carriage. Then, to cover his tracks, he wrote a note incriminating Jemnaz in petty thievery of some silver, adding that he, Manakin, had gone to London in pursuit of the boy. To give credibility to the lie, Sir Rupert neatly pocketed several apostle spoons. The boy, of course, would never be found: as for the Marquess of Manakin, there would be much conjecture and a very cold trail.

Pandora had certainly not meant to fall asleep, for her brain was teeming with the plot she had cooked up for that evening; thus she awoke with a start when her abigail nudged her.

"Didn't mean to startle you, Miss Pandora, but I thought you might like a bit of supper."

"Thanks, Nora, but I couldn't eat a thing," she protested, not even looking beneath the covers of the dishes, "for there's much to do for the evening ahead."

"Then I suppose it's time to bathe and dress," Nora replied in a subdued voice as she set the dinner tray to one side.

"Now, you have nothing to worry about," Pandora assured her as she bounded out of bed on a sudden surge of energy. "I'll be right there, pistols at the ready—and believe me I know how to use them now. There is no way our villain can escape."

"Oh, I'm not afraid for myself—well, not much." With a grim determination she set about Miss Tremantle's toilette, and for the most part refrained from dire pronouncements. "However," Nora began in lowering tones as she helped Pandora into her costume, "About this Marquess—"

"Sir Rupert Montescue," she quickly corrected, having earlier taken her abigail into her confidence. "Let's not elevate him above his station."

"Whatever you call him, he's a thieving blackguard, who'd just as soon slit your throat as look at you." She made a clucking sound like a mother hen as she fastened the towering headgear onto Pandora's curls. "I do wish you would heed the real Marquess's advice."

"Nonsense!" She gave a toss to her head, which necessitated a refastening of the headpiece. "I do not wish to think on him just now." She managed to hold still while Nora secured the extravagantly pointed hat, whose flowing scarves of gold silk were clearly patterned with red diamonds.

"The perfect bait, don't you agree?" Pandora said, twirling before the glass and admiring the fall of her gown. It was a long-sleeved creation of red and gold silk covered by gold tissue, bearing the red diamond motif. Should any questions arise concerning her costume, there was the scepter, topped with a large red diamond, and from this a streamer held the title "QUEEN OF DIAMONDS." She deviated from the playing card in the gown's low-cut décolleté, which revealed a lovely expanse of creamy white skin. And about her neck: the ruby!

"Well?" Pandora turned from her reflection to address Nora, who was shaking her head.

"Do you really think we can fool Sir Rupert? For though we are the same height, our coloring is quite different."

"The scarf will cover your hair, and the mask, your face: besides, it's just for a short stroll in the garden. The most important thing is that he see the ruby. I can guarantee he will attempt to follow you down the garden path . . . as it were." A delicious smile settled on Pandora's lips as she added, "And when he attempts to burgle the jewel yet again, I literally unmask him—for I'll be hiding behind the rose trellis—and then present him to the real Marquess of Manakin."

"Oh, but Miss, so many things could go wrong. What if he accosts you now?"

Covering the ruby with her scarf, Pandora replied, "He won't see the ruby until later, when you will be wearing it; and besides, right now I am merely making an appearance that he might know who I am. Oh, and I might let him see just a glimpse of the jewel. That is of course before we switch roles."

"But what if—"

"No buts! We must act with resolve. Help me on with my mask, for I hear the musicians tuning up, and I am anxious to be about this night's business! And you are not to worry: I'll follow you like the shadow of a cat."

"Yes. The cat with nine lives," Nora said, adjusting the scarlet domino mask on her mistress. "Humph! When the Viscount—"

"Marquess," Pandora corrected once again.

"When the *Marquess* discovers what you intend on doing, he shall be furious with you."

"Oh, he knows I'm about something, and while he's spending the evening figuring out just what it is, I shall have the villain exposed." Waving her scepter as if it were a magic wand, she added, "But there's a lot that gentleman does *not* know: for example, he undoubtedly still believes I think him the Viscount Cardew!"

"And best you leave it that way," Nora scolded, following her to the door in a last-minute attempt to straighten the precarious headpiece.

"Yes, who knows, maybe he *did* strangle his poor fiancée!" Pandora rejoined on a ghoulish note.

"Oh, not him, Miss! But don't you be forgetting all his years in India."

"Heaven forbid I should! Winthrop was just telling me the other day that he'd done more reading on him while in London, and that the *Morning Post* referred to him as the *Legendary Sahib of Manakin.* Of course Winny believes Sir Rupert to be the Marquess, and the Marquess to be the Viscount. He shall have the very devil of a time sorting through it all. Well, I'm off, but shall be back in a trice." Then pausing at the door, she added, "Don't fret: remember, I'll have my Forsythe pistol with me, and no harm shall come to you." With this remark ringing in her abigail's ears, Miss Tremantle passed into the hall and down the stairs to the party.

She paused at the entrance to the ballroom, and made a futile attempt to quiet her pounding heart, for as she neared the hub of activity, she was of a sudden beset by an attack of nerves. What if something *did* go wrong? she wondered. Oh, she should not have listened to Nora's pronouncements! Nothing could go wrong. It was a quarter to nine, which gave her plenty of time to mingle, then make the switch with Nora. It would be the simplest thing imaginable.

On this heartening note, Pandora made her way into the lavishly decorated ballroom, nodding at a myriad of unrecognizable masked faces, feeling much more at ease, and a little excited over the evening ahead. At midnight Aunt Beatrix would present Chloe, everyone would relinquish their masks, and the merriment would slowly wind down. Pandora smiled with satisfaction, knowing that by then Cardew would have had his comeuppance and Montescue his just reward. It was a thought as delicious as the brimming glass of iced champagne that the footman was at that very moment presenting to her. Lifting it off the silver tray, she then proceeded towards the French doors that let onto the trellised gardens. From this vantage point she could view the festivities, and, she hoped, locate Sir Rupert.

Pandora had always loved this room. Its vast size and crystal chandeliers lent a magical quality to it, and when the candles were lit, the prisms of the chandeliers threw light in hundreds of shapes on the cream-colored walls and sparkled dazzlingly in the mirrors. Masses of flowers had been placed about the room in brass urns, and garlands hung over arched windows and the French doors that led onto the garden. Several sideboards groaned under the weight of all the delicacies that Cook had been laboring over for the past few days, and crystal fountains sent eddies of champagne into silver-lined moats. There was also a bevy of liveried footmen circulating with yet more liquid refreshment. No one need go thirsty!

But where was Sir Rupert? And what sort of costume would he be wearing? Luckily, like the Marquess, he was of a height not easily dismissed. Pandora's gaze swept the colorful guests for some sign of one or the other, but so far she'd seen nothing remotely resembling either gentleman. She'd spotted three Louis the Fourteenths, two Marie Antoinettes, and a magnificently attired Charles the Second—all extravagantly wigged, patched, and clothed in richly embroidered satins. Winthrop, in clanging armor, was executing a rather stiff minuet with his beloved, who, in her pink shepherdess costume, with its nipped waist and puffed sleeves, was enchanting to behold. It was then she spotted her quarries. They were at opposite ends of the ballroom, one in cavalier costume, the other dressed totally in black, as if he might blend with the night; undoubtedly Sir Rupert!

Finishing off her champagne and depositing the empty glass on a footman's tray, she edged her way around the dance floor to the gentleman in black, and with a curtsy, purposefully informed him of her identity, and would have boldly asked for a dance, had he not wordlessly swept her onto the floor for a high-spirited country dance. But it was not Sir Rupert! Even had he not tipped back his black domino to reveal his flashing eyes, she would have recognized the feel of his arms as they encircled her, would have known instantly that peculiar magic he exuded that left her feeling slightly lightheaded, as if she'd had one too many champagnes.

"Your costume is quite fetching," said Cardew, drawing her closer. He added softly, "I presume it is part of your ploy to entice our cavalier friend." With a nod of his head, he indicated Sir Rupert, who seemed to be making a study of the couple as they danced past him.

"I don't know what you're talking about," Pandora replied sweetly, thankful that her scarf was securely draped around the ruby, "though I thank you for the compliment on my costume."

"For one who disapproves of gambling, you certainly chose a remarkable disguise: one that is sure to attract our friend's notice. But then, since I am sure that's what you intend, I shall simply claim every dance with you."

"Nothing of the sort!"

"My, how you do bristle, my little Queen of Diamonds."

"I am not your *little* queen of anything," she shot back.

He eyed her with considerable humor, and after a pause said, "No, I suppose *little* is not the proper adjective. Perhaps *towering.* I believe that was one of the words Sir Horatio used to describe his headstrong daughter."

"Oh, really?"

"*Impetuous* was another. Tsk, tsk. Such a disagreeable look about your mouth. I should have a care if I were you, or it might freeze in those lines, then whatever shall become of you?"

"Save your fancy words, and leave off discussing my mouth—"

"Though on occasion it *has* delighted me, as I'm sure you can recall."

"I have a lamentably poor memory, Lord Cardew; however, I do know this charming dance is concluding, and I really must circulate." Disengaging herself from him, she added, "And you wouldn't want to make a scene, would you?"

No sooner had she whirled around then the orchestra struck up a lively waltz, and Montescue in a swashbuckling fashion doffed his plumed hat, and crossing the floor, drew her into a rough and eager embrace. The gunmetal coldness in his eyes was visible despite the green velvet domino.

"What a clever costume," he remarked as they swung across the dance floor.

"I thought you might like it, especially knowing your penchant for games of chance."

"Ah, yes. I've always been one to take a calculated risk, if the prize warranted it, Miss Tremantle."

"You have seen through my disguise . . . and I through yours; thus I would have a word with you later. Perhaps we can strike up a bargain." She smiled to herself, pleased with the sudden tension in his body.

"What, might I ask, are you up to?"

"Just what I said: a bargain. For you see, *Sir Rupert,* I know who you are, but am capable of forgetting, if you catch my meaning."

"Why, I believe you intend a little blackmail," he rejoined, not missing a beat of the music.

"Did I say that? Let us call it remuneration for what you did to my father . . . and to my brother . . . *and* to me. Tsk, tsk. Don't look so surprised." She reprimanded him playfully with her fan. "You were once called the Duke of Diamonds, and undoubtedly have a trove of gems and absolutely pots of money. And you surely know that the high card takes the trick, and being Queen of Diamonds, I graciously accept my winnings."

"Ah, but the ace has not been played, and you've not a shred of proof that I am this *Sir Rupert.*"

"Oh, I have good reason to think you are: why else would

you drug my brother, then come round with tales of spoilt brandy?"

"What a feverish brain you have to concoct such stories." He pulled her close as the final strains of the waltz rang out. "Pity no one will believe you." As Montescue removed his domino Pandora could see the full malevolence of her opponent. Their repartee was at an end, and though she felt a sudden prickle of fear, dauntlessly she pulled back the scarf, revealing the ruby.

"*That* was a mistake you shall regret, my dear," he promised menacingly.

"And it is all the proof I need: shall we say, my trump? Meet me in the rose garden in twenty minutes!" With that parting shot, she hastened from the ballroom, leaving a displeased, but not undone, Sir Rupert in her wake.

Not wishing to seem overanxious, Pandora purposely delayed the reappearance, fussing over the drape of silk scarf which concealed Nora's curls.

"Now all you have to do is keep Sir Rupert at a distance; well, of course, once you've lured him into the garden you needn't worry, for the light is quite dim, and I daresay his eyes will be on the ruby."

"But what if someone else should approach me?" Nora asked as she ran a nervous hand over the jewel at her throat.

"You act as if you don't see them—go in the opposite direction; but whatever you do, make sure you catch Sir Rupert's eye. I doubt it will be hard to do," she said, reassuring her abigail, "for I left him quite eager for our next encounter." Pandora added this quite breezily, and patting her voluminous pocket, she reminded Nora that she carried the pistol, and would not let them out of sight.

"Just mingle, and when you've gotten Sir Rupert's attention, head straight for the garden," Pandora instructed as she knotted one of Nora's kerchiefs about her own head. She was dressed in serviceable cambric, which she hoped would render her all but invisible.

"I hope Sir Rupert doesn't try to dance with me, for I don't know how."

"I wouldn't worry about that," Pandora assured her on

a light note. "Sir Rupert does not like my dancing style!" On this note, Miss Tremantle and her abigail made their way downstairs.

"There he is!" Pandora whispered as she directed Nora into the ballroom from the shadowed alcove that let onto the garden. "After he has spied you, come out and down the garden path. I'll be just behind the trellised roses. Now go!" She gave an encouraging pat to Nora's backside, then quickly headed toward the trellis, her heart pounding ridiculously, but one hand firmly gripped about the pistol. The cool night air that carried the caressing scent of roses was lost on Pandora, as was the beauty of the moonlight-dappled path. Finally she heard the rustle of approaching skirts.

"Miss . . . Miss Pandora?" Nora's voice wobbled from the other side of the trellis.

"Shh! Wait right where you are," Pandora whispered. "Stand near the sundial, and remember, I'm right here!" As the moonlight slipped behind the clouds, Pandora realized it would be almost impossible to see clearly. She peered up the graveled path, which was no more than a funnel of darkness, but then out of that black labyrinth came the fast click of boot heels—closer and closer. Pandora slipped between the small opening in the trellis and slowly withdrew her pistol. She could barely see Nora's outline. The crunch of heels grew louder, and suddenly a figure was upon Nora, whose muffled cry was effectively silenced.

"Give it to me, you little fool!"

"Stand back, and put your hands up, Sir Rupert Montescue!"

Pandora stepped into a sudden shaft of moonlight, and leveling her pistol at the man who had attacked Nora, repeated herself.

"Good God! So *that* was your crackbrained plan!" Lord Cardew stepped forward, ruby dangling from one hand, with the most irritating smile on his lips Pandora had ever seen.

"You! You've ruined everything!" she sputtered.

"Not everything—I'm only shifting the bait. And you can put your weapon away, Miss Tremantle, and perhaps even change back into that very fetching costume. Meanwhile, I—"

"I'm not putting this pistol down until you give me that ruby!"

"Surely you wouldn't shoot me in the rose garden, would you?"

"Oh, miss, do as his lordship says," Nora gestured towards the pistol.

"You should listen to your abigail, for firearms seem to set you on a course of disaster."

"The disaster is in your court, for this time *I* have the upper hand. Now give me my ruby."

"Your ruby? I seem to recall having this conversation before. Only that time I foolishly let you have the jewel back. My, my. Such a fuss over a stone."

"If you don't give it to me . . . I'll . . ."

"Oh, miss, you mustn't shoot him *again!*"

"She won't. Besides, it's my turn to play with the jewel." He pressed another of his maddening smiles on Pandora, then turning smartly on his heels, added, "I purposely let you play your scene with Rupert on the dance floor, but enough is enough. What I'm doing now is for your own good."

"Stop!"

"You'll have to shoot me, my dear," he tossed over his shoulder.

Picking up her skirts, Pandora hurried after him, Nora fast on her heels. "But what are you going to do?" Pandora asked Cardew.

"Dangle the thing in front of Manakin's nose, then leave."

"Are you mad?"

"Perhaps, for it will be me he's after, and not you. Also, with the ruby in my keeping, I can rest assured you won't be scheming any other plots."

Reaching his side, Pandora grabbed his sleeve, "I should like to see you in Hades for this night's work. I . . . I actually think you like humiliating me."

"*Humiliating* you? Ha! You little ninny. Hardly that." He glanced down at the hand on his sleeve, "It's just that for some idiotic reason I've decided to protect you from yourself. And I must say, I'm glad you've pocketed that pistol."

Abruptly Pandora released the Marquess's coatsleeve, and addressing Nora, said, "Thanks to the Marquess's bungling, we might as well switch costumes again, for Aunt Bea is bound to wonder what happened." Then lifting her skirts, she brushed past Cardew, only to pause and add, "You were right, of course; it would have been terribly messy shooting you in the rose garden."

"Ha! To hear you, you'd think *I* was the murderer instead of the Marquess."

Pandora paused a moment, then carefully added, "No, not the murderer, but you certainly are the Marquess of Manakin."

"You are full of surprises, aren't you?" He regarded her with a hooded look, then quietly asked, "Just when did you figure out who I really was?"

"Some days ago. It neither raises nor lowers you in my esteem. Though I have to admit your adoration of Lady Lorena and your dogged pursuit of Sir Rupert is . . . admirable." An odd sense of loss suddenly pervaded Miss Tremantle, as she slowly added, "Your betrothed must have been amazing to have inspired such devotion on your part."

"Lady Lorena? *Amazing?*" He shook his head as if beset. "No, Miss Tremantle, Lorena was hardly that. However, I would not have wished her murdered. Some might say it was her own doing; for you see, she was involved in a liaison with Sir Rupert even while planning nuptials with me." He shrugged his shoulders wearily. "So you see, my dear, I lack the one sterling quality you had mistakenly attributed to me. And now if you ladies will excuse me, I'm off to bait our villain."

"But . . . but . . . then why are you after Sir Rupert?" She was clutching his coatsleeve again, feeling an unaccountable relief surge over her.

"Let's just say I have some principles, despite my odious, wretched, unruly behavior. And," he added, gently disengaging himself from Miss Tremantle, "I do not appreciate the likes of Sir Rupert using my name." With an abbreviated leg, he turned and continued up the path.

Pandora stood some moments considering his words, then grasping Nora's hand, said, "Come!"

"But miss, your costume!"

"We're just going to peek in the ballroom: no one will see

us. Besides, I've got to see what happens!" Drawing Nora closer to her, they crept towards the French doors, then quickly flattened against the cool stone walls.

"There!" Pandora whispered, leaning forward. "Look at the brass that man displays!"

"It's a ruby, miss," Nora whispered back, still pressed against the wall.

"Yes, and he's practically twirling it from his watch fob, though Aunt Bea is too taken in conversation with him to even notice!"

"We'd better go now, Miss Pandora."

"In a minute." Releasing her abigail's hand, she inched forward only to jump back. "Sir Rupert's joined them, and there's no way *he* can miss that ruby!"

"Yes, yes. Now, let's go!" Nora implored, tugging on her mistress's hand. "You must change if you are to be down by midnight."

After a pause, Pandora said, "I suppose you're right; besides, I've seen enough." Enough, she mused, to know that this Viscount, this man she wanted so much to loathe but couldn't, was indeed the legendary Marquess from India. That he had made a hasty departure before she had returned to the ball was disappointing, but the fact that Montescue gave her wide berth only pointed to Cardew's unerring judgment. Was the man *never* wrong? Pandora fumed a bit at this possibility, but by the time the ball was over, and she was once again in her bedchamber, she had to admit that his concern for her welfare more than pleased her.

Pandora had sent her abigail to bed, insisting she could undress herself; besides, she wished to write in her journal before retiring.

The Abbey was quiet, and only the scratch of her pen and occasional owl hoot could be heard. Laying her plume to one side, she listened for the owl, but instead heard a soft crunch on the gravel carriageway. *Footsteps?* she wondered. *At this hour?* Extinguishing her candle, she crossed to the window, and carefully pushing back the drapery, looked below just in time to see a man hurrying across the path towards an awaiting carriage. It looked like he had a large sack slung over his shoulder, one which he unceremoniously dumped on the floor of the vehicle. At that moment a shaft of moonlight fell across the man's face: it was Sir Rupert!

Snatching up her reticule, Pandora stealthily made her way down the back stairs; and though impetuous by nature, she took a moment to catch her breath and consider her next move. Why was Sir Rupert about at this hour of night? And what was he carrying? Determined to find out, she crept past the darkened kitchen to the side entrance. A cool breeze from the opened door sent prickles up her spine, but none so chilling as the smooth dark voice that came from behind.

"Miss Tremantle?"

As Pandora spun about, Rupert clapped a hand across her mouth, then quickly dragged her out the door to the awaiting vehicle. Yanking open its door, he threw her inside, and was upon her in the instant, strapping a foul-tasting gag on her mouth, then wrenching her over, he commenced to bind her hands and feet. At length he settled back on the seat opposite her, his breath coming hard and heavy.

"You seem addicted to these nocturnal perambulations, my dear. Pity. For I warned you you'd regret your foolish actions, and since I am a gentleman of my word, suffice it to say this is not going to be a first-class ride for either you or that interfering brat." Indolently he dusted off his jacket, then pausing before stepping down from the carriage, he added, "And this is strictly a one-way trip."

Chapter Fourteen

The early hours of the following morning probably precipitated more chaos than Chatford Abbey had known since the Dissolution of the Monasteries: for it would appear that before the sun was decently up, everyone in the household had either galloped off for parts unknown, or was in the throes of threatened swoons.

This cacophony commenced when Winthrop, up for a dawn ride, came upon the following note left by Sir Rupert to account for his and Jemnaz's sudden disappearance:

Mr. Tremantle:

Since you are the man of the house, I felt you were the one to inform that as I was about to retire I heard some noise in the stables, and upon investigation, I saw Jemnaz galloping off. Having seen him nosing about the silver earlier this week, I checked this out also, and discovered the Apostle Spoons had been taken—undoubtedly by the boy. Thus I am pursuing him to London, where he undoubtedly plans to sell the silver.

Manakin

Not believing the tale, Winthrop set off for London after the man he still believed to be the Marquess of Manakin. But it was Nora who, arising quite early and discovering her mistress missing, awakened Chloe and set everything in motion. Nora managed to babble out just enough to alarm Miss

Deeds thoroughly. And if *this* wasn't enough, the note which Winthrop had slipped beneath her door capped everything:

Dearest Chloe:

As you will see from the enclosed missive from Manakin I have but one choice: to catch up with him and set the confusion to rights. I am assured of Jemnaz's innocence.

Yrs truly,
Winny

Chloe, looking up from the note to Nora, declared, "We must hasten to the Orange Crown and seek the Viscount's advice. Surely he will know what to do!"

It was this very carriage ride, however, that set the alarms to clanging; for Mrs. Pattybone, Chloe's fusty old abigail, was about her morning toilette when she happened to glance out the window and see the carriage as it disappeared around the bend in the north road. Immediately she checked on her charge, and finding her gone, and fearing the worst—for Chloe and Winthrop often jested of Gretna Green—she searched out Miss Pandora. Upon discovering this latter lady not only gone but her bed not slept in, Pattybone sought out Nora, Mr. Winthrop, and even the Marquess of Manakin—all to no avail, for every chamber was vacant. Pattybone's feverish brain scrambled the evidence: *Of course,* she thought, *a double elopement! Miss Pandora and the Marquess, and Miss Chloe and Mr. Winthrop; all aided and abetted by the feckless Nora!* Oh, merciful heavens, how could she contain this dire news? For Mrs. Deeds would raise the very roof if she knew her precious darling had run off with Mr. Winthrop! What to do? What to do? Certainly not ring the alarm bell. Not just yet. Thus in deep thought, the plump little abigail commenced to pace the carpet in Miss Deeds's chamber, staring from time to time out the window, where early morning sunlight languidly dappled the lace curtains.

Just as she had determined that she could delay no longer, there was a sound of hoofbeats clattering down the north road. As the carriage swung into view, Pattybone could clearly see Miss Chloe in her russet-colored riding habit with a man she assumed to be Mr. Winthrop. Clambering forward, and practically toppling from the window, the old abigail shrieked out a greeting. This had the unfortunate effect of awakening Mrs. Deeds, virtually catapulting the night-capped lady from her curtained bed and into the hall.

"Good heavens! Whatever is happening?" Mrs. Deeds hollered, as if beset by villains. This in turn summoned Miss Beatrix, in a similar state of dishabille, who upon seeing her hysterical sister, grabbed her by the shoulders and gave her a good shake. The subsequent appearance of Mrs. Pattybone only added to the din and confusion which greeted Chloe, Nora, and the Viscount as they rushed onto the scene.

"Mama! Aunt Beatrix! Pattybone!" Chloe cried out in a voice loud enough to be heard over the ruckus. "What has happened that you should rent the air like the Three Furies?"

"Oh!" her mother ejaculated, realizing that she was scarcely attired to receive the Viscount. A look of pure horror struck her sleep-creased face, suggesting that she was about to suffer something terminal.

"The Viscount!" exclaimed Beatrix, equally undone, clapping her chubby pink hands to her round cheeks. Then regaining some semblance of sanity, she said in as normal a voice as she could muster under the trying circumstances, "Lord Cardew! I trust there is some pressing cause for your early morning call?"

Before the Viscount could respond to the chaos of this scene, Mrs. Pattybone piped up with, "Then you *didn't* elope, did you, Miss Chloe?"

"Elope?" Statira's voice wobbled, as she looked frantically from her daughter to the Viscount.

"Yes, elope," the abigail repeated. "Mr. Winthrop is gone, and I saw Miss Chloe steal away at dawn, and—"

"Oh, I am undone! Give me your hand, Beatrix!"

"Nonsense. Can't you see that Chloe's done no such thing? Compose yourself, Statira."

"Let me explain," Chloe pleaded.

"We are not properly clothed for explanations!" Beatrix somewhat heatedly pointed out. "Whatever it is, it can wait until breakfast. You have *not* eloped, and that is all that counts!"

Statira, glancing at her own white nightdress, let out a gasp, and fled to her chamber.

"I think we should let Miss McClellan attend to herself," the Viscount said diplomatically. "And I had best send Chandro after Mr. Tremantle."

"Mr. Tremantle?" Beatrix repeated, looking nonplussed. "Winny hasn't ridden somewhere he oughtn't again, has he?"

"Aunt Bea, it's a long story," Chloe said, patting her hand.

"Did you have a finger in this pie?" her aunt asked, looking suddenly suspicious.

"No, of course not! However, things are in the very devil of a mess. The Viscount is here to straighten everything out."

"Unfortunately, there's no time for the telling," Lord Cardew said. "Though I do wish to assure you that Miss Tremantle and Miss Deeds shall return unharmed."

"Return unharmed? But Chloe is *already* here," Beatrix said, clasping and unclasping her hands. "Oh, heavens, what does all this talk mean?"

"Perhaps it is Miss Pandora and the Marquess who have gone to Gretna Green, then," the old abigail's voice rattled out like bones in a crypt.

"Gretna Green?" Beatrix repeated the name as if it were a curse. "Nora, what does this mean? Pattybone, Pattybone, did you say *Gretna Green?*"

"She is mistaken, ma'am," Lord Cardew said briskly. "And upon our return, all will be set to rights."

"Most definitely," Chloe assured her aunt, "Lord Cardew didn't want you to worry over our departure."

"Oh, this smacks of scandal broth!" Beatrix rejoined. "And, I daresay, it might well send Statira into permanent vapors. For it is not the thing at all for Chloe to go about unchaperoned."

"Nora will be with me, and besides, we must go after Pandora. Lord Cardew has figured it all out."

"Miss McClellan, I would beg of you a quill and some paper. There truly is little time to lose." The brilliance of the Viscount's smile sufficed to win Beatrix over, and thus without explaining the whys or wherefores of the entire imbroglio, which he felt certain included a double abduction of Miss Tremantle and Jemnaz, he managed to sweep aside all objections to his proposed plan. Cardew did, however, stress the importance of retrieving Miss Tremantle, and to that end, and most specifically for her reputation, he would require that Miss Deeds and Nora follow by carriage. He skirted the abduction issue, and let Miss McClellan believe that Winthrop and possibly the "Marquess" were in pursuit of Jemnaz—who naturally had been wrongly accused of thievery. The precise reason for her niece's headstrong flight was glossed over, as Cardew quickly penned his note to Winthrop.

Dear Mr. Tremantle:

Jemnaz is not in London! The Marquess has disappeared, and I am in pursuit of your sister—on the road towards Gretna Green.

Yrs,
Justin Cardew

Chandro, who had been obediently waiting in the hallway, quickly entered when his name was called. Snatching up the note, and giving the Viscount a wink, he chirped out in English "And now you take Miss Tre-mantel off the shelf and marry her!"

It was at this untimely moment that Statira, fully clothed and revived, entered the room, only to shrink against the wall as the black heathen dashed by her. Beatrix, on the other hand, would have fallen into transports, had the Viscount not discouraged it by his rapid but formal leave-taking, which included making a splendid leg and ushering Miss Deeds and Nora out the door.

Although Lord Cardew thought he had accounted for everything, his hastily penned note to Winthrop, while not in gross error, put the gentleman in a state of considerable agitation. Upon receiving the missive, Mr. Tremantle read it twice, as if to decipher some special code, then pointing to the line, *"I am in pursuit of your sister—on the road towards Gretna Green,"* he demanded Chandro explain Lord Cardew's intentions. The Indian boy, wishing to please the troubled gentleman, repeated his favorite refrain, "The Viscount takes our Miss Tre-mantel off the shelf and marries her!" He then presented the distraught Mr. Tremantle a ludicrous grin.

"What!" he practically exploded. For Lord Cardew to practically *announce* that he was absconding with his sister to Gretna Green was not to be countenanced. Never! It was one thing for his Chloe to trill about such an adventure, and for him to cajole her in this harmless fantasy. But by God! he would call Cardew to accounts before he would allow his only sister to ruin herself in such a way.

"Gretna Green? They are getting married at Gretna Green?" he repeated the question to make sure.

"Yes, sahib." The boy nodded his head enthusiastically. "He brings her off the shelf and marries her!"

Thus it was that Winthrop Tremantle, in a fair fury, and goaded on by the vision of his sister being spirited off the shelf and into Gretna Green, took to the north road at a fast clip.

The gentleman who had taught Chandro that quaint turn of phrase, *on the shelf,* was even at this moment enjoying his first proper English breakfast since arriving from Bombay: grilled kidneys over toast and a pint of dark ale. As usual Sir Horatio had gone out of his way to stop over at his favorite inn, the Swansfoote, a place noted for its exceptional cuisine and clientele. It was here that he intended on fortifying himself before facing his sister-in-law, Beatrix McClellan. Having arrived the night before, he had sent word on that he would indeed make his niece Chloe's ball: that Sir Horatio had miscalculated the date was not surprising, especially considering the arduous journey he had undertaken.

Difficult and long though the trip had been, Sir Horatio was otherwise in exceptional fettle. He was immediately recognized by the innkeeper and several of the servants, and was ushered into the front chamber, as befitted him. There was never any question of Sir Horatio's station. He carried his six feet with an authority that brooked no nonsense, and the full head of silver hair framing a high forehead further distinguished him. His wanderings in India had kept him lean and fit, though his attire was slightly dated. Still, one had to admit he looked prepossessing in his close-fitting, single-breasted coat of superfine and his breeches of nankeen cloth which met his scuffed and well-worn jockey boots.

Had Sir Horatio chosen a different spot to partake of grilled kidneys, his morning would undoubtedly have turned out to be rather ordinary. Such was not the case. But at least the gentleman was able to consume his breakfast in peace before the drama commenced.

Some distance down the road, and quite unbeknownst to him, his daughter, Pandora, bruised and aching all over from the rough-and-tumble journey, had finally succeeded in freeing her hands from the coarse rope that had bound them. Spitting out the last remnants of her filthy gag, she set to restoring the frightened child. The ride had been hard on Jemnaz, and time and again she'd heard him whimper in the darkened carriage as it lurched and pitched along the north road. The sound tore at her heart, leaving her feeling—perhaps for the first time in her life—completely helpless. But although she had made a muddle of things, she was determined to do everything in her power to free them both—for she still had the pistol!

Quickly she removed his gag, untied his hands and feet, then drew him into an embrace. For a moment he succumbed to her ministrations, but then pulling himself away declared that now that she had freed him, he would save her life, run the villain through, and send him to perdition.

Despite their perilous situation, Pandora found herself laughing. "And what will you use for a sword, my valiant knight?"

"I would use the power of Kali!" Jemnaz managed a victorious grin. "If I knew how," he admitted with a shrug of his brave little shoulders.

"Oh, we'll think of something," Pandora said on a decidedly bright note. "But tell me, why did Sir Rupert kidnap you?"

Jemnaz's dark eyes grew wide, "So he was *not* the Marquess after all! Humph, I thought not. For you know he did find the Snow Leopard Jewels: the entire box of them!"

"The Snow Leopard Jewels . . . in a box?" The carriage lurched suddenly, and it was all Pandora could do to keep from crashing into the door.

"That man does not know how to manage his horses!" Jemnaz muttered as he scrambled forward to secure his position on the seat. "But, yes, Miss Sahib, for these jewels were on the covers of many books. Very clever way to disguise them. Old Indian proverb says that man is blind, seeing only what he expects to see: but only the wise man looks beyond the surface to see what is *really* there."

"Heaven help us if that makes Sir Rupert wise," Pandora quipped.

"Oh, no! He was expecting to find jewels; but that is just the cover of those holy books. He is blinded to their true meaning."

Pandora gently patted the boy's head, "My father was right about you, you *are* one of India's true jewels. For it is you who are wise."

"In English I think you call this a *compliment.* But in my country we do not have this custom so much." Bracing himself as the carriage careened around a curve, he added, "In India it is expected to develop wisdom, and always even the poorest looks for the unseen hand of God. Such is our way, Miss Sahib." He bowed his head, then looking at Miss Tremantle with a mischievous grin, added, "No more compliments: we must think on how to unsmart Sir Rupert that he might get his Karma quickly."

Pandora nodded in agreement, and rubbing her chafed wrists, said, "Yes, let's hasten our villain's Karma. So . . . since he only sees what he's expecting, then when he comes for us he'll be looking for two bound and gagged figures, right?"

"Right!" Jemnaz answered gleefully. "But we will surprise him, and . . . and . . ."

"And if you had Kali's powers or a nice fine sword, you'd run him through."

"This is so."

"Do you think he'll see this pistol if I point it at him?" Pandora smiled broadly as she withdrew the weapon from her reticule.

"Wonderful!" Jemnaz cried, clapping his dark hands together. "This time you pop the *bad* man and send him to Kali."

"I rather imagined trussing him up and presenting him to Lord Cardew instead."

"Humph. Oh, well, I suppose either way his Karma will travel to him." Bracing himself as the carriage swerved into a sharp turn, the boy glanced out the window, and quickly added, "And I think the time is now, Miss Sahib! See? We are slowing down before an inn."

"Splendid: Winny's pistol is loaded, cocked—and I promise not to hit you!"

"I still say, pop the bad man!" With an impish grin, Jemnaz tucked himself into the corner as the vehicle came to a shuddering halt. This was followed by Sir Rupert's string of commands; namely that the horses were to be walked, groomed, then fed and watered. On no account was his private carriage to be touched. He would have a light repast in private quarters, and would be departing later that afternoon.

Pandora pressed herself against the velvet seatback, and leveling the pistol straight ahead, waited to see which door would be opened. Surely he'd check on them, if for nothing but curiosity. In this she was right. However, since he was expecting his victims bound and gagged, he stepped quickly into the interior. He faltered visibly upon finding a gun pointed at his head, and Pandora had the pleasure of seeing him blanch ever so slightly.

"Jemnaz says you handle your horses poorly." With a wave of the pistol, Pandora indicated Sir Rupert was to be seated. "Though I am not terribly surprised, since all forms of life seem inconsequential to you. All except your own." She smiled graciously. "But our little Indian friend says that your Karma has caught up with you, and I'm sure your years in India have taught you something about this belief."

"Pop him off to Kali!"

"Shut up, you little heathen!" Sir Rupert's eyes flashed. "I should have finished you both off long ago."

"Oh?" Pandora raised the gun a trifle higher. "Without the Snow Leopard Jewels? All that work for nothing? Oh, no, Sir Rupert, I think you should at least have time to perhaps glance through one of the volumes." Turning to Jemnaz, she said, "Have the innkeep open up his best chamber: order enough tea and scones for us all. Tell him the *Marquess of Manakin* is in a black mood, and would like the room as soon as possible."

"Yes, Missy Sahib!" The boy scrambled out the door, babbling joyously in Hindi.

"What sort of game are you about?" Sir Rupert asked, as he edged towards the door.

"I wouldn't try that, if I were you. I *am* a crack shot, despite what you think, and would not hesitate shooting you." With a wave of the pistol, she added, "And this is not a game, though you may view it that way, if you wish. Quite simply I shall give you measure for measure. A messenger shall be sent to fetch Lord Cardew, who as you know is the real Marquess, and while we await his arrival, Jemnaz and I shall enjoy tea, and you shall be bound, gagged, and perhaps hit upon the head for good measure.

"It could be days before your knight arrives."

"More's the pity," Pandora yawned.

"People will wonder. There will be talk!"

"My dear Sir Rupert, as for people wondering and talking, they have been doing that since the beginning of time, and most especially about the Tremantles!" Without taking her eyes off her quarry, she added in a chipper voice, "Ah, here comes Jemnaz!" Her eyes narrowed, and in an earnest voice, she said, "The gun, although hidden in my reticule, shall be aimed at your very black heart, so I suggest you put on your most charming hat and lead me up to tea, for it has been such a trying journey, and I am fairly famished." Gesturing with the weapon, she added, "After you, Sir Rupert."

Sending Pandora a murderous look, he stepped from the carriage, but as he passed the ostler, he tossed several coins into his outstretched hand, then proceeded up the stone path that led to the Swansfoote Inn.

Miss Tremantle, with one hand on the hidden pistol and the other firmly clasping Jemnaz's hand, followed directly behind Sir Rupert; she had time, however, to note that the establishment, with its thatched roof and mullioned windows, had been maintained quite nicely. Feeling Jemnaz squeeze her hand, and catching the victorious look in his dark eyes, Pandora couldn't help but wonder that perhaps this entire affair had gone too smoothly. For although Sir Rupert was initially furious, he was now playing his part a bit too convincingly. She chided herself for such thoughts, and managing to hold her impatience in check, waited while the innkeeper's daughter located the keys to the chamber. The girl, meek and mousy haired, silently led them up the broad oak staircase. A pungent woodsmoke filled the air, and as they entered the room, Pandora's quick glance took in a broad hearth, hunting horns, and the head of a stag. Tea and scones, they were quietly informed, would be along shortly. Pandora then requested a basin of warm water, wash rags, and several towels to be sent up immediately. And although the serving girl thought it strange that this lady of quality should be traipsing about in a torn and filthy costume, accompanied by a small black boy, she refrained from letting it be known. She did, however, say that her brother would be carrying up the water.

Thus, when a sharp rapping on the door was heard, followed by an unintelligible deep grumble, Jemnaz jumped up to answer it, but was knocked aside as the oak door swung abruptly open, revealing Tribbs! In the instant he had collared the boy, and had his knife positioned for the kill.

"No!" Pandora screamed, starting forward. But her movement was checked by Rupert, who seized the opportunity and dashed the pistol from her hand, sending it skittering across the floor. She lunged for it, but he grabbed her about the waist. Then pinning her across the broad table, he let out a deep, satisfied laugh.

"Who shall die first? You, or the brat?" He lowered his face to hers until she could smell his fetid breath. She saw his iron gray eyes, devoid of all emotion but greed, and felt his thick, rough hands as they tightened about her neck. "The boy, I think; for that leaves you for other things." Suddenly cupping her chin, he leaned closer, and as his lips met hers, she bit him, hard and fast. In his astonished recoil, Pandora wrenched from his grasp. He lunged again, grabbing her foot. She kicked, then scrambled forward. Her outstretched hand closed about the pistol too late, for Tribbs, having tossed Jemnaz aside, laid his boot heel upon that very hand. Pandora screamed as the gun went off and Tribbs in a great howl, fell back, clutching his wounded foot. Immediately Pandora retrieved the pistol, and with a bruised and shaking hand, leveled it once again at her adversary.

"I'll shoot!" she cried, stumbling to her feet, clutching the gun with both hands.

"And she would, were the chamber loaded," Lord Cardew announced, advancing into the room, "though I had hoped to settle with you myself." He sent Pandora a cordial smile, then added, "And I should also like very much to settle up with you too when this is all over." Raising a questioning eyebrow in Tribbs's direction, he asked, "Wasn't your aim a bit off with that one?"

"Well! I'll have you know I was not aiming for him," Pandora replied.

"Better and better. You amaze me."

"She's an interfering little sl—"

"Kill him yourself!" Pandora said, cutting Sir Rupert off; then lowering her pistol, said in a softer voice, "I believe Jemnaz would say you have *Karma* with him." With this, the boy hurried to her side, then together they backed against the far wall.

Montescue moved forward. "Say your prayers, dead man!"

"And you, yours."

"I've no need," Sir Rupert said. Producing a dagger, he edged cautiously towards Cardew, who countered this move with one of his own. Like solitary chess pieces they began to challenge each other, back and forth, their eyes locked in combat, never wavering. Then of a sudden, Sir Rupert jumped Cardew, and knocking him to the ground, pressed his glistening dagger against his throat, which would no doubt have drawn blood had Cardew not heaved the villain off. Then magically producing a blade from his walking stick, Cardew sent Sir Rupert's dagger spinning from his grasp and into the hall. As he scrambled for it, Cardew lunged after him, clipped him on the jaw, and sent him sprawling over the edge of the landing. Stepping back a pace, his shoulders hunched but his breathing still even and steady, Cardew said, "Get up!" His hands were knotted, one about the dagger's handle, the other free for battle. They were at the head of the stairs, and were it not for a cluster of guests, who had gathered to investigate the commotion, his lordship might have maintained his advantage. But in that split second that Cardew's concern wavered from his prey to the crowd, Rupert shot to his feet, and barreling into Cardew, sent them both crashing through the banister and onto the ground floor. The startled guests gave them a wide berth and pressed against the walls, in rapt fascination at this unexpected diversion.

The men rose, their coats and fine neckcloths ripped beyond repair. They stood amidst the dust and broken crockery: their breathing was labored, and deadly intent stamped them both. Sir Rupert suddenly lunged, but Cardew countered this attack and began to dance the impostor around a table and into a corner. Sir Rupert, in a last, desperate move, overturned the table, sending biscuits and ale crashing after it, but the Viscount nimbly cleared this in a single leap and toppled his opponent, holding his blade over the man's heart.

There was but a moment of deadly silence, wherein the urge to finish off Sir Rupert was almost overwhelming. Slowly, however, the Viscount stepped back, and instructed the innkeeper to have the man and his wounded accomplice put in restraints and to send word to the Bow Street Runners that the infamous Duke of Diamonds had finally been apprehended.

As the servants hustled the villain at gunpoint into a back room, the innkeeper declared that he was sure all of London would hail the Viscount as hero—but what of his busted banister?

Distractedly clapping a goodly sum into the proprietor's hands, his lordship turned his attention to Pandora, and was immensely gratified at the way she ran down the stairs and after the briefest of pauses, hurled herself into his arms, quite mindless of the gaping crowd. She mumbled something tearful into his shoulder, and would likely have continued these watery proceedings were it not for the arrival of her brother, whose voice—high pitched and slightly unstable—drew an instant audience, at the ready for further entertainment.

"Unhand my sister, you Lothario, you!" He strode forward amidst the crowd's renewed buzzing, and peeling off a single glove, made to slap the Viscount in the face, when a voice unexpectedly made the young man freeze in the very act.

"See here, Winny! What the devil are you doing?"

Winthrop whirled about, his demeanor noticeably altered: the hauteur of the Noble Hero melted into that of a Prankish Bad Boy. "Papa!" he uttered after a speechless moment, "whatever are you doing here?"

"I asked first!" the older gentleman countered, entering the throng from the doorway of the downstairs parlor. Successfully he wrenched the glove from his son, who backed up and began to grapple for words.

"Well?" Sir Horatio prodded, slapping the glove against his leg as if it were a switch.

"G-G-Gretna Green!" was all he succeeded in saying.

At this disclosure, chaos reigned supreme: Pandora sustained the shock of seeing her beloved father, and ignoring Winthrop's gibberish about Gretna Green, had just thrown herself into Sir Horatio's arms, when Chloe and Nora, breathless from their breakneck carriage ride, entered the hostelry. Immediately everyone's attention swung to them.

"Winny!" Chloe cried, entering the drama, though not perceiving her uncle. "Why are you going on about Gretna Green?" she asked. She might have gotten an answer, had not Chandro chosen that moment to make *his* appearance! Upon seeing Sir Horatio, his Sahib Savior, he burst into a torrent of Hindi, touched the floor several times, was then joined by Jemnaz, and together they fell upon the gentleman with squeals of joy.

Chloe, thus drawn from her interrogation, repeated the much-favored question, "Uncle Horry! What are *you* doing here?" As if on cue, everyone gathered about the gentleman and commenced to babble.

Sir Horatio's booming voice silenced the throng. "Believe it or not, I thought to have a quiet day prior to enjoying the undoubted pleasures of my family, rag-tag group that you are!" He paused to take particular note of Pandora's torn ball gown before slowly adding, "Beatrix will not be joining us, I take it."

"Oh, no, Papa," Pandora replied on a laugh. "We have enough confusion without that!"

"Aha!" Sir Horatio exclaimed on a relieved note, then turning toward the Viscount, added, "I say, you are the only one who hasn't fallen over me as if I had returned from Hades!"

"Sir Horatio, I am attempting to contain myself, but as always, I am your servant!" He inclined his head in a small bow.

"Nonsense!" Sir Horatio glanced at his gold watch and said, "Innkeep! I say, we'll have luncheon in my chamber: turtle broth, mutton with mint sprigs, pickled salmon, some of that aspic you served last night—oh, and plenty of vegetables for my lads here." He put an affectionate arm around the Indian boys. "They don't hold with eating animals. And who knows, maybe they're right." Then with an expansive gesture, he added, "We'll repair to my private parlor where we shall sup like royalty, and perhaps straighten out all this mess about Gretna Green! I say, Winny, surely Beatrix is not apprised of all this?"

"Oh, Uncle Horry!" Chloe burst out, linking arms with him as they ascended to the upper floor. "Everything is more scrambled than eggs; though I cannot imagine why Winny was talking about Gretna Green!"

"I thought . . . that is . . ." Winthrop, fast on their heels, was thoroughly fuddled at the goings-on.

"There is a logical explanation for everything," the Viscount said in a smooth and amiable voice as the little group filed into Sir Horatio's chamber—much to the disappointment of the interested patrons.

"Then you weren't trying to steal my sister off to—"

"No, I was not," Cardew interrupted with some amusement. "You understandably mistook my hastily written note; I merely meant I was traveling on the road *toward* Gretna Green in order to . . ." With a sigh, he added, "But it is a long story, and I suggest, if Sir Horatio agrees, that we all have a spot of wine first; for the balance of this tale will thus be more easily digested."

"Splendid suggestion!" the older gentleman said, as he motioned for one of the servants to fill everyone's glass to the brim. Once accomplished, he insisted on toasting Viscount Cardew, whom he rightly suspected had had a hand in setting things straight. The wine was acclaimed to be a superb vintage, and several glasses were consumed before luncheon was spread before them.

"Well," Sir Horatio said at length, as the turtle broth made its appearance, "let us have the report from the Marquess of Manakin."

"Marquess of Manakin?" Winthrop repeated. "D'you mean to say that Viscount Cardew is the Marquess of Manakin? But then who is . . . who is the Marquess of Manakin at Chatford? An impostor?"

"Impostor?" Horatio echoed, eyebrows traveling up his broad brow. Then regarding the Viscount said, "Someone trying to pass himself off as you? Ha! That explains the broken banister!" He gave Cardew, who was seated next to him, a hearty slap. "So that's why your frock coat is mussed. Had a bit of a mill, eh? And I thought p'raps you were starting a fashion!" He dipped his spoon into the soup, as if they might have been discussing the weather.

"Bit of a mill?" Pandora said in astonishment. "Why, Sir Rupert not only kidnapped Jemnaz and me, but he tried to kill Lord Cardew!"

"Kidnapped?" Horatio's spoon dropped with a clatter. "Kidnapped, my pet? What is all this?"

In the swiftest and simplest manner, Cardew summed up the misadventure to a stunned and silent audience. But when he mentioned Sir Rupert for the second time, Horatio banged the table with his fist.

"Sir Rupert? Rupert Montescue? The chap I met in India? Do you mean *he* did all that?"

"I'm afraid so," Cardew replied.

"Posed as you, wormed his way into my house, and all for the Snow Leopard Jewels? Don't misunderstand me, I have spent years searching for those holy books, and they are of high value, but nothing is as precious to me as my Pandy. But what of the Runner I hired to watch over the family? Oh, but when I think of Sir Rupert kidnapping my daughter and little Jemnaz, I become quite enraged!"

"The man shall dance on the gallows. As for the Snow Leopard Jewels, they are quite safe," Cardew assured him. "And even as we speak my men are searching Sir Rupert's carriage. Mr. Rice, however, did not fare so well, though I understand he shall eventually recover."

"It is all as scrambled as eggs," Chloe said, repeating her earlier pronouncement. "And I am sure when we return to Chatford, and Mama hears of this—"

"Statira? At Chatford?" Sir Horatio blinked in disbelief.

"She came for my ball, and I know she hated every moment of it," Chloe said with a sniff, valiantly holding back sudden tears.

"Oh, my pet! I missed your big event! Dashed stupid of me." Her Uncle reached across the table and patted her hand.

"Oh, that's all right, Uncle Horry, b-but Mama, who foolishly lost all her money, has . . . has promised me to . . . to . . ." Dissolving into tears, she was quite unable to finish her sentence.

"To a man she cannot abide!" Winthrop, rising to his feet, declared impassionedly. "But Father, Chloe and I are destined to be together! And Aunt Statira refuses her blessing, saying that it will be Lord Larkin Pettigrew or no one!"

"Pettigrew? Of the Pettigrews of Bath?" Sir Horatio made a face as if the soup had gone bad, and added in a constrained voice, "Over my dead body shall she wed that miser! And do not worry about Statira: I shan't let her go to debtor's prison!"

Pandora, relieved that this drama was being resolved, became aware of the Marquess's steady gaze on her. The chatter of the family fell away, and to her consternation, she felt a blush steal onto her cheeks. Suddenly Lord Cardew rose to his feet, and appearing somewhat agitated, prepared to say something. The assembly grew silent, but just as he was about to speak, his men, loaded down with satchels, staggered in.

"We found all manner of riches!" the fat one said, depositing his booty at the Marquess's feet.

"I am sure," Cardew said, clearly not wishing to discuss jewels at this moment.

"Oh, Mama should like that exceedingly!" Chloe, fast recovering from her tears, said on a laugh. "It might even put Lord Pettigrew in the shade."

"I shall run him through, and make a widow of you," Winthrop warned.

"Ah!" Sir Horatio said, fondling one of the jeweled books. "The Snow Leopard treasure. Ha! Had I remembered the legend, there would have been no need for worry!"

"The legend?" several people echoed.

"Yes, for according to the ancient legend, only the pure of heart can ever lay claim to these holy Islamic books. I'm no saint, mind you, but sufficiently whitewashed. *If* an evil one so much as touches a jeweled cover, he is doomed to perish. The Muslims, unlike the Buddhists or Hindus, are a touch fanatical. I expect rather like we Irish," he added with a chuckle. "Ah, but just think, when I find the other four volumes, I'll have the complete set for the museum."

"Papa," Pandora began, "Surely you're not thinking of returning to India, are you?"

"Why not?" He glanced up from the jeweled book to his daughter. "My biggest worry has been you. But I obviously needn't have fretted, for your days on the shelf are clearly numbered, eh, Cardew?"

"Sir, I would have a word with you," the Marquess said, as he distractedly ran a hand through his rumpled hair.

"Oh, sahib, the Marquess takes Miss Tre-mantel off the shelf, and saves the beautiful lady!" Chandro's recitation was the proverbial straw breaking the camel's back.

"Yes, by God!" Lord Cardew said impatiently, then rounding the table, he grasped Miss Tremantle by the wrist, and lifted her off her chair and into his arms. "Miss Tremantel is officially off the shelf, as I've been trying to say for some time! And were I totally crazed, I *would* abduct the very beautiful lady to Gretna Green."

"About Gretna Green—" Winthrop said, but never got to finish.

"Be hanged with it! It shall be St. Gregory's and done up in the first stare, and then perhaps a honeymoon in Bombay—"

"Or the south of France, Lord Cardew," Pandora suggested.

"Call me *Jus,*" he corrected softly.

"Jus?"

"Yes, short for Justin," he responded smoothly. "I'm wearying of 'Lord This' and 'Lord That.' "

"I expect it is confusing for you; but it is certainly not my fault that you choose to take fake titles."

"Oh, I *am* Viscount Cardew," he assured her with a grin.

"Stuff," she muttered affectionately, as he pulled her closer. Then looking earnestly at him, she added, "And I cannot, for the life of me, imagine why you should wish to be leg-shackled to a lady who shot you in the arm, tried to rob you, and has caused you no end of misery." Her eyes danced mischievously, and ignoring the babble of questions this confession precipitated, she surrendered to his embrace.

"I will endeavor to endure your capriciousness, if you don't mind marrying a man with a shadowed past." He kissed her forehead, and their audience grew silent.

"Well . . ." She drew the word out and, drumming her fingers on his chest, added, "I have what we Tremantles call the Fatal Family Flaw, in that I frequently speak and act without thinking." She looked up at him through her lashes.

"A quality that has held me in amazement of you since our first encounter. Dash it all, Pandy, will you marry me or not?"

"Oh, yes! Yes, of course!" she replied as he pulled her to him in a bone-crushing embrace. She repeated this sentiment to his coat lapel, and was rewarded with a rough and wonderful kiss. Somewhere far off she heard her father say, "And when they *do* get to Bombay, they can pick up little *Indira.*"

The Marquess wasn't sure he had heard that right, but as the kiss ended, he did hear Chandro pronounce in perfect English, "Indira is my sister, and True Jewel Number Three." The boy giggled, then added, "Sahib says Miss Tremantel will be our mother, for she is most bea-utiful!"

"He's right about that," Cardew murmured, oblivious to these endearments being bandied about in public. "For you are indeed beautiful, but more than that, you are *my impetuous Pandora!*"

Whatever response she might have made was effectively silenced by yet another kiss, sweeter than the one before, and promising oh so many more.